Reader's adored *Jennifer Brown's Journey*.
Here's a small selection from the shedloads of 5-star reviews:

Loved loved loved this book! Would highly recommend it and it's easy to relate to Jennifer Brown! It's funny but also endearing. This book will get you hooked and you'll be begging for the second part! I can't wait for it to come out! ⭐⭐⭐⭐⭐

Becky Smith

'A complete delight from start to finish. I honestly read the entire story in one 3 hour sitting! Jennifer Brown is so relatable and impossible not to like. It's so refreshing to have a female character with some real personality and I cannot wait to read the next two books in the series. A fantastic debut novel by Angie Langley. Totally brilliant! ⭐⭐⭐⭐⭐

Nathalie Derrick

A fantastic read, picked it up this morning and have just finished it in time for tea! Funny, moving, encouraging. A great read for a lazy day either in the sun or later in the year tucked up next to a roaring fire. Can't wait for the next one. ⭐⭐⭐⭐⭐

Pam Pamther

I thought this would be a girlie book but I loved the whole story and can't stop recommending it to other men. Enlightening, entertaining, refreshing. ⭐⭐⭐⭐⭐

Peter Hawes

Absolutely brilliant book! Really well written, funny and heart-warming. Highly recommended. Can't wait for the next instalment! ⭐⭐⭐⭐⭐

Diane Blackman

I very much enjoyed reading the tales of Jennifer Brown. It was an insight into the challenges and achievements of an everyday life of someone I think every woman would relate to in some way. Life events told with passion, empathy and most importantly, wit. I look forward to the next installment! ⭐⭐⭐⭐⭐

Joan Dunlop

I haven't enjoyed a book as much as this in a long time, beautifully written and a real page turner, I didn't want it to end. True escapism, I cannot wait for the sequel! ⭐⭐⭐⭐⭐

Lyn Mills

ANGIE LANGLEY

Jennifer Brown Moving On

Riverside Publishing Solutions

Angie Langley asserts her moral right to be identified as the author of this book.

Published by Riverside Publishing Solutions
www.riversidepublishingsolutions.com
Copyright © 2019 Angie Langley

Jennifer Brown Moving On paperback edition
ISBN: 978-1-913012-10-6

Also available as Kindle edition
ISBN: 978-1-913012-11-3

Printed and bound in the UK.

I dedicate this book to Howard Sargeant

Contents

Jennifer Brown Moving On

25. Discovery	148
26. Speed Dating and Canoedling	153
27. Capes and Kaftans	160
28. Not-So-Special Agent	161
29. My Weekend is a Bust	175
30. A Staggering Blow	185
31. A Pact. Then a Fact	192
32. New Year, New Zealand	198
33. I Mean Business	203
34. A New Zealand Fleece	207
35. Look Back, But Not in Anger	216
36. Portrait of a Lady	230
37. Suffragette City	235
38. D Day	241
39. D is also for Destiny	244

Acknowledgements

Writing *Jennifer Brown Moving On* has been a joy and made easier by the constant feedback and support from the many *Jennifer Brown's Journey* readers who have taken time to write to me and who continue to inspire with their kind words and wonderful reviews.

I would like to thank the talented Maurice Stevens for his superb illustrations which bring alive Jennifer's character in such a charming manner.

A huge thank you to my publishers Duncan Potter and Paul Beaney from *Riverside Publishing Solutions* for their continued support and professionalism.

Most of all I'd like to thank Howard Sargeant my brilliant editor who is not only kind, patient and courteous, but is also one of the nicest people I know.

'Life had imposed a series of adjustments on me
and here I was again, shedding my skin and,
if not moving forward, at least moving on'

1

Knickers in a Tin

'Tickets!'

I was jolted from my dream – a trim, tanned version of myself on a sunset balcony in Santorini sipping champagne with Gerard Butler in a white linen shirt open all the way to his abs – by the ticket collector on the 10.15 to Waterloo, a forty-year-old misery guts who looked like the love child of Rosa Klebb and my old workplace jobsworth, Not Allowed Nigel.

'Bugger!'

Not in my jacket pocket. Not inside my phone case. Not immediately obvious in my handbag.

Four rows away, the miserable sod was giving some poor teenager a hard time.

'No, I'm going to have to charge you the full fare if you haven't got your railcard.'

Sodding hell.

This day in the city was already costing me a bloody fortune. I could ill afford to pay for my train ticket a second time.

It didn't help that I had the mother of all hangovers, thanks to my best mate, Will and his taste for tequila slammers. I'd suspected all along that a birthday bash at the Spice Garden would challenge my delicate constitution. This morning's thumping head and boiling innards were confirming my suspicion that tequila and tikka masala wasn't exactly a match made in heaven.

Worse than the physical fallout from the evening was 'the dread' – the creeping fear I'd said or done something awful that I couldn't now remember but would soon be confronted with if I ever plucked up the courage to take a peek at my Facebook account.

I had a vague memory of Will handcuffed to something by the stripagram guy – knowing Will, the 'something' was probably the stripagram guy – and I remember being relieved that Jonathan Dashwood-Silk, Will's boss at Intext and my old boss, had gone outside to take a call and had mercifully not witnessed the whole sordid scene. Will was on a shortlist for promotion to Senior Account Manager. I didn't reckon sleazy shenanigans with whipped cream and a fake policeman with a glow-in-the-dark truncheon was going to do him any favours with HR.

I upended my handbag on the table and the elderly lady opposite cracked a smile as the contents spilled out: make-up bag, purse, charger. Spare knickers.

The guard was at my shoulder.

'Tickets.'

I beamed up at him. 'Sorry. Give me a minute. It *is* in here. Somewhere.' Hairbrush, travel mousse, half-eaten cereal bar.

The guard sniffed, checked his watch, gripped his ticket machine. *Think, you dozy mare. Think!*

I remembered. The young guy busking on the platform who looked frozen on such a cold rainy January day.

The tone-deaf rendition of *Don't Look Back In Anger* that had skewered my brain. The doe-eyed canine companion that had melted my heart and made me, on an impulse and on the hoof, hand over my Let's Eat bacon wrap and cappuccino. The empty paper bag. And inside it my crumpled ticket.

'Got it!'

The guard sniffed, pulled a face (the phrase *like a bulldog licking piss off a nettle* leapt into my brain), then turned and marched off down the aisle in search of another customer to terrorise.

When did we start calling passengers 'customers'?

My elderly travelling companion smiled over at me.

'I used to carry paper ones. In a tin.'

'Sorry?'

'Knickers.'

She glanced down at the black lacy spares I was stuffing back into my handbag.

'Not as stylish as those. But practical. You had to be ready for anything in the sixties.'

She gazed out of the rain-lashed window, a seventy-year-old suddenly seventeen again. 'We did have a lot of fun. Exciting times. New music. Crazy fashions. People walking on the moon. You never knew what was going to happen next.' The train pulled into Hazlemere. 'Well, this is me. Bye, dear.'

Through the window, I watched her scurry across the platform to get out of the pouring rain, looking every inch a spinster on her way to a WI meeting.

I thought of my mum. I couldn't remember her saying she'd ever worn paper knickers. And if she had, she certainly wouldn't remember it now. There were fragments of memory, but they were smaller each time I saw her.

Thank God for Leon, the unerringly sweet *Big Issue* seller mum had befriended in the street and invited back for a sandwich and a cup of tea a lifetime ago and who was now her full-time carer. A silver-haired 85-year-old former regional bridge champion and a dreadlocked dude in red leggings and a rasta hat. Barbara Cartland and Bob Marley in the fruit and veg aisle in Sainsbury's.

I glanced at my watch. Forty minutes until the train reached Waterloo. Then a short hop on the underground to Marble Arch and my big lunch date.

Tequila was still trampling all over my digestive system so, when the trolley guy came along, I grabbed a bottle of water to redress the hydration balance. After ten minutes, the fog in my head started to clear and I steeled myself to check Facebook for incriminating evidence. Reassuringly few photos had been uploaded by partygoers, and only one of me, an action snap in which I'm giving Handy Dick my best *Just you bloody well try it, sunshine* glare as I reach for a second helping of tikka masala.

As the train pushed on towards London, the bottled water I'd been frantically glugging summoned me towards the onboard facilities. The engaged sign I didn't see should have worked hand in hand with some sort of locking system but, together with the overflowing bins and timetable irregularities that have become the fate of the British rail customer, this little bit of technology was predictably faulty, too. With the result that the open door revealed a middle-aged man in full flow, sheepishly but animatedly begging me to close the door with a panicked wave of his free hand. I coloured up and pressed the button again. But the door wasn't playing ball and, instead of staying closed, chose to play its own game of 'now you see him, now you don't', in a scene that might have been lifted from a 15-rated episode of *Fawlty Towers*.

I decided this particular customer's distress trumped my own and I retreated to my seat to cross my legs and reflect on the previous evening's activities.

Sleazebags aside, it had been fun catching up with my old office colleagues: Helen, who'd become my landlady for a few months (and was now engaged to New Age hippy boyfriend Paul and giving chapter and verse on their 'organic' wedding to anyone who would listen); the three middle-aged female admin staff I collectively (and cruelly) referred to as the HRTs, whose sniffy superiority towards me had now, post departure, been buried under genuine warmth; the impossibly suave and handsome Jonathan Dashwood-Silk, my old manager. It was as if I'd never left.

But I had. A lot of water under the bridge since. There'd been a couple of new incarnations of me since my days as the worst typist on the planet at Intext.

I'd been housekeeper to a saucy sexagenarian angler and, during that time, had become a passable cook and household organiser, as well as an accomplished domestic diplomat.

That portfolio of skills had secured me a job as estate manager at a crumbling Elizabethan manor house. Now three months had passed since I'd left Thornhill Hall. I'd stayed on long enough to see the household begin to recover from the sudden death of George Winstanley. Dear George. Dear, troubled, conflicted George. It hadn't taken me long to understand that his marriage to the beautiful but fragile Camilla was a union in name only and that his heart belonged to his long-term, not-so-secret lover, Cécile. That this bohemian arrangement suited all three parties and that I had no business disapproving. That heart and head can be rationalised to suit the circumstances.

And that's what I was doing, here, on this train, on the rainiest day of the year. Rationalising. A new adventure for a Jennifer with a new sense of confidence. If I looked over my shoulder, I could still see the ditzy secretary whose atrocious spelling could turn the blandest memo into a comedy script. But she was receding further and further into the hazy distance. Here was a new Jennifer.

She didn't have all the answers, but the path she'd chosen was, she told herself, the sensible one. She was looking to the future and being pragmatic, perhaps even a little selfish. For once.

But what about the man with the warm eyes and the velvet vowels? The thought of him still did strange things to her stomach and it was a thought that came into her mind more often than she wished. More often than she knew was wise. And wisdom had to be the order of the day for the new Jennifer.

Thinking with her head.

Telling her heart to bloody well mind its own business.

2

The Finest of Dining

I'd forgotten just how mental our capital city can be.

Twelve million people, all striding, steaming, sprinting in all directions, most of them crossing my path in the atrium of Waterloo tube station. Added to which default fever pitch, some twozzock had left an odd-looking package on a platform at Embankment and now the Northern Line was bristling with square-jawed armed-response types in kevlar vests and black baseball caps.

I'd have to take a cab. More cash leaking out of my purse.

After thirty-three minutes in the dampest of queues, I dived into the back of a taxi, wrestling with a recalcitrant umbrella and hoping the heavens hadn't done a Crystal Tips number on my hair.

'Where to, love?'

'Le Gavroche.'

The driver made a faint whistling noise through his teeth. 'Blimey. You won the lottery or something?'

'A friend is paying. At least I hope she is.'

'Nice one.'

A minute of companionable silence.

'Daft name for a posh restaurant.'

'Is it?'

'Yeah. Named after that street urchin in *Les Misérables*.'

'Right. I didn't know that.' I don't do musicals. Not even Oscar-winning ones. 'Street urchin. Well, I'll fit right in.'

He glanced at me in the rear view mirror. 'Don't knock yourself.' An East End barrow-boy smile. 'You're a very attractive woman. If you don't mind me saying.'

I sort of minded. But sort of didn't.

I don't imagine this bit of Mayfair has a particularly high urchin footfall.

The cars parked on Upper Brook Street looked like the kind that get polished a lot (by a footman) and not driven much. A mix of old-money Bentleys and new-money Italian-stallion jobs in scarlet and canary yellow. I thought of my little blue Peugeot and the squeak somewhere below the petrol cap that the boys at the garage keep telling me they can't hear.

Cécile stood to greet me warmly. Effortlessly elegant in the kind of crisp linen that only works well on toned French buttocks, she fitted right into the thick-carpeted, red-panelled sophistication of Michel Roux's bar. To the manner born.

Could the manner be acquired? With help, perhaps.

Cécile's kisses on the cheeks ('Four – I'm from Paris, remember') were full of genuine affection.

'Jennifer. So lovely to see you.'

'I'm delighted to be here. Well, delighted to be with you. A little intimidated by this place, though.'

'Relax. Imagine it's a little piece of France. We don't stand on ceremony in our restaurants like you Brits do.'

'It's just not what I'm used to.'

'Nonsense. You are a capable woman with a track record of estate management. An impressive record. Women like us belong in places like this. If not us, then who?'

She poured champagne into two sparkling crystal flutes and handed me one. She raised her own.

'To our absent friend.'

Her eyes glistened with tears and I felt a lump rise in my throat.

'Yes. To our absent friend.'

Cécile took a sip and regained her composure. One, two, three – back in the room.

'Now. Let's get you into the wine business. Properly.'

'Sounds great.' *Sounds terrifying, actually. But nothing ventured …*

'After all, you won't always have a generous and indulgent friend on hand to boost sales.'

She looked me in the eye and smiled. I blushed at the memory of my first and only experience of working in the wine trade – a tasting of Cécile's that I'd gone to as a guest but which she'd talked me into working at as an 'exhibitor' when one of her staff hadn't shown up at the last minute. I'd spent a sweaty five minutes scanning Cécile's notes on 'legs' and 'bouquet' and 'finish' and feeling sick with nerves. But I'd been delighted at the huge numbers that had flocked to my table, keen to taste the entire range, only to discover the response was less to do with my charming sales patter and more to do with my failure to keep the tasting measures within modest limits. I'd been throwing Cécile's best Bordeaux at them by the bucketload. Free. Money down their necks.

Then my old boss, Jonathan, attending the event in his capacity as urbane connoisseur of all aspects of fine living, had ridden in on a white charger and saved my bacon by ordering thirty-five cases of Cécile's top stuff, the biggest order she'd ever had from a walk-up buyer.

'No. I guess I won't always have a helping hand.'

'In Sales, confidence is key. And *you* can project confidence, Jennifer. I've seen that. But I flatter myself I know you well enough to know that, in order to feel truly confident, you need a foundation of knowledge. You need to know what you're talking about.'

God. She's professional, beautiful, kind. And, to top it all, she reads me like a book.

'Which is why I think we need to organise a fast-track apprenticeship. A crash course. A month shadowing me in the office here in London before we get you over to Bordeaux to see how the wine is put together, then a bit of solo flying. How does that sound?'

I wasn't sure how I felt about the solo flying.

'Sounds wonderful. The solo flying …'

Cécile slid two files across the table.

'In the fullness of time, I'd like you to manage these two accounts.'

A quick glance revealed two names: Harry Sinclair and Sheikh Saeed bin Sohal. The first name put me in mind of my mum's old insurance man, who now ran a pub in Portsmouth. The other sounded like he might run a place like Dubai.

The food was produced, the waiters performing a precise routine choreographed to perfection, and we continued to chat through my *soufflé suissesse* (apparently one of old Michel's signature dishes) and my *filet de boeuf grillé*, while Cécile nibbled her way slowly through a minuscule *pâté maison* (no bread) and a *salade de crevettes*.

So that's how you keep those elegant limbs so willowy.

Cécile was generous but no idiot. There would be a probation period that would last six months – a month in London, three months in Bordeaux, and a follow-up two months in London. I had, of course, no right to expect a permanent position straight off the bat (who gets *that* these days?) and, in any case, the provisional nature of the position was more than made up for by the prospect of three months in Bordeaux – the glory months of June, July and August – and a starting salary that made even George Winstanley's generosity look positively parsimonious. I was a lucky girl indeed.

But a lucky girl who would be working in London. With, in London, nowhere to live. Let's not spoil the best lunch I've ever eaten and usher in indigestion by worrying about that little detail now. A bridge to cross later.

My head was spinning as we stepped out into the rarefied air of Mayfair, with me holding the door for Cécile and, unintentionally, for a lacquered grey-haired member of the Gavroche clientele who paid me a backhanded compliment.

'Thank you, dear. You're all so wonderful here.'

My plain navy suit had marked me out as 'staff' and, in my demeanour, there was clearly still something of the lackey.

Need to shake that.

The train back to Hampshire was standing room only until Woking Central, after which I bagged a seat opposite an elderly couple who'd just been to see the matinee performance of *Phantom*. For the thirteenth time. They were eager to share their experience with anyone who still had a pulse.

'Absolutely marvellous, dear. But no one will ever play the lead like Michael. Which you'd never have guessed if you'd only seen him hanging off the back of a bus on roller skates in *Some Mothers*. He was sublime. Wasn't he, Derek?'

Derek nodded. Part avid *Phantom* fan, part bulldog in an insurance ad.

'We've got the programmes going right back to the premiere in 1985. Haven't we, Derek?'

She whipped out the latest glossy that would be filed away on the shelf with the other dozen.

I managed a 'Nice' before my bacon was saved by the arrival of Portsmouth station. She was humming *Music of the Night* as I stepped onto the platform.

Then it hit me. Bob and Brenda. My late dad's brother and his wife. Who just happened to live in Bexleyheath. An eminently commutable distance from Cécile's office in fashionable, gentrified Shoreditch.

3

Britannica and the Waves

A strong northwesterly was blowing its way across the south coast when I woke the following morning to the sound of six-foot waves crashing along the shoreline. I snuggled down under the duvet, enjoying the novelty of not living by the alarm clock. *I could get used to this.*

But there was much to think about.

An hour later and I was munching on toast and marmalade as I flicked through the rich tapestry that is daytime TV. The sight of Hyacinth Bucket dusting her Doulton Crinoline Ladies prompted me to get on with it, grab the phone, and call Auntie Brenda.

'Bexleyheath 2731, Brenda Brown speaking'.

My delightfully batty Auntie Brenda's telephone manner hadn't moved on since that nice Mr Eden was running our affairs overseas.

'Hello, Auntie Brenda. It's Jennifer. Ronnie's daughter.'

'Jennifer, dear. How lovely to hear from you!'

She sounded genuinely pleased. I felt genuinely shabby. This overture was coming in the wake of a sustained period of radio silence from me. And here I was, finessing an invitation to move in. But, the truth was, without it, this wonderful opportunity with Cécile would crash and burn.

'We were only saying last month, WEREN'T WE DEAR?'

I pulled the receiver a foot from my ear as she hollered to Uncle Bob in the next room.

'WE WERE ONLY SAYING WE HAVEN'T SEEN YOU SINCE YOUR FATHER'S FUNERAL.'

At this volume, I hardly needed Mr Logie Baird's marvellous invention. If I opened the window, I might catch her side of the conversation as it blasted its way across the Surrey Hills and the South Downs to the furthest reaches of Hampshire.

A muffled response from Uncle Bob.

'NO DEAR. THAT WAS 2006. MR GIBBS FROM THE ROTARY CLUB. YOUR BROTHER PASSED AWAY IN 2008.'

And so it went on. A comedy sketch. Phone ping-pong.

'WE DON'T TRAVEL FAR THESE DAYS, DO WE BOB?'

Then a conspiratorial whisper to me.

'Not after he knocked some poor lad off his bike on the A20. On our way to the Chislehurst car boot.'

'BUGGER WASN'T WEARING A HI-VIS!' Bob hollered back. Nothing much wrong with his hearing.

Brenda ploughed on, owning the conversation, changing tack.

'How's your mum, dear? Haven't heard from her in a while.'

Her question caught me off guard.

'She's ... struggling.' I felt a lump rise in my throat. I dissolved it with humour. 'She doesn't make many calls these days. Just the odd one to the emergency services, to ask if a Victoria sponge needs to be cooked at one-eighty.'

'Poor love. Bob plays the grumpy old sod quite well, but don't be fooled. He's very fond of his sister-in-law. Very.'

Brenda – stop it or you'll have me bawling down the phone.

I changed the subject. The circuitous path my career had followed and the new phase it was embarking on.

'So you'll be moving to London. And we can see more of you. What a treat for us! In fact, if you could bear the company of a couple of old codgers, why not move in here? I'll get Bob to clear all his auction rubbish out of the spare room.'

'That's very kind, but ...'

'If you've got younger, cooler friends you want to bunk with, that's fine. But if you haven't, come and stay here. Look, I know how cruel the cost of living is in London. It's alright for us – we bought our house in 1968. We're on the overground line right into London Bridge. Thirty-five minutes. You can pay us a bit of rent if it makes you feel better. But it's really not necessary.'

Huh. I thought I'd be the one doing the conning. But dear old Auntie Brenda had pulled off something clever and lovely. She'd sniffed the air when I'd mentioned my new job, smelt the real reason for my call, and saved me the ignominy of having to ask outright for what was, by any standards, a massive favour. She'd got in first with a generous offer that solved my problem and saved my face.

Like Cécile, she'd seen right through me.

Half an hour later, strolling along the shingle, I was imagining the flurry of activity needed to clear the spare room of Bob's 'auction rubbish.'

Uncle Bob had been a pack rat all his life, physically incapable of passing up a bargain, even on something he could find no earthly use for. He was the kind of man who went into town for a pound of mince and came home with a stainless-steel grass rake, two 1940s advertising signs for the White Star Line, nine albums of Brooke Bond PG Tips collection cards, and the Encyclopaedia Britannica in sixteen volumes. On my last visit, four or five years ago, he'd spent the afternoon in the garage stripping down the engine of a 1950s moped he'd bought at auction for a tenner. He'd been like a boy with a Christmas train.

'Ten pounds! For a classic! Can you believe it?'

Brenda had rolled her eyes. She knew the script. There'd be a day or two of enthusiastic activity before he'd get fed up and move on to the next object of boyish excitement and this classic would go the way of all bargains and join the heap of unfinished 'projects' at the back of the garage.

I made my way to the jetty, sidestepping the foamy waves that lashed the shore and sifted piles of shingle on a neverending rinse programme. The wind was getting up and my aching ears were making me wish I'd worn a hat. I pulled two tissues out of my pocket and stuck one in each ear and pulled up the collar of my fleece. Practical, if not pretty.

A chocolate Labrador bounded past me, his handsome owner ten paces behind. As he approached, I flashed him my winningest beam and he, clocking the paper hankies dangling from my ears, gave me the polite but nervous smile reserved for persons escaped from a secure health facility.

4

Shaping up

I had a few weeks' free time before moving in with Bob and Brenda.

I put the time to good use by swotting. I hoovered up back issues of *Decanter* magazine and camped out in the Havant branch of Majestic, scanning the shelves for Bordeaux, taking notes, pumping the bearded hipster manager for sales info and swilling free samples with the artfully furrowed brow of someone who doesn't just drink whatever's on special in Asda and hasn't just discovered that *terroir* isn't a small dog that digs for rabbits.

At home, I was devouring the French sections of Will's copy of Hugh Johnson's *World Atlas of Wine* and becoming painfully aware that the task ahead – acquiring enough knowledge to make wine my job – would involve going back to school for large doses of geography, swathes of history and a hefty chunk of science.

And part of the job would also be *looking* the part. My old faithful navy suit was as tired as my complexion and not the attire that would cut the mustard in Shoreditch.

But my eye for fashion tended to drag me towards rails of safe stuff – things I knew (or thought) would suit me. Which meant I usually got back home with a bagful of the same old thing in a slightly different shade of navy.

I decided that, if I was going to push the envelope stylewise, I'd need some professional advice.

'Any particular style in mind, madam?'

The personal shopper was a twenty-three-year-old Bond girl with porcelain skin unencumbered by pores. The kind of young woman who spends Sundays on a yacht with broad-shouldered screen idols kneeling at her feet clutching ring boxes.

'Erm … something … professional.'

Her on-trend brows dipped as she took me in slowly from head to toe, her plump, painted lips pursed thoughtfully as if she were deciding what type of 'profession' I might be referring to and was hovering between something based in the portakabin reception of a third-rate double-glazing company and an altogether older profession operating at street level.

'For an executive job. In Shoreditch. London.' Why did I feel like a kid trying to impress a grown-up? *Stop it, Jennifer Brown!*

Her emerald eyes settled on mine incredulously, but I lifted my chin an inch and held her gaze. She lowered hers once more, studying my shape from all angles.

'Hm. We need to try to create a silhouette.'

She sighed, as if the task of turning base metal into gold might be easier to pull off, then flounced away wordlessly, leaving me standing in the middle of the floor like an abandoned child. I half thought to trot along after her but stopped myself, took a deep breath and tried to summon the persona of the professional employing the hireling, which is essentially what this set-up was.

How easy life must be if you belong to the class that runs the world. If your schooling and your family life and your whole existence fixes in you the belief that the world is yours to own, that any problems can simply be bought off with money or connections, and that every space is populated by people whose natural role is to serve you.

Bond Girl returned with an armful of the kind of labels that probably languish in the dressing room in Scarlett Johansson's beachfront mansion in Malibu. No price tags.

'Erm, I was hoping for something a little less … ostentatious.' Which was code for, *Get me something affordable, you cow.*

Her plump lips settled into a grimace and she flounced off, doubtless heading towards that section of the store where the bri-nylon housecoats lived. I decided to head her off at the pass and, hotly regretting my decision to enter the personal-shopper battle arena at all, began nosing around myself for real clothes with actual price tags.

I spotted a smart black suit that I could imagine being broadly in Cécile's personal orbit. The price tag was steep but not ridiculous and the reality of it emboldened me, so that, when Bond Girl returned, I'd mustered enough confidence to dismiss her selection and send her off with the commission to fetch the black number in my size.

Initially a little put out, she quickly warmed to her task and became a helpful assistant, assembling underwear and accessories that complemented the suit and my 'generous curves', a fabulously backhanded compliment but one that, feeling the balance of our relationship had been restored, I was in the mood to take.

When Bond Girl handed me the credit card receipt, I knew it would take me six months to pay the lot off.

But I figured I was worth it.

***

During my few weeks of downtime, I also resolved to see more of my mum. She was now virtually housebound and every time I thought of her, and of how small her life was now, I felt a sharp stab of guilt for not doing more for her and for having a life of my own that was full of opportunity.

I phoned and got Leon. Dripping with remorse, he gave me the latest instalment. The day before, when the two of them had been out on a rare shopping trip and Leon had popped into a record shop to check out their vintage vinyl with the injunction that Mum wait for him outside, she'd hopped onto a bus and ended up in Chichester, sixteen miles away. There she'd buttonholed a traffic warden and asked him the way to Brighton Pier, and he'd got the wind up and called the police, whereupon a 'nice young policeman' had driven her all the way back home to Portsmouth and a frantic Leon.

'I was only in the shop for two minutes!' Leon said, affronted that this had happened on his watch.

I pulled my collar up against a biting March wind as I climbed the narrow lane that led to Mum's house. The thought of the warm comfort of her kitchen made me pick up the pace. As always, before opening the back door, I peered in through the kitchen window. But these last few months she was hardly to be found in her old station at the table, pinny-clad and busy with some plum-based confection. Daytime TV was now her world.

'Hi, Mum.'

I kissed her powdery cheek. She looked up at me. Three seconds of blankness while she rummaged around at the back of her memory cabinet for the file containing my face. She was seized by panic.

'Oh, dear. You're early. I haven't wrapped your present.'

I felt my eyes moisten. I squeezed her hand gently.

'Christmas was weeks ago, Mum. We're in March.'

She stared for a second, then shook her head.

'Oh, well. You'll just have to have it unwrapped this year.'

I smiled through my tears. 'That's fine. I don't mind.'

She turned her attention back to the TV screen, where a chef I'd never seen before, on a channel I'd never heard of, was doing something elaborate and exotic-sounding with a guinea fowl.

I made tea and poked about in the kitchen. For as long as I can remember, my mum's kitchen has been a rich source of homemade cake. Confection was part of coming home. Mum, tea and cake. The three things went together. And, in the village, everyone knew Iris as the woman who made the killer plum tart.

But baking was another forgotten feature of Mum's life. The fridge was devoid of tart and the cake tin was rusting at the back of the pan cupboard. The only sweet treat I could find was a half-eaten battenberg from the Co-op.

Leon appeared, with a bag of shopping and a fistful of cash. Mum's latest hobby was scratchcards.

'She's won three times this week!' he grinned.

It was bizarre. My mum, who used to say that gambling was the ungodly curse of the working class, was now one of the National Lottery's best customers.

Three hours and several cups of tea later, Mum dozed off in the chair. I gently prised the remote from her papery hand and, with the flick of a button, sent the shopping channel into oblivion.

I said goodbye to Leon and silently thanked the lucky stars that had brought him into her life, and mine. I shuddered to think what state she'd be in without him, or what kind of life I'd have as her full-time carer. The guilt I carried around was mitigated by the knowledge that the arrangement appeared to suit Leon well. He had a roof over his head for the first time in years and, as her carer, drew a small income that satisfied his modest requirements. And he had the perfect blend of endlessly patient and relentlessly cheery that made him the ideal companion to an elderly woman. In a different life, he'd have made an excellent nurse.

***

'You lucky cow!'

Will topped up my glass of Chianti and shovelled more prawn linguine into his animated mouth. He talked through pasta.

'Three months in Bordeaux! That'll be bloody gorgeous!'

'I can't speak French.'

'Oh, bollocks. They all speak bloody English.'

'No, they don't. And this is wine. Even the Brits speak French when it comes to wine – *cru*, *appellation*, bloody buggering *terroir*!'

'You'll be fine. You always bloody are.'

Typical Will. My dear friend and old colleague was always the perfect antidote to self-doubt. A raw, brash injection of confidence just when I needed it.

'You just need to bag yourself a French bloke early doors. Do wonders for your sex life *and* your language skills.'

'Hm. We'll see. Anyway, what about you in the bloke department?'

'Kavi.'

'What?'

'My new bloke. Kavi. He's Indian.'

'Another one off militarycupid.com?'

'No. I'm not on that anymore. Too many bogus brigadiers for my liking. I met Kavi over a hot chicken biryani.'

'Nice.'

'He spilt most of it down the sleeve of my new shirt. Have you ever tried getting turmeric out of white satin? Well, don't bother. It's bloody impossible!'

I shook my head.

'Fifty-six quid! He's worth it, though. We had our first official date – you know, with him *not* being my waiter – last week. Pina coladas at the top of the Spinnaker Tower, looking out across the Solent.'

'Sounds idyllic.'

Will winked at me.

'I am, as you know, the Queen of the Romantic Date. Anyway, what about you?' He glanced at my cleavage. 'Who's admiring the view from your gorgeous balcony?'

'Shut up. Nobody.'

'Oh, shove it. Jonathan could never keep his eyes off your assets. You should give him a call, by the way – I think he's struggling a bit under the new regime.'

I hadn't spoken to my old boss in months. I wondered what was up. Will ploughed on, massaging my ego.

'And I can guarantee you that every heterosexual male in this restaurant is looking at you right now and wishing he could have a little … private time in your company.'

It wasn't true, but Will's kindness was always very welcome. And always offered whenever I was feeling at a particularly low ebb. My current rampant self-doubt about how I'd fare in the world of wine had now been joined, thanks to Bond Girl, by a fear of simply not *looking* up to the job. All the old body-image insecurities were crowding in again. Two years on and clearly I still hadn't rebuilt the walls that Pete had bulldozed when he'd made the move to an altogether fresher piece of property.

Will sloshed the last of the Chianti into my glass and, looking over to the waiter, air-wrote on his hand.

'Take that guy.' He nodded over to the waiter, a slim-hipped silver-haired gent who, though undeniably fine-looking, was old enough to be my dad. Not exactly the ballpark I was looking to play in.

'He's had his eyes on your puppies all night.'

'Stop it. Not all men are sex-crazed sleazebags like you.'

Will stood up and lifted his turquoise velvet jacket off the back of the chair.

'I am simply a man with a healthy appetite. As the exquisite Kavi will discover when I have Skype-sex with him this very evening.'

'I don't even want to know what *that* involves. But I'm glad you've got someone. You deserve it.'

I must have looked pathetic because Will actually teared up. He stepped forward and hugged me close and kissed my hair. Then he looked me in the eye.

'And nobody deserves it more than you, my darling. And it will come. It has to. Good things *do* happen to good people. You're off to Bordeaux for the summer. That's a great start. The start of something good. Trust me.'

It was my turn for tears.

'Think of me when you're on some gorgeous sun-drenched terrace tucking into *foie gras*. I'll be standing in the pissing rain in the queue for a Greggs sausage roll.'

I smiled and wiped my eyes.

'Just remember, though – if you ever see *couilles de mouton* on a menu, stay well clear.'

'Why? What is it?'

'Sheep's bollocks.'

5

Lunch and an invitation

I couldn't shake what Will had said about Jonathan having a bit of a tough time at work, so I texted my old boss and suggested a catch-up lunch at the Pier Grill in Southsea, a favourite of mine since my days as a waitress there, in a previous life.

Well, like me, the Pier had undergone something of a transformation in recent years and was now Happy Buddha, a Thai joint with an all-you-can-eat lunchtime buffet.

I sat on a purple velour chair in the bar area, next to a thick-waisted man in a replica Portsmouth FC top waiting for a takeaway he clearly hoped would cure what looked like a raging hangover.

Jonathan was predictably late and predictably handsome with a light tan recently acquired from a short break in Monserrat. He strolled across to the bar looking like Richard Gere in *Pretty Woman*.

'Sorry I'm late, Jen.' He kissed me on the cheek and sat down. Two middle-aged women at a table ten feet away were lifting their jaws off the floor.

'A mix-up with the time of a conference call.'

He took in the purple and gold flock wallpaper. 'Interesting choice.'

I was just about to explain that I hadn't known about the refurbishment when a pretty waitress with an eighteen-inch waist, glossy black hair and dreamy eyes arrived with menus. True to form, Jonathan held her gaze for a few moments more than necessary.

'What would you recommend?'

When the wine arrived, he poured us each a glass and we clinked. He sighed and his face took on a wistful look.

'I miss the old days, Jennifer Brown. It's not the same without you.'

'I'm sure the spelling in your memos is a lot better these days.'

He smiled. 'It's not your work I miss. It's *you*.' He reached across the table and put his hand on mine. This wasn't charm – he knew full well I was immune – but genuine affection. So genuine it stirred up all the old guilt I'd felt two years before when I'd handed in my notice at Intext Software Ltd and gone off to play housekeeper in the Hampshire countryside, leaving him to cope with my replacement, Zilla, the temp in snakeskin trousers who'd now become permanent.

I tried to lighten the confessional mood, hiding the fact that Will had hinted that all was not well at Elsinore. 'Oh, I'm sure you're coping fine.'

He took a big glug of sauvignon blanc. 'More than ever, we're about targets. Bottom lines. Efficiency.'

'Shorthand for redundancies.'

He lifted his glass again. 'The side of the job I've never relished.' He took another glug and looked out of the window. Beneath the dazzling smile, the flowing hair and the expensive suits was a rather gentle soul who hated confrontation, negativity, nastiness.

Again I tried to lift the mood.

'How's Steph?' I pictured the leggy blonde with the Hollywood uplift and the rosebud lips as I wrapped my own lips round another forkful of crispy duck.

'Fine. Still keen to move in. But, you know me. I'm not great at …'

'Commitment.'

'I've never been the committing type. Although ...' He flashed me his best Richard Gere smile. '... the love of a good woman might easily change that.'

I flashed him my best withering stare. 'We wouldn't last a week. Besides, I don't fancy you.'

He pasted on a look of mock offence. Then he turned the spotlight back on me.

'So what's new in the world of Jennifer Brown?'

'I'm spending the summer in Bordeaux.'

'Terrific. Think of all the delicious wine you'll be drinking.'

'I won't be drinking it. I'll be selling it.' And I told him all about my new job with Cécile, the training in the London office, the stint in Bordeaux and the prospect of managing clients. Jonathan seemed a little amused at my elevation into the world of wine, considering my disastrous performance that had prompted his rescue at Cécile's London show the previous year. But he was also impressed. And genuinely pleased for me.

'I wish you success. In all things.' He lifted my hand and kissed it.

Then his phone buzzed and the screen lit up – an image of a sleek young woman who was certainly not Steph – and he snatched it up with an apology.

'Sorry. I really must take that.' He moved a discreet distance away and I took the opportunity to check my own phone – a text from Auntie Brenda asking if I still liked Ovaltine.

Jonathan returned, composure restored, and ordered another bottle of wine and we relaxed into a long, lazy, companionable lunch.

As we were settling the bill, he threw a curveball at me.

'I'm going to a wedding next week.' A sheepish pause. 'Don't suppose you fancy being my plus one?'

I narrowed my eyes and he read the look.

'Steph's away in Milan. And I won't enjoy being on my own in a roomful of smugly happy couples. Please.'

Most women would salivate over an invitation to spend the day hanging on the well-tailored arm of Jonathan Dashwood-Silk. But, for me, it would be seven hours playing second fiddle to a more attractive friend and withstanding the puzzlement of younger, sleeker women who wondered why this adonis had come to a wedding with his cleaning lady.

But he was practically begging. And I had nothing in the diary.

'Okay. Where is it? And, more importantly, *who* is it?' I pulled on my jacket.

'It's a very private affair. The registry office in Chichester then a small reception at Northfields – just a couple of dozen guests. David's closest friends.'

'David?'

Jonathan took out his car keys. 'David Harwood. He's our new CEO.' My cheeks started to burn. 'He always asks after you.'

My stomach was gripped by emotions I thought I'd left behind at Thornhill Hall, the site of my last meeting with David. I'd been Estate Manager and he'd been an unexpected member of a party booked in for an executive awayday. The man I'd first bumped into, literally, when he'd been a client at Intext and I'd been the world's worst typist. The man I kept bumping into. The man with the warm hazel eyes and the velvet vowels. And now he was getting married. And now I'd agreed to be a guest at his wedding.

On FaceTime with Will, I tried to play it cool.

'Jonathan tells me David Harwood's your new CEO. How's he getting on?'

'Seems to be well liked. Why?'

'I'm going to his wedding, as Jonathan's guest.'

'Bloody hell! Northfields. You'd better get your roots done.'

'Shut up. Jonathan was a bit coy about David's fiancée. What's she like?' I felt my face flush slightly, which Will clearly spotted.

'My oh my, Jennifer Brown.'

'What? I'm just curious.'

'Hm.'

'So?'

'So what?'

'So what's she like?'

'Nobody's met her. Sarah Something-Or-Other. Interior designer.'

'You haven't seen her?'

'No. But last week Trisha saw him getting into a car with some blonde at the wheel, so I guess that was her.'

'Right.'

'It'll be a very posh do. At Northfields.'

'Yes.'

'The best of stuff. Food. Wine. You'll be able to flash your new wine patter.'

'I will.'

'But get your roots done.'

After three large vodkas, and feeling like a silly teenage stalker but also feeling unable to stop myself, I trawled through social media looking for posh blonde Sarah. When we give in to the baser bits of our nature, the results are rarely welcome. I found a profile on LinkedIn that made me feel shitty in the extreme.

Sarah was an exquisite-looking early thirties with a sunkissed complexion that looked like it had never needed makeup and never would. She ran an interior design business with a client list that read like a *Who's Who* of fashionable society. She'd won a silver medal in Dressage at the Athens Olympics.

Beautiful, successful, athletic.

I felt sick.

***

Gareth's hands circled my chair.

'You always give me a lot to work with, Jennifer. I like that.'

He nodded, clearly agreeing with himself, and his heavily lacquered black quiff bounced up and down. He spun the chair round to face the mirror and began plucking at my hair, pulling it back off of my face.

'So what are we doing?'

'I was thinking, something sophisticated but not too short.'

I'd known a few hairdressers who were a little too enthusiastic with the scissors. And, with his skinny tweed culottes, his orange linen blouse, and his air hostess scarf, you'd be forgiven for thinking Gareth was the kind of guy who fancied himself a style visionary. An experimentalist. A revolutionary. Which he sort of was. But he kept it on a leash. And, importantly for me, he always listened. And he always made me look good.

'What about colour?'

'Erm …'

'I'd go for an ash blonde balayage. To keep it natural. No?'

'Sounds good.'

He snapped his fingers and a sixteen-year-old model in a tight black vest trotted over, then stood to attention, awaiting orders.

Gareth was a genius. But he was also a cheeky sod. He caressed my forehead with his fingertips.

'Ever thought about Botox?'

6

A Quick Change

Chichester registry office was a good choice for the upmarket wedding of David Harwood and Sarah Something-Or-Other, I told myself, as sunlight seeped through the curtains of my bedroom window on the morning of the wedding. A glorious Spring day.

For some.

Birds were singing, bees were buzzing, and Mother Nature was casting her magic spell on all living things.

Except me.

David was tying the knot.

I had a knot in my stomach.

I made some extra-strong coffee, pulled back the curtains, and spent an hour sitting in the window, staring at the beach, trying to feel positive.

Early morning runners were out in force, breaking their stride to give a wide berth to a thick-necked bloke with an eager Rottweiler straining on a chain. I've never been of the running persuasion – a slow twenty minutes on a treadmill is my limit – but I imagine I'd be quite nippy with a muscular killhound snapping at my buttocks. One young runner in all the gear, absorbed in his music, didn't see the hound until the last minute and sprang out of the way with a level of alarm that suggested an impromptu evacuation of the bowels.

The sight snapped me out of my reverie and back to the task in hand. A considerable task. A shameful task. The task of looking amazing. Most days, I looked fine. This much I knew. This much I'd managed to convince myself of, rebuilding the wall of self-esteem brick by brick since Pete had bulldozed it a lifetime ago.

But this wasn't most days. This day, this particular day, I needed to be, or at least to *feel*, amazing. Amazing for one day only.

I shouldn't have cared. But I did. To my shame, I cared an awful lot.

The lovely man with the warm eyes and the velvet vowels was marrying someone right off the cover of Tatler. You can't beat the bride on her wedding day.

But you can come bloody close.

Wishing I hadn't spent over an hour mooning out of the window, I fired up my go-to eighties Spotify mix and ramped Billy Idol up to full throttle.

Nice day for a white wedding.

My 'generous curves' were looking their absolute best in my new ivory silk suit, a gorgeous gem of a find from Estelle's in Winchester. More than I'd wanted to pay (natch) but I was always, I told myself as I admired the effect in the mirror, worth it.

The irony of the day did not escape me. A wedding I'd rather not be going to, of a man I'd turned down but whose mental image still played havoc with my insides, was costing me a bloody fortune.

Old Dashwood Silk arrived bang on time for once, looking immaculate in dove grey Armani, crisp white shirt and pale blue silk tie.

He lowered his shades and took me in as I pulled open the passenger door of his white Morgan Roadster and climbed in beside him.

'Scarlett Johansson.'

'What?'

'Dressed like that. That's who you remind me of.'

Smooth bastard.

'Shut up and drive.'

But yes. You're right.

After an hour of West Sussex countryside, we reached the
pretty cathedral city of Chichester, in the foothills of the glorious
South Downs.

A boutique hotel, Number 14, in the town centre was the venue
for a pre-wedding drink. As the Morgan's tyres crunched over
the gravel of the car park, I was feeling every inch the lookalike
Hollywood star. The misgivings of the morning had been swept
away by self-confidence and anticipation. It was going to be a
beautiful day.

Then I looked across the car park and a rock fell into my stomach.

David Harwood was standing beside a sleek black limousine,
opening the door for his bride-to-be. As she stepped into the
sunshine, there was no doubt Sarah Something-Or-Other was a
stunning bride. Her lithe limbs and flawless face were shown to
their best advantage by the gorgeous outfit she'd chosen for her
special day. An outfit she'd picked up from Estelle's in Winchester.

I turned flaming red cheeks to Jonathan, who was busy
straightening his tie in the rearview mirror. He saw my face.

'What's wrong?'

'I … er… I feel a bit queasy. You go on ahead. I need to … I just
need to nip to the chemist.'

'The chemist?'

I gave him my best *Women don't have to explain these things stare.*

'Yes!'

He cracked the code. 'Right. Sure. See you in there.'

I stood in the middle of a Chichester street thick with Saturday
shoppers and wondered what the hell to do next. The street wasn't

offering many options: an M&S Food, a Greggs, a British Heart foundation shop, and the constituency office of some horse-faced bloke I'd never heard of.

Charity shop it is.

A frantic ten minutes of flicking through other people's cast-offs threw up a straight choice between a white trouser suit from someone's *Saturday Night Fever* phase and a long red floral dress with padded shoulders out of *Dynasty* by way of *Eastenders*.

I imagined Jonathan in oak-panelled opulence looking at his watch as I struggled with both outfits behind the ill-fitting curtain in the corner of the shop, my nostrils filled with a smell like last week's hiking socks.

'I'd go with the dress, love.'

I peered through the gap in the curtain at the elderly volunteer whose badge identified her as 'Val.'

'Here, this'll go with it.' She handed me a red fascinator with what looked like a dead poppy stuck to it.

'Definitely the red. White can be a bit … unforgiving.'

Time was flying by, and Val was going all Gok Wan on me, so I snatched back the curtain, handed Val a tenner, and, four minutes later, staggered into the refined surroundings of Number 14 looking like Peggy Mitchell's dowdy younger sister.

I scurried over to Jonathan. He gave me a puzzled *What the fuck?* look and I nodded towards Sarah Something-Or-Other, looking every inch the equestrian golden girl bride, and he got it.

'Oh. Right.'

He collared a teenage waiter with a tray of champagne and grabbed two flutes. He handed both to me.

'Get these down you.'

The ceremony at Chichester registry office was a sober affair. A girl on a baby grand (did the registry office have one or had David brought his own?) gave us Debussy's *Claire de Lune* as the couple made their way forward and, when vows had been exchanged, a middle-aged man galloped through Shakespeare's *Let me not to the marriage of true minds* with all the emotion of a loss adjuster.

But I had to admit Sarah looked quite stunning in the ivory silk suit whose twin sister now languished in a blue plastic bag at reception. And David looked genuinely happy.

After a restrained photography session, the couple headed back to the hotel to greet their guests ahead of the reception.

And I took a deep breath (and drained the contents of a third flute) to steel myself for the part of the day I'd been dreading.

Jonathan shook David's hand warmly and airbrushed Sarah's cheek before introducing me.

'I'm sure you'll remember my old secretary.' He nudged me forward.

'Of course. How could anyone forget Jennifer Brown?'

David looked both surprised and delighted to see me again. He kissed me warmly on the cheek.

His new bride's polite smile almost masked her evident puzzlement over my fashion sense but she was far too well bred to make a thing of it.

'Lovely to meet you.'

'Congratulations. You look lovely.'

She smiled with genuine warmth. 'Thank you. That's very kind.'

Clever, beautiful, successful *and* nice.

The cow.

The afternoon passed in a whirl of fine food and urbane chatter. The speeches were gracious and polite, including Jonathan's, which could, in all sincerity, remark on the bride's beauty. And there wasn't a man, or woman, in the room who could argue with his assessment.

But when Jonathan gave the bridal toast – 'To David and Sarah. The perfect couple' – David's eyes seemed to seek mine for a second before he turned an adoring gaze at his gorgeous wife.

I had a split-second vision of me standing and shouting out, 'No! This is a mistake. David should be marrying ME!' but when I came to, he was kissing his bride and I was staring at the bubbles in my fourth glass of fizz.

I excused myself and escaped to the conservatory to take a breath, the protective colouring of my BHF frock blending seamlessly with the potted geraniums.

After the happy couple had headed off for their honeymoon – ten days kicking around Antigua and Barbuda on a crewed schooner – I felt a well-tailored arm on my shoulder.

Jonathan pulled me in and gently kissed the top of my head.

'Only you would do such a selfless thing, Jennifer Brown,' he said tenderly. 'That's why I'll always love you.'

7

B and B's

A week later, I packed my bags and moved out of the little rented flat by the beach that had been my home for the past six months.

I spent the afternoon with Mum and feigned a shared enthusiasm for the latest QVC deal of the day.

When it was time to leave, I told her I'd give Uncle Bob and Auntie Brenda her love.

'Who?'

'Dad's brother, Bob. And his wife, Brenda. Don't you remember Bob?'

'Of course I remember him. He died years ago.'

I told Leon I'd Skype him the following week. Perhaps Mum could wave to me on the screen. Leon thought that would only confuse her more, so I promised to call instead, 'on a proper telephone'.

Then it was time to say goodbye to another very special friend. Someone who'd seen me through all the ups and downs of the past ten years. Someone who'd listened to my troubles without judgment, put up with my erratic driving and tried to keep me on the right track even when I knew I was heading in the wrong direction. Yes there'd been times when she'd let me down, but they were few and very far between.

'For Christ's sake, Jen. It's only a bloody car!'

'I know it sounds stupid, but I can't help how I feel.'

'I could understand you if it was a Porsche. But it's a clapped out old Peugeot with a rusty exhaust and a ghost living near the petrol cap.'

Will was right, of course. It was just a thing, not a person. It was stuff. And we shouldn't get attached to stuff.

I tried to rationalise my feelings about the first and only car I'd ever owned. But they weren't rational. They were fond. Heart ruling head. Again. Memories. Endless journeys to Intext and my work friends. Picnics with Pete. My adorable dogs, Betty and Eric, buzzing around on the back seat.

But the order of the day was pragmatism. A car in London is a passport to misery. And if I needed one in France, I'd sort something out. I certainly couldn't trust this old girl to get me to Bordeaux in one piece. The cost of taxing and insuring something that served no purpose just didn't add up.

So my little blue Peugeot had to go.

But the villainous swines at the garage had made me an offer so insulting my eyes had been hot with tears of rage

'Three hundred quid!'

'Relax. Your old queen in shining armour is here. Breathe. We have a solution.'

I wiped my eyes.

'Kavi needs a runaround. For takeaway deliveries and pootling about in at the weekend. If you throw in the satnav, he'll give you six hundred.'

***

Bob and Brenda's 1920s brick-and-pebbledash semi was tucked away in a quiet street. A typical suburban home. Bow windows and a low garden wall. An aspidistra in the window.

Auntie Brenda flung her arms round me as if I were her own long-lost daughter. She hadn't changed a bit. A short, compact, elegant lady with top notes of Estée Lauder Youth Dew. A double set of pearls and matching earrings in case the Queen dropped in for a cup of tea and a Garibaldi.

Uncle Bob lurked behind her in the doorway, in beige cardigan and brown cords, his small features an uncanny reminder of my dad. He grunted a welcome then headed back through to the 'lounge' to catch the last ten minutes of *Cash in the Attic*.

Brenda closed the door behind me and ushered me into 1972. Rather like the 60-year-old punk I sometimes saw on the bus, who found a fashion style he liked when he was 17 and stuck with it, Bob and Brenda had remained faithful to the decor that must have seemed the last word in modern when the first Morris Marinas were rolling off the assembly line – bold floral upholstery in oranges and yellows, striped Axminster carpets that were strangely all the retro rage again, and furniture in teak, an outrageously exotic wood from the far east that Britain adopted as its own and that was also enjoying a resurgence under the 'mid-century' banner.

I wondered if Cécile's Shoreditch office had caught the retro bug.

But Brenda had stamped her own indelible mark on the style. Ranks of glass-fronted cabinets crammed with Charles and Di mugs and Golden Jubilee plaques and Queen Mum commemorative coins announced that this was a royalist household. And reminded me of my mum's old nickname for Brenda – *Queen B*.

And the faint aroma of old wood mingled with cigar smoke suddenly transported me back to my childhood. My dad and Uncle Bob settling into their armchairs for a seven-hour marathon of cricket coverage, the telly sound off and Test Match Special on the radio. I could almost hear again the reassuring Hampshire vowels of John Arlott, everyone's favourite cricket commentator.

I didn't know a googly from a backward short leg (still don't) but I didn't care. Something about the scene – the cricket whites, the cigar smoke, the absorption in statistics that made no sense to ordinary humans – gave the nine-year-old me a deep sense of peace.

Cigars were nominally banned from the house now (the smoke upset Custard, Brenda's beloved canary whose cage lived in the corner of the lounge) and old Bob was banished to the shed to pursue his pleasure. But you didn't have be Poirot to sense he occasionally had a crafty puff indoors when Brenda was out, probably on Thursday afternoons when she popped down to the community centre to play canasta.

Brenda saw me sniff the air.

'He thinks I don't know. I've told him it'll kill him one of these days. And kill my Custard. But he doesn't listen. Thinks I'm a nag.'

There was more cause for her to nag in the dining room. Spread out all over the table were the hundreds of parts that went to make up a 1:32 scale model of Sir Francis Drake's flagship *The Golden Hind*.

'I've told him if he doesn't get a move on and finish it, I'll bin the bloomin' lot quicker than he can say Spanish Armada.'

Brenda had gone to some lengths to smarten up the spare room for my stay. She'd bought a new matching duvet and curtain set in vintage rose pink. She'd added a pretty bow to the lampshade and there was a new knitted cover on the tissue box on the bedside cabinet.

There was even a little cushion on the pillow, recently embroidered at her crafting class. 'Home Sweet Home.'

A very kind and tender touch.

And Bob had done a good job of clearing the room of clutter. At least on the face of it.

When I opened the built-in wardrobe, it was stacked high with shoe boxes, secondhand books of indeterminate age and value, and biscuit tins going back to the '30s. Judging by the weight, they were all empty, the objects of a collection amassed, presumably, for its own sake.

I squeezed half my stuff onto an exposed section of hanging rail. The rest could live in the case. I didn't mind. I was grateful to have a low-rent bunkhouse a reasonable commute from my new job.

Time for bed. I needed to be on top form tomorrow for my first day in wine.

8

Settling Into Shoreditch

My unwanted six o'clock alarm call came in the shape of a full-throttle *Today* programme blasted through from the neighbouring bedroom. Two thousand miles away, across the Mediterranean, I imagined slabs of sandstone detaching themselves from the walls of Jericho.

I would discover that B&B were nothing if not creatures of habit.

Breakfast was consumed at precisely seven-fifteen and consisted of Kellogg's cornflakes, two slices of white toast from an uncut loaf, Anchor butter, and thick-cut marmalade from Sainsbury's.

Tea, never coffee.

And, as befitted a couple who'd lived through levels of privation I will hopefully never know, nothing was ever wasted. Leftover toast was blitzed in the food processor to make breadcrumbs, while used teabags nourished Bob's prize chrysanthemums.

My benefactors were not hard up. In fact, they were not slow to tell me how well off they were, what with Bob's generous civil service pension and Brenda's 'little bit she'd put aside' over the years in case of emergencies. The mortgage had been paid off decades ago and what few holidays they allowed themselves consisted, without fail, of six nights in a static caravan near Eastbourne.

But, like baby boomers everywhere, they'd been brought up not to waste a single thing.

Brenda was a kind, thoughtful and delightful hostess. My perspective of her had been a little different when I was younger. Mum always told me Brenda thought she'd hit the jackpot when she met Bob. Apart from being a lovely man, he was from the nice part of Winchester and Brenda felt she had to posh up. Mum often poked gentle fun at her sister-in-law's new mode of speech – the voice now an octave higher, the frequent references to 'Bob and I' (not 'me and Bob'), the sentences sprinkled with 'marvellous' and 'super'. That, and the royalism, explained why Mum referred to her privately, and with great affection, as *Queen B*.

As I gathered my things together for my first day at Artisan Wines, Brenda's maternal instincts kicked in and, wiping her hands on her apron, she walked me to the front door. In a way, I suppose this *was* my first day at school. Wine school. In London's capital of cool.

'Don't speak to strange men on the underground.'

Brenda smiled ironically, more self aware than I gave her credit for.

'I won't.'

The journey from Bexleyheath to London Bridge took thirty minutes, plus a five-minute hop on the underground to Old Street. This was to be my morning commute. I was a drop of water in the tidal wave of suited bodies surging onto a hundred trains and, once installed, staking their place as close to the doors as possible for a quick getaway at the other end.

Becoming slowly aware of an off-colour aroma emanating from me, I rifled through my bag and found the egg sandwich Brenda had shoved in when I wasn't looking. I glanced around to see who else's nostrils were bothering them. But I needn't have worried. Hardened capital commuters have perfected the art of self-cocooning non-engagement. One young bearded hipster reading a book three feet from my face had developed the ingenious technique of turning each page with his mouth. Next to him, a

modern-day Sloane Ranger applied her make-up effortlessly as the
train swayed and jolted. Every second counted.

I took a deep breath and pushed open the heavy glass doors
that took me into the industrial-chic interior of Artisan Wines, an
old warehouse transformed into premium office space in London's
trendiest *quartier*.

A slim, pretty, nineteen-year-old receptionist with heavily
contoured eyebrows and fake acrylic nails looked up at me from her
desk. With her tinted black hair and plumped-up lips she looked
like a Bratz doll. Then her face broke into a smile that would melt
the iciest of hearts and I was instantly disarmed.

Kellie took a while to find my name on Cécile's list of
appointments for the day (which didn't do my blood pressure any
favours), largely because she kicked off by looking at the previous
week's diary. A mistake Intext Jennifer might easily have made.
When she blushed at her own stupidity, I liked her even more.

She walked me through a large open-plan office and I felt the
familiar pang of self-consciousness as several pairs of eyes glanced
over at the new 'kid' on the block.

Cécile was standing by the window of her glass-walled office,
chatting on the phone, looking immaculate in velvet-and-lace
Valentino cut to perfection. She smiled and beckoned me inside
and gestured to an empty armchair. While she wrapped up her call I
took in the uncluttered workspace, the business-ready ultraportable
laptop, the Hermes handbag.

'Lovely to finally have you here.'

'I'm delighted to be here.'

'So … the plan. To shadow me. Then, ultimately, to build your
own portfolio of clients.'

'Okay. Sounds good.' *Sounds buttock-clenching, but fine.*

'But first, I think it would be good to get you some basic training
with one of my sales staff. What do you think?'

'I think I'd be grateful for basic training.'

She smiled. 'Relax. You can do this.'

'That's what I keep trying to tell myself.'

Lee held the sales record at Artisan Wines. A clean-cut thirty-something in a slim-fitting mid-grey suit, he looked every inch the ace salesman. He had an easy smile, a charming manner and a penchant for practical jokes (stepping over an imaginary wire and seeing who would copy him caught Kellie out twice in my first week). But with his work head on, he was a wizard with clients and I picked up a lot, making notes whenever he was on the phone and watching him interact on Skype.

'The trick to making a sale is making the customer *want* to buy. And you do that by making them believe that what you're selling is too good to miss.'

'FOMO.'

'Exactly. Luckily for us, we have top product. Which we can genuinely believe in. Clients see that. So it practically sells itself.'

Lucky indeed. And his words made perfect sense. I could see that selling wasn't rocket science and Lee's smooth patter was very persuasive.

But putting it into practice myself would be a very different kettle of fish.

The more time I spent professionally with Cécile, the more impressed I was by her. She could read a twenty-page report and distill it into a couple of sentences and could switch from VDPs and AOCs to bounce rates and costs-per-click in the blink of an eye.

And I learned more about her as a person.

As the daughter of a British diplomat and a French ballerina, she'd had a rarefied upbringing, spent mainly in Paris. But the family had a 'place' in Saint Emilion, the medieval village half an hour from Bordeaux, and that's where her summers had been spent.

She'd walked, cycled and swum in the lake at Blasimon, a name that still had the power to make her misty-eyed. And she'd haunted the glorious vineyards of France's most famous wine region, fascinated by the magic that turns soil and fruit and sunshine into something delicious. It was no surprise that the region captured her heart.

Her heart was also captured by young men. First came Jean-Yves, the son of a vineyard labourer. But her parents discouraged a liaison with someone from the manual class and shipped young Cécile off to an elderly aunt in Arles with instructions to focus on her education and her future as an advocate in Paris.

But she seemed destined to thwart her parents' wishes when, a couple of years later, her heart was captured by Charles Davenport, a young army captain she met at a formal dinner in London hosted by her father. She threw up her studies and, within six weeks, had married Charles and settled into a new life in England as an army wife.

She felt her disobedience was being punished when, less than two years into the marriage, Charles died suddenly of a heart attack, triggered by an allergic reaction to a wasp sting.

'They called it Kounis Syndrome. One person in a hundred thousand. That person was my husband.'

Charles's best friend, George, supported his friend's young widow and helped her manage Charles's finances. George Winstanley slowly became her mentor and, perhaps inevitably, her lover.

With George's support, Cécile regained her confidence, rebuilt her badly fractured relationship with her parents, reclaimed her French heritage and her love of Bordeaux, and carved out a career in the wine trade.

Then her beloved George died and her heart was broken again.

But here she was, aged sixty, a still-beautiful, highly successful businesswoman.

An example of strength, skill, survival.

I could think of no better role model.

I gradually eased into life at the office and enjoyed Lee's company. And I developed a real soft spot for Kellie.

She lived with her dad and two younger brothers in a high-rise block a ten-minute walk and a world away from the office. She'd been forced to take on the role of mother and housewife at 17 when her mum had buggered off with a BT engineer who came to sort out the internet and discovered more hotspots than he'd bargained for.

While her dad spent every waking hour flying up and down the M1 in an HGV to keep the family canoe afloat, Kellie put her younger brothers out to school every morning, and every evening made their dinner, supervised their homework and taught them how to use the washing machine. And held down a full-time job.

I bloody love women.

***

Three weeks in and I had my first glimpse of Harry Sinclair, one of Cécile's top clients and one whose account I was being groomed to take over.

Cécile had given me the gen on Harry.

He was affectionately known as El Dorado (the Golden One) for his knack of making money hand over fist. He'd made his fortune off the back of the financial crash in '87, investing heavily in commercial property. He knew the right people, and a few of the wrong people. Now in his sixties, and wealthy beyond measure, he could easily retire but would never slow down while there were still deals to make.

And to his considerable portfolio of interests and investments, he'd added fine wine. With Cécile's advice, he'd amassed one of the most impressive private collections in Europe.

At precisely two minutes before the appointed time of 11 am, Harry strolled into Cécile's office in sharp suit and shades, with skin the colour of wealth.

He greeted me graciously by name without being introduced and kissed Cécile warmly on both cheeks, four times in her Parisian way, then quickly settled down to business.

I sat quietly while Cécile and Harry discussed the merits of the last five vintages and their investment potential. I paid attention to how Cécile finessed new 'products' and to how Harry reacted to her suggestions.

He shook my hand warmly as he left and wished me well in Bordeaux. Here was a man who did his homework. The personal touch was important to him.

It would need to be important to me.

9

Fur and Feathers

Weekdays were full on and I was getting the hang of life as a wine professional and a London commuter.

But I did look forward to weekends and the chance to drop down a couple of gears.

This particular weekend, Bob and Brenda announced they were off to Canterbury. Bob had his eye on a sixty-piece Royal Worcester dinner service that was coming up for auction. It would fit nicely with the other eight sets currently gathering dust in the garage.

'We need to set off early. Bob isn't the driver he used to be. I sometimes wonder if he can see the road at all.'

As they pulled away, I hoped they'd make it to Canterbury in one piece (and made a mental note never to get into a car with Uncle Bob behind the wheel).

At the end of the driveway, the car juddered to a halt. I wondered if Bob was searching for the road. Brenda got out and shouted up to me.

'You will remember to feed Custard, won't you, dear?'

'Don't worry. You just enjoy yourselves. And stay safe.'

Brenda gave me the doleful look of the condemned woman and climbed back in. Then Bob's orange Austin Allegro lurched out onto the public highway.

Custard was Brenda's pride and joy. A surrogate little one. They'd never had children (a problem with Bob's plumbing, Mum had always said) and Custard the canary went some way to filling that unfortunate hole.

The feathered fellow currently flitting around in the corner of the lounge was the fourth Custard iteration. On average, canaries live ten years, Brenda told me, but the previous little chap had held on for thirteen, a lucky number for him.

But, a creature of habit, Brenda had never changed the name.

As the orange Allegro disappeared from view, I felt a guilty sense of elation at what felt like freedom. A whole Sunday to myself. No *Archers Omnibus*, no *Countryfile*, no *Antiques Roadshow*.

I could go mad. Watch trashy TV, order a Hot and Spicy from Domino's, put away a whole tub of Ben and Jerry's.

But first I had to earn it.

I emptied the dishwasher, put the bath mats on to wash, straightened the cushions in the lounge, and tidied away a pile of clothes lying over the back of Brenda's armchair.

One of these was a full-length fur coat – one of Bob's latest antique fair acquisitions, sold as having belonged to fifties icon and all-round glamourpuss, Diana Dors, with an apparent letter of authentication to prove its provenance and, with it, its age and pre-ban credentials. It hardly seemed the kind of thing Brenda would wear so, like pretty much everything else Bob picked up in the line of antique, vintage, and plain-old knackered, it had been bought on a whim. A purchase made for the sake of it.

I slipped it on. It didn't look half bad. There was still something of the Dors about my figure and the coat complemented my curves rather nicely. I felt at home in it.

Sensing that some of the coat's Hollywood glamour was beginning to rub off on me, I settled down in its luxurious folds to bingewatch *Breaking Bad*, a recommendation of Lee's.

Halfway through the episode where Walter shows Jesse how to make the purest crystal meth, I remembered my promise to feed Custard.

As I filled up his little seed tray, I found myself pitying him, a creature built for the skies spending what might be thirteen years cooped up inside a metal cage no bigger than a microwave, with only plastic mirrors and toy bells for company.

A little (controlled) freedom couldn't do him any harm.

I checked that all windows and doors were firmly closed. Then, feeling a little like a modern-day St Francis of Assisi, I flicked open the tiny wire door of his cage to give him a taste of liberty.

It might have been the unexpected sight of a fur-clad five-foot-one mammal on two legs, but something clearly spooked poor old Custard and he shot out of the cage as if fired from a cannon, slamming straight into the gilt-framed mirror that hung over the fireplace.

SMACK!

A ball of senseless yellow feathers dropped like a stone onto the Axminster.

I stood for four long seconds with my mouth wide open. Then I dashed over and stared at the comatose canary and examined him for signs of life.

Not a single flutter of a single feather.

This could be curtains for Custard.

I grabbed my phone and Googled concussion in birds, a search that threw up more than one video of vodka-fuelled hen-night shenanigans, plus the gnomic quotation 'the bird that flies at the window means death is knocking at the door.'

A mirror wasn't a window. But was it close enough?

I began to feel sick.

I finally alighted on an RSPB article with what seemed like sound advice – put the stunned bird in a box lined with soft cloth and place him somewhere quiet to recuperate.

I snatched a bra from the drying frame in the hall, scooped up Custard, wrapped him in the double D, and lowered him slowly into an empty cornflakes box from the recycling bin and laid him in the airing cupboard under the stairs, hoping for a reboot.

That was Plan A.

Plan B? Hope that the Pets At Home on Dartford Road had a replacement canary that would pass muster.

Plan C? Make a full confession.

Two tense hours went by, the interval the RSPB bird whisperer told me was decisive. If your wobbly warbler hasn't recovered by then, he isn't going to.

I peeked inside the cornflakes packet.

His little feathery chest was rising and falling like a good 'un. Relief.

I cupped him in the lacy double D, carried him over to the cage as if he were a live grenade, and laid him gently on the cage floor.

By the time the orange Allegro was stuttering up the drive, the fur coat was hanging innocently in Brenda's wardrobe and the little fellow was up on his perch, whistling away like Roger Whittaker on speed.

The auction had been a bust. To make up for not bagging the Worcester, Bob had filled the space in the car with a six-month supply of the loo rolls on offer that week in Lidl, plus another toy bell to add to Custard's collection.

Brenda greeted her surrogate child with all the clucking indulgence of a mother hen.

'Have you been a good boy for Jennifer?'

Thank God birds can't talk.

Bob walked past her to inspect a bird-shaped smudge on the mantel mirror.

'You're slipping in your old age, love.'

'What?'

'This mirror's bloody filthy.'

10

Excursion Intrusion

Cécile had news.

She was in talks with a wine company in New Zealand about a possible business relationship. The kiwis were currently schmoozing a 'high net worth individual' in Gstaad, the Swiss ski resort favoured by the world's beautiful people, and had invited Cécile out for an overnighter to talk shop. Private jet. Luxury chalet. Hot tub overlooking the Saanerslochgrat peak.

'Would you like to accompany me?'

Does a dingo do his do-do in the desert?

'Sounds wonderful. If you're sure I won't be in the way.'

'Not at all. I'll be glad of the company. And it's all part of your training.'

My old faithful suitcase would do for Blackpool and the Costas but it was far too knackered for this gig.

Plus it was the size of a four-man bobsleigh.

I imagined Cécile had a piece of Louis Vuitton of every size and for every occasion. I explained my predicament to Brenda over our dinner of liver and bacon.

'I've got just the thing.'

She jumped up from the table, scurried up to the bedroom, and returned seconds later with the answer to my fix – a paisley-pattern carpet bag she'd bought for her honeymoon in Bournemouth. In 1967.

It looked like a bag Mary Poppins might use as carry-on luggage, but it had a certain retro chic and I thanked Brenda sincerely for her kindness.

***

After coffee and pastries in a stylish lounge in an eerily deserted corner of the airport devoid of queues, we were whisked across the tarmac and onto the gorgeous little plane.

Speedy boarding indeed.

Cécile turned to me. 'Is this your first time in a Learjet?'

'Me? Oh no. It's the only way I fly. I usually take one to Waitrose.'

She smiled. 'My first time, too. But *they* don't need to know that.'

We clinked our champagne flutes and tucked into the most delicious smoked salmon I'd ever tasted as the jet banked over the English channel and set a course for the Swiss alps.

Gstaad is a picture-perfect alpine village set in a wide valley between pine-covered foothills dwarfed by the drama of the Bernese Oberland. Being there is like stepping inside a Christmas card, even in May.

Our limousine deposited us at the entrance to the Gstaad Palace Hotel, the venue for our meeting. As I breathed in crisp alpine air and took in the opulent scene, a scarlet Ferrari pulled up beside me and a woman in Ray Bans and a fur coat (not unlike the one that had freaked out poor old Custard) stepped out and stood for a few seconds, waiting to be noticed.

This was clearly *not* my kind of place.

After polite introductions, we were seated for a working lunch of truffle cheese fondue in the hotel's *La Fromagerie* restaurant. While Cécile and the bigwigs batted about words and phrases that might as well have been a conversation in biblical Aramaic for the amount of it I followed, I smiled and nodded sagely, noting that the crisp white Chenin Blanc I was trying not to guzzle was cutting nicely through the creaminess of the cheese. *Check me out!*

Their esoteric discussions continued well into the afternoon. Then, after another round of handshakes and smiles and a flurry of exchanged cards, the meeting was finally at an end. We were, Cécile told me, one step closer to a business relationship with the kiwis.

Outside in the winter wonderland, darkness had descended and this impossibly swish spot had pulled on an evening gown of twinkling fairy lights. The pistes were closed for the day and those few well-heeled young skiers who were catching the rump of the season had decamped to the village's bars to down cocktails or glasses of hot punch.

Our overnight accommodation was the epitome of luxury living – a secluded and expansive chalet in the traditional style spread over three stripped-oak floors and sprinkled liberally with sumptuous leather sofas and armchairs, fur-covered beds and open fireplaces. Silver candelabras adorned the gleaming twelve-seater table in the middle of the dining-room. In the corner, a grand piano. Steinway. I wondered if Burt Bacharach would be tinkling the ivories as part of this executive package. Looking around at the level of opulence, I wouldn't have been a bit surprised.

I unpacked Brenda's carpet bag in a bedroom the size of a gym hall – fur rugs, crackling fire, three-acre bed. The level of luxury was starting to make me feel uncomfortable.

'What do you think?' Cécile was leaning against the door.

'I don't know. It's lovely …'

'But …'

'I just feel a little … guilty.'

'I know what you mean. An ill-divided world and all that.'

'I know you're used to it.'

'I am. And my business, *our* business, is part of that luxury world. We sell expensive things to rich people.'

She looked me squarely in the eye.

'But that doesn't mean it's *all* we are. And it doesn't change *who* we are. As long as we don't let it. We can move in this world with confidence but not allow it to rule us. And make us blind to other things. Noble things.'

I hoped she was right.

For my part, I wasn't sure I'd ever be entirely confident moving in this world, certainly not to the extent Cécile was, but I resolved to try. And not to beat myself up any more about spending twenty-four hours in the lap of luxury. The trick (and the pleasure) was to appreciate it as a privilege and never see it as a right.

And I had a whole evening of appreciation to myself.

Cécile was meeting an old friend for dinner (I didn't ask). An evening confined to barracks was no hardship for me when the barracks were so splendid. These were my reflections as I soaked away my guilt in the biggest hot tub in the Western world, champagne in hand, gazing out at the Saanerslochgrat peak. Tomorrow evening, I'd be back in a Bexleyheath semi with tea and a gypsy cream, watching reruns of *Last of the Summer Wine*.

I decided to exercise my bragging rights so I called Will on FaceTime audio.

'Guess where I am?'

'Lying under a handsome, rich, well-hung wine buyer.'

'Don't be filthy. Hang on. I'll show you.' I switched to video and pointed my phone at the peaks. 'Those peaks, my friend, are the Bernese Oberland. And I'm viewing them from the terrace of the most luxurious chalet you've ever seen in your life. I'm in the hot tub.'

'Impressive. But you might want to press the Switch Image button. I'm getting a fabulous view of your double-D peaks.'

By midnight, my eyelids were drooping and Cécile still wasn't back from her dinner. I didn't know whether to be worried or not. I didn't want to call, for fear of interrupting something, and of coming across as the flapping tenderfoot I knew myself to be, so I wandered through the chalet's numerous rooms for ten minutes, wondering what to do.

Should I lock the front door? I didn't imagine Cécile had taken a key. And what about the alarm system? It had a control panel only slightly less forbidding than the bank of instruments in the cockpit of a Boeing 767, so I was going nowhere near that.

I decided to go to bed and stop worrying.

As I was dropping off, I heard movement downstairs and, through my semi-slumber, felt relief that Cécile was back safe.

Then a sound made my eyes snap open. Someone was turning the handle of my bedroom door. A feeling in my water told me this was *not* Cécile looking in to check I'd brushed my teeth and the feeling was confirmed when a gloved hand stole round the edge of the door. Petrified, I lay stock still and half-closed my eyes. A tall male silhouette emerged silently into the room and I clamped my eyes shut and feigned the breathing of the deeply asleep.

The intruder moved slowly round the room and I was aware of him lifting objects as he went. For a couple of seconds, I considered leaping out of bed to confront him. But what if he was armed? Or manically high on something?

It struck me that the downside of privacy and seclusion is that no-one can hear you scream.

After what was probably only thirty seconds but felt like ten minutes, the figure left the room, pulling the door quietly to. Another thirty seconds later, I heard him rifling through drawers and cupboards downstairs.

I snatched up my phone. Cécile answered in the afterglow tones of someone whose evening has been a success.

'Sorry it's so late. I'm just coming up the drive.'

I spoke in a whisper.

'Someone's broken into the chalet.'

'Are you alright?'

'I'm fine. He was in my bedroom but I pretended to be asleep. He's downstairs now.'

'Don't leave your room. I'm phoning the police.'

With typical Swiss efficiency, in less than a minute the drive was filled with sirens and lights. I heard a French window yanked open and the thud of a heavy landing, presumably following a leap from the balcony.

The Swiss detective gave us an almighty dressing-down – all the more almighty delivered in German – for leaving the door unlocked. Then, satisfied we'd learned our lesson, he walked us round the chalet with the local agent from Red Carpet Rentals, noting what items had been stolen. The list included the candelabra from the dining room (natch), a top-of-the-range Bose bluetooth speaker, and a silver carriage clock in the art nouveau style.

This had been a discerning thief. And one with a penchant for retro chic.

He'd also nicked Brenda's carpet bag.

11

A Date and a Disaster

Before I knew it, it was my last few days at the office.

Ever since I'd told her about my scare in Switzerland, and about how shitty I'd felt explaining to Brenda about the theft of her precious honeymoon heirloom, Kellie had been very attentive, plying me with tea and asking after my welfare at two-hour intervals.

And, out of the blue, came an invitation to her flat. That evening.

'I'm not much of a cook but I'll knock something up. And you can meet my dad and my brothers.'

I was spending my pre-Bordeaux evenings sweating over sales reports and (still) trawling through Hugh Johnson to get all the *appellations*, *crus* and vintages into my thick skull. Time was precious.

But this was a kind-hearted gesture from a young woman I'd really warmed to and who'd come to regard me as something of a mother figure (which I hoped wasn't a reflection on my motherly figure).

Plus the invitation gave me a perfect excuse to give Brenda's toad-in-the-hole (approximate calorie count: three thousand) a deft body swerve. Win win.

Kellie's flat was on the tenth floor of a tower block in the kind of multi-ethnic community East London does very well. Not glamorous or photogenic but alive with colours and smells and sounds that make you feel like you haven't seen enough of the world.

And it was a *community*. In the three of four hundred yards between the main road and Kellie's block, seven people greeted her by name. I counted them. Some younger than her, most very much older, all with a smile and a joke. One, a West Indian man in what looked like a demob suit, with a nice line in flattery.

'This your glamorous sister?'

He winked and walked on and we both guffawed.

'What a great neighbourhood!'

'It *is* nice. Great people. And the flat's okay. Bit small.'

We walked into the building. There was a handwritten *Out Of Order* sign stuck on the lift door.

'It's alright until this happens.'

'How often does the lift break down?'

'About twice a week. A guy comes out, pulls open a panel and does something with his screwdriver, and it comes back on. Two days later, it's knackered again.'

'And you're on the *tenth* floor?'

'Sorry. Works up an appetite.'

Yeah. And it's no wonder you're a size eight.

The tiny hallway was a jumble of school bags, jackets and shoes and the battle sounds blasting from an Xbox confirmed that Kellie's brothers were home.

'They'll come out of their room when they're hungry.'

'I suppose even a virtual army marches on its stomach.'

Kellie's dad, Kenny, was as bulky as his daughter was skinny, with wardrobe shoulders and arms the size of ham hocks. I didn't imagine anyone on the estate messed with him.

Kellie disappeared into the kitchen as her dad rose from a recliner, shook my hand warmly, and told me (in a voice a couple of octaves higher than I'd expected) that his little girl thought I was 'a diamond.'

'Well, I think she's a darling. She's made this last month run very smoothly for me.'

'She's a good girl.'

'She is indeed.'

He gestured to the sofa and lowered himself back into his recliner, under a poster for the film *Heat*, with De Niro and Pacino facing each other up.

'Do you have a team?'

'Sorry?'

'Football.'

'Right. No. Never really interested me. You?'

'West Ham. Need you ask. I'm a regular Alf Garnett.'

I smiled. In looks, Kenny was a million miles away from the bald, moustached, bespectacled misery guts from the 70s sitcom.

'Don't get to the games much these days. I'm on the road a lot at weekends.'

'Yes. Kellie's told me how hard you work.'

'Not as hard as she does. She's a bloody angel. Pardon my French.'

'The two of you make a bloody good team. Pardon *my* French.'

Kenny smiled. 'You're not wrong.'

I glanced round the room. He followed my eyes.

'Not exactly the Ritz.'

'It's very comfortable. And your neighbours seem lovely. And look at that view!'

The winter sun was setting over the Thames, snaking its way east to Greenwich, Tilbury and the sea.

'Yeah. And, up here, no twitching curtains.'

Sensing the preparation of food, the boys had emerged and were banging about in the kitchen, much to Kellie's irritation. There were animated voices.

She came through to the living room with two plates of pasta bolognese and set them down on the table in the corner.

'The boys want pizza. I'll take them to Papa John's. We might go bowling after. Is that okay?'

Kenny and I exchanged a glance. He smiled and shook his head in mock exasperation.

'I can read you like a book, my girl.'

'I don't know what you mean.'

The front door slammed and Kenny and I were alone. 'I'm sorry. This wasn't my idea.' He stood up and went into the kitchen. 'It's fine. It's actually very sweet.' Kenny returned with an open bottle of Asda Chianti and two glasses.

'She means well. She just misses her mum.'

'Yes.'

Kenny poured the wine and clinked my glass. 'Here's to scheming and well-meaning daughters.'

'I'll drink to that.'

We both saw the funny side of Kellie's shameless matchmaking effort and, with the awkwardness out of the way and with us both instinctively knowing there was no romance in the air, we relaxed and had a pleasant evening.

Kenny was, as my mum would have said, 'a big soft soap with a big heart'. He opened up a lot about his marriage. Hadn't had the faintest idea anything was wrong until he got his wife's note, telling him she'd been unhappy for years, bored with their life together, and wanted some excitement for herself. This, she imagined, could be found in the arms of a twenty-eight-year-old BT engineer.

'Do you think she'll ever come back?'

'No idea.'

'Would you take her back?'

'Probably. That's how much of a soft sod I am.' His smile was rueful. 'What about you? Would you take your fella back?'

Not even a nanosecond of thought.

'No. No chance. I'm a completely different person. No room for him in my life now.'

'Nobody else on the horizon?'

I thought about David Harwood. His wedding. Whether he'd been a wasted opportunity.

'No.' I lifted my glass. 'Being alone isn't so bad.'

'No. Not if you've got good friends.'

***

My last day got me out of the office.

Lee was doing some of his 'bread and butter' selling – the low- to mid-range wines to local businesses, the kinds of places whose accounts weren't hitting the big numbers but whose custom was regular and kept the business ticking along nicely. It was good, he said, to get out of the office and do some old-school selling.

'Keeps you on your toes and makes you grateful for the big stuff,' he told me, as he lugged his wheelie down the steps at Old Street tube.

Our first stop was a wine bar in Clapham. Exposed brick, stripped floors, twenty-something bar staff in tight black T-shirts. Clientele happy to pay fifteen pounds a glass for something they believed was special.

Lee was pitching a 2015 reserve from Léoville Barton, the 'second' wine from this prestigious chateau and one that, with our economies of scale, came in at sixteen pounds a bottle and sold in places like this for anywhere between sixty and eighty.

I watched him uncork it with his 'waiter's friend' and a very practised hand. The manager liked it but was initially non-committal. Lee swirled it with the flick of the wrist I was still practising with water in B&B's kitchen and, as he swirled and sniffed, he dropped in an anecdote about the time he'd visited the vineyard and helped with the harvest when he was twenty. That seemed to do the trick and the result was a solid order.

Lee was good.

As we made our way back to the Tube, I quizzed him.

'Was that true? About the harvest?'

'Absolutely. I never tell an out-and-out lie in order to make a sale. Which isn't to say I don't embellish a bit.'

The thing that impressed me most about him, as we criss-crossed the city with his wheelie full of samples, was his sheer positivity. He never went in without a broad smile, he always engaged fully with the client – even the most dismissive and sour-faced – and he always expected a sale. And usually got it.

'You have to be pleasant *and* persistent. The sell isn't made with shyness and reserve. I'm always polite – I back off if they're clearly not interested – but I cajole and tease and nudge until the deal's done. I'm an Olympic nudger.'

Our last call was a high-end hotel off Grosvenor Square. Ornate plasterwork, marble floors, antique furniture polished daily.

An austere sommelier caught sight of Lee's wheelie and strode past us, not even acknowledging our presence.

Lee's phone rang. 'Sorry. I'll have to take this. Can you open a bottle of the 2004 so old Vinegar Face can decant it?' He stepped outside.

My hands started to shake. The 2004 was £27 a bottle to us. £150 to the affluent diners in a joint like this.

I stabbed my thumb with the cutter but eventually got the foil off, less cleanly than I'd have wanted. I got the screw in relatively straight and the lever anchored on the lip of the bottle neck. Then I heaved.

Nothing.

Sweating, I looked around. A silver-haired diner in a lavender blazer with a white rose in the lapel glanced my way. I took three small steps to the side to be out of his eyeline, gripped the bottle between my thighs and tugged, feeling my face turn the colour of the bottle's contents.

As the cork finally yielded to my unbecoming tug of war, the kitchen door was shouldered open and struck me squarely on the left buttock, firing the bottle from my hand and spilling the waiter's cargo – a tray of silverware – all over my back. The Léoville Barton exploded on the marble floor and my incompetence took the form of a claret stain four feet across and spreading.

I turned in numb horror to see Lee dashing over.

'Don't worry. I've done that more times than I care to remember.' He beckoned a waitress over and asked for a mop. She hurried off and returned with a bucket and two cloths. I stood in a mute stupor, holding back tears, while Lee and the waitress, on their knees, mopped up a chunk of my wages.

They'd removed almost all trace of my ineptitude by the time old Vinegar Face put in an appearance.

Lee piped up. 'I'm really sorry. My hand just slipped. It happens to the best of us, I guess.'

'You guess wrong,' glowered old Vinegar Face.

'I'll come back some other time.'

'Good idea.'

We bumped the wheelie down the hotel steps, past the liveried commissionaire.

'You needn't have taken the blame for my stupidity.'

'It wasn't stupidity. It was bad luck. Some corks are sent to try us. It might happen to me tomorrow. Don't worry about it.'

I grimaced. 'I'll try not to.'

'Seriously. Let it go. You'll open hundreds of bottles during your three months in Bordeaux. You might drop another half dozen. But you'll get experience and, with it, confidence. That's all you're lacking.'

I'd needed his calm reassurance. Having him as a coach, a mentor, had been not just helpful but necessary this past month.

How would I cope in a foreign country, with a foreign language I could barely speak, in a business that still felt pretty foreign?

There was only one way I was going to find out.

***

As I put the final few items inside my big case, Brenda clucked round me maternally.

'And always keep your handbag close to your chest. Don't leave it dangling.'

'I've travelled all round the world, Auntie Brenda. I'll be fine.'

'And what about the sun?'

'What about it?'

She was gone. Sprinting up the stairs two at a time. I shot a quizzical look at Bob. He shrugged as if to say, *I don't even* try *working her out these days.*

From the bedroom above we heard a shriek. She came barrelling down the stairs, a sunhat from the Joan Collins stable in one hand and, in the other, the Diana Dors fur coat that had freaked out poor old Custard.

Well, what was left of it.

The glamorous garment was a loose mass of cascading shreds. A sort of leopardskin Hanging Gardens of Babylon.

She launched into Bob.

'You said you were going to treat it for moths! With camphor cakes!'

'It was hanging in your wardrobe, so I thought *you'd* done it!'

'Where would *I* get hold of camphor cakes?!'

'Balls!'

'What?'

'Camphor *balls*!'

12

Shaken. Then Stirred.

'You all right, love?'

The waiter balanced his tray of lager with the skill of a juggler as another monster wave slammed into the side of the *La Rochelle*, fighting her way across the bay that is home to some of the Atlantic Ocean's fiercest weather.

I forced a smile and willed my stomach to hold onto its contents. 'Fine.'

'Biscay's a bit of a bugger if you're not used to it. Fresh air might help.'

'Thanks.'

He strolled off to deliver his order to the lads in replica Spurs tops whose steady intake of Stella was soaking up the worst of the ship's game of pitch and toss.

I gripped the edge of the table and tried not to look at my half-eaten and ill-advised plate of strawberry cheesecake as it slid off the table and landed cake-down on the floor.

The waiter strolled over and picked it up and wiped up the mess. 'Sorry.'

He smiled. 'It's fine.'

'How do you do manage to stay upright?'

'Sea legs. Twenty years in the Merchant Navy.' He passed me a wad of napkins and a sick bag.

'Take the plane next time?'

'Probably.'

Flying had been the plan. Then I'd bumped into Trev, my old friend from French conversation classes who worked for Brittany Ferries. Kind, thoughtful, permanently single Trev had pushed the offer of a free crossing from Portsmouth to Bilbao with such delight at the opportunity to help that I hadn't had the heart to tell him: a. that I hated sailing, and b. that Bilbao wasn't exactly round the corner from Bordeaux. But, eager as ever not to cause offence, I accepted his kindness.

And here I was. Stuck in a perfect storm with no George Clooney to save the day and a bunch of Spurs supporters growing more head-splittingly vulgar by the pint.

'Not long now.' My waiter deposited a glass of water by my elbow. 'Believe it or not, this isn't bad for Biscay. And when you've done it a few dozen times, you actually enjoy the rollercoaster ride.'

The word 'rollercoaster' brought to mind my experience a few years before on the Master Blaster on Clarence Pier, when the ride operator had clocked the billow potential of my skirt and fired us high into the clear blue sky at maximum velocity, re-acquainting me with my lunch and treating the whole of Southsea to a fine view of my salmon pink V-kinis.

By the time the *La Rochelle* was easing its bulk into Bilbao, the Spurs boys were feeling the pain of their Stellafest and I was thanking a God I didn't believe in for keeping my innards from becoming outtards.

It was a two-hour bus ride from Bilboa to Hendaye, just over the border in France, where I'd pick up a train to Bordeaux.

At Hendaye station, I got into a fight with a ticket machine.

A thick northeast accent piped up behind me. 'Try using euros, pet.'

I looked at my hand. I was feeding pound coins into a French machine. I turned round to see a smirking man in chinos with, behind him, a line of half a dozen quietly seething French travellers.

'Don't worry. They'll wait. The trains are all over the place today, anyway. Industrial action. Bloody frogs always on strike about something. Fancy a coffee? I'm Tony. But my mates call me Geordie. An army nickname that stuck.'

'On holiday?' Geordie took a sip from his double espresso.

'Actually I'm here for work.' I explained about my mid-life change of career and my misgivings about my aptitude. 'How about you?'

'Visiting my ex-wife. Our son turns sixteen next week. Don't get to see him much these days. He's more French than English now. So I've got to make a big effort with this stuff.' He patted a phrasebook on the table that looked a lot like the one in my handbag. 'Not easy for a simple lad like me.'

I detected a sadness beneath the cheeky-chappie twinkle and in the hours we had to wait for our train, I learned its origin. Tours in the Falklands had shaken him up. Then came Bosnia. He'd seen too much of the mindless evil that people can inflict on each other.

'I used to bottle it up. Hardly ever talked. Then when I did, what came out was anger. And my wife was usually in the firing line.'

He shook his head.

'She was absolutely right to divorce me. Nightmares, flashbacks. It was too much to ask anyone to put up with. We're piecing something together again. But it'll only ever be friendship now.'

He smiled.

'I'll have to settle for that.'

'That's worth a lot. There's no way I could make space in my head for a friendship with *my* ex.'

'It *is* worth a lot. Life's much better now. Better than I thought it could ever be when I was out of my face on cheap cider and sleeping in doorways. We're all of us only three steps away from being on the streets.'

I pictured myself standing at Viv's door with my suitcase. A lifetime ago.

'You're right. Life's a lot better now.'

As my train sped through the flat Gascony countryside towards Bordeaux, I thought about Geordie and his PTSD and I was transported back to my childhood. We didn't have a name for it then but the blackness that had settled on my dad's soul was born of multiple tours in Northern Ireland.

The initial excitement of his return always dissolved within a day or two, replaced by fear and confusion and the sounds of the raised voices downstairs that my bedroom radio could never drown out.

Then came the frequent benders. The lock-ins. The lost weekends.

But there were normal days. Fun days in the park. Picnics. Rounders on the beach. And I grew up thinking this constant, violent up and down was just what married life was.

The announcement that we were approaching Bordeaux jolted me back to my reality and I prepared myself for the last leg of this ridiculous journey, the thirty- minute train ride to Saint Emilion, my final destination.

As you pull into the medieval village with its spire, its honeyed sandstone, and its ever-present vines, it's easy to see why the UNESCO World Heritage people gave it the thumbs-up in 1999. The Romans planted grapes here round about the time the Emperor Hadrian's brickies were throwing up a wall in the north of England to keep out the troublesome Picts and all the other rabble-rousing ancient Britons.

And wine is everywhere. Now one of the biggest names in Bordeaux, it wasn't (my Hugh Johnson notes tell me) featured in the famous 1855 classification of Bordeaux wines that still dominates the industry in the region to this day, only getting its classification a hundred years later. But it hasn't hung about since then and its expert blends (merlot-heavy and with cabernet sauvignon, cabernet franc and a bit of malbec) are famous the world over.

I'd arrived in wine central.

I wondered if the somnolent sixty-something bear with the drooping moustache was the man I'd been told to look out for. I tapped on the window of his little white van and the bear stirred.

'Ah! Madame Jen-nee-fair!'

Benoit leapt out of the van, grabbed my considerable luggage, deposited it in the back, and hopped over to open the passenger door.

Soon we'd left the ancient cobbled streets of the village behind and the windscreen was filled with rolling hills and vast fields of emerald-green vines stretching as far as my Biscayed eyes could see.

Benoit kept up a rapid-fire commentary on the scenery, his marriage and (accompanied by frequent smacks of his ample abdomen) his love for his wife, Sylvie, particularly for her prowess as a cook. Judging by the evident tension on the buttons of his blue-check shirt, Sylvie was a real crowd-pleaser in the kitchen.

With my high-school French now supplemented by a year's worth of weekly conversation classes with my old friend Trev, I was picking up about twenty percent of Benoit's banter. Not a bad strike rate.

But, as we all know, receiving is much easier than transmitting and so far I'd only managed 'Oui' and its more exotic variant 'Ah! Oui.'

It wasn't exactly Proust.

Benoit mopped his brow, pointed heavenwards and said something about the weather. Something framed like a question. Which required an answer.

'Ah! Oui,' I ventured and flapped my hand in front of my face in the manner of a Southern belle. 'Je suis chaude.'

The van swerved and the look on Benoit's face told me his flabber had been thoroughly gasted. Then he erupted with laughter.

'Non, non, non! C'est pas ça qu'vous voulez dire! Ah non!'

More gales of laughter.

I pulled the phrasebook from my handbag and flicked through it frantically. I couldn't imagine what the problem was. I'd even remembered that, because I'm female, any adjective describing me needed to have an 'e' on the end – so 'chaud' becomes 'chaude'. I was quite pleased with myself for remembering a rule learned thirty years ago.

Benoit continued to wipe away tears of hilarity as I lifted my eyes from the phrasebook and caught my first glimpse of Château Paulus, picture perfect in the afternoon sun, its pale stone walls and narrow shuttered windows like something from a landscape by Cézanne.

As we pulled up to the chateau's imposing façade, my phrasebook offered me a cross-reference that made the blood sprint to my cheeks – under *chaud* in the section on *Weather* it said *see also Sex and Relationships*.

A chuckling Benoit unloaded my bags from the back and, newly sick to my stomach, I realised my mistake.

I'd wanted to say 'I'm hot.'

I'd actually said 'I'm horny.'

Benoit was still chuckling as he carried my bags inside and a tall, thin man with salt-and-pepper hair stepped forward to shake my hand.

'Philippe Moreau. Pleased to meet you, Jennifer. You've made a good impression on Benoit, I see.' Philippe's English was as good as my French was ropey.

'I'm afraid I've made a terrible faux pas,' I said, a lump rising in my throat at the thought of my gaffe. I explained the howler.

'Oh, please. A little error of expression. We all make those. If we can make people smile with our mistakes, I think that's a special success.'

Philippe's easy manner and gentle voice put me immediately at my ease and he guided me through to a shady terrace where a willowy woman was seated at a table littered with paperwork.

'You must be tired after such a long journey. I'm sorry our trade unions caused you problems. In France, militancy is never far from the surface and disruption is part of our everyday life.'

I was reflecting that my French would never be as good as Philippe's English even if I stayed in Saint Emilion for a thousand years as the willowy woman stood up from her papers to greet me.

'This is my wife, Madeleine.'

'Hello. Welcome to Château Paulus. We're delighted you'll be working with us.'

In skinny jeans and cotton shirt, Madeleine had something of Cécile's easy elegance about her. She was achingly pretty, with luxuriant chestnut hair, and pale skin that brought out the green of her eyes. But, where Philippe's English was the work of years of study and practice, Madeleine's English was native.

'I'm from a little village near Cheltenham. Came here in '91 as a student. The usual summer grape-picking gig.' She trailed her hand in the water bubbling from an ancient limestone fountain. 'And I just never went back.'

I looked across the terrace and out over vines rising up to the horizon.

'I can understand why you stayed.'

'The place casts a curious and powerful spell. The place and the people.' She shot a look of pure love at her husband and he reciprocated in a way that made me feel I ought to leave them alone.

Madeleine stood up. 'But where are our manners. Let's get you out of this heat and settled into your apartment.'

A small terrier I hadn't noticed roused itself and came over to greet me.

'This is Napoléon,' she said, pronouncing the name the French way and in an accent that sounded native to my ears. 'You'll be seeing a lot of him.'

The little dog's bubbly manner and warmth towards me made me think of my Betty and Eric, the beloved pets I'd been forced to leave behind when Pete had made it clear I was surplus to requirements.

God, I missed my little friends!

My 'apartment' was a generous space in a *new* wing of the chateau (new about three hundred years ago) and consisted of a spacious bedroom, a large bathroom, a light and airy study, and a drawing room the size of a tennis court.

Total area: 124 square metres.

The size of a four-bedroom house in the suburbs of Paris.

Pale yellow walls. White-painted floorboards. Grey-blue dresser. Iron-frame bedstead.

Basically, a collection of plates from the catalogue of quintessential French style.

Then Madeleine steered me round the chateau and I sipped from a cooling *kir royale* as she gave me the tour and filled me in on the household.

The chateau was small by Bordeaux standards and full-time vineyard staff consisted of herself, Philippe and Benoit, supplemented by Gabriel, a Polish man who came over in the spring and stayed until late autumn. Benoit's wife, Sylvie (she of the button-bursting cooking), worked as housekeeper.

So I'd be a very welcome extra pair of hands.

Although more modest than its glamorous Bordeaux cousins, Paulus was still a fine establishment with wide staircases, long corridors and ample public spaces generously furnished with oil paintings and fine antique furniture.

On the first floor, Madeleine lowered her voice as we walked past a heavy oak door.

'Madame Hélène. My mother-in-law.' Madeleine raised an eyebrow. The relationship was clearly not an easy one.

'Sylvie fusses over her. Which makes life bearable, just, for the rest of us. You'll meet her tomorrow. She's not joining us for dinner tonight.'

The considerable delights of Sylvie's dinner were blurred by my intense fatigue – I remember a mouthwatering pâté and a crème brûlée that tasted like clouds – and, within seconds of retiring to my apartment, I fell fast asleep.

Fully clothed.

13

Beauty and the Beast

I awoke to bright sunshine and a female voice cursing in French in the kitchen below.

The household was already astir and I'd slept in. Not a great first impression. I leapt out of bed, took a quick shower, and showed my face.

Sylvie was flicking her dishtowel at Napoléon and the puddle of urine at the kitchen door explained why.

She turned to greet me and the terrier cocked his leg again. Sylvie lifted a pan of water and flung it at the little mutt, who seemed as fearless as his namesake. He scarpered off to terrorise the chickens in the yard.

Sylvie, a pleasant-looking woman in her late fifties whose own figure testified to a passion for food, spoke so fast I found it almost impossible to follow. But bonds can be built without words and Sylvie's soft eyes and kind demeanour told me here was a friend.

She deposited a bowl of fresh coffee on the table in front of me, followed seconds later by a croissant, a chunk of bread and a dish of a marmaladey-looking orange preserve.

'Ça va?' She lifted her own bowl of coffee with a curious-looking but effective crab-like grip and swallowed deeply.

'Oui. Ça va.' I started to attempt the grip then, sensing disaster, went in with the two-handed hash of the coffee-bowl novice. It was strong stuff. I blinked.

'Il est fort, mon café. Hein?'

'Oui. Fort. Mais bon.'

Wow. I'm rocking the old French this morning. A dose of politeness and two *adjectives.*

Sylvie jumped up and went back to her vegetables – shining carrots, an exotic lump I fancied was celeriac, and tomatoes so ripe and aromatic they almost made you weep with delight at Mother Nature's wondrous bounty.

I stood to lend a hand but she waved me back to my chair.

'Tranquille.' She smiled, then nodded to the bread and jam. 'Mangez.'

I obeyed. The croissant was feather-light and fresh. And the preserve, the colour of apricots but the taste of plums, was such a delight I couldn't let it pass without comment. I buckled up and prepared to unleash a flurry of top-notch French.

'Le préservatif est très bon.'

Sylvie dropped her knife. Then she turned her soft eyes and warm smile on me.

'C'est pas le mot juste. C'est pas ça qu'vous voulez dire.'

I'd heard those words before.

What the bloody buggering bastarding hell have I said now?!

'Préservatif c'est autre chose.'

She picked up a large carrot from her worktop and made the gesture of someone applying a sheath of thin rubber to an excited male appendage.

I clamped my hand over my mouth and Sylvie guffawed and patted me warmly on the shoulder.

'Alors, c'en est une bonne!'

I'd complimented her not on her jam but on her condom.

Philippe showed me round the winery. He explained how, while the majority of their grapes were harvested by machine, the best were handpicked.

'Bordeaux wines are the result of subtle blending. We have here a very complex geology, with sand, clay and limestone, and this *terroir* gives Saint Emilion wines their distinctive characteristics.'

At his mention of limestone, some terms from O-level Geography jumped into my head – *karst, dolomite, escarpment.* I was going back to school.

'Vines grow better on poor soil because they must dig for their food. Because they work harder, they get more flavour. Just like chicken.'

'Chicken?'

'Yes. The breast of a chicken looks nice, but it doesn't taste so good. Because it's a lazy part of a bird that doesn't fly. But a chicken's legs are always moving. Working. So the leg is tasty. A chicken's thigh is the best part. For flavour. Because it works the hardest.' Philippe smiled. 'Vines are like chickens.'

'That's a phrase I wasn't expecting to hear today.'

'Then I have surprised you. That's good.'

A car horn sounded and we both looked across the courtyard. Madeleine was sitting at the wheel of a black Citroën SUV.

'We have meetings in the city. Including with the bank.' He grimaced. 'Please look around. Explore the winery and the vineyard. Find questions for us to answer at dinner.'

I set off for the vines with Napoléon dancing round my feet and I wondered if he should be on a lead and if a cocked leg would spell disaster for this year's vintage. But he was suddenly ten yards ahead of me and my only option was to keep an eye on him.

For ten minutes the little dog and I strolled companionably along avenues of chest-high leaves on ancient gnarly vines sprouting from what looked like chalk. Then, when we reached the end of the road, Napoléon picked up the pace and made a break for the wire fence that marked the border between the vineyard and an area of woodland beyond.

My little friend shot through the fence and disappeared into the trees.

Christ! I'd been here less than twenty-four hours and I'd managed to tell the estate worker I was horny, accused his wife of putting condoms in her jam, and now I'd lost the owners' bloody dog!

The terrier's yapping grew fainter then disappeared altogether. Then everything became strangely, unnervingly still.

My breathing became shallow.

The snap of a branch broke the silence and a pheasant flew up into the air. I saw a dark shape moving behind bushes ten yards away.

'Napoléon! Come here, you little sod!'

A voice behind me whispered a command.

'Stand still. Don't move.'

What was happening? Was I being mugged? It didn't seem likely in the middle of a wood that bordered a vineyard. But I was too terrified to speak. Or move.

The dark shape moved slowly and showed itself. Wide shoulders. Thick, coarse fur that would rip your skin. Huge black wet snout sniffing the air.

Black eyes staring straight into mine.

'Stay still.'

I held my breath.

The boar held my gaze for five long seconds. Then he turned his ample posterior on me and sniffed the ground.

'Is safe now. Just walk back. Slowly.'

I took several tentative steps backwards, all the while eyeing the beast who'd taken my breath away. Then an aroma somewhere off to the right caught his attention and he disappeared into the bushes.

I exhaled deeply and turned around. My boar whisperer was a man. A very handsome man indeed.

'We are lucky. He have tusks like razor. Charge like bull. Slice you here.' He touched my thigh with his finger. 'Cut big blood.

Then ...' He made the international gesture of a throat being cut. 'That would make curtains for you.'

I looked into his heavily lashed eyes. 'How did you know I was here?'

'I watching from vines.'

Napoléon came trotting up to him and nuzzled his ankles. Like butter wouldn't melt.

'This boy, he laughing at you. Only do what is told by Madame.' My handsome interlocutor shook his head at the dog and smiled.

'Are you Gabriel?'

'Yes. And you are Jennifer.'

He held out his hand and I took it. Gabriel. Not so much angel as Greek god. *Steady on, Jennifer Brown.*

I've heard it said that, in matters of the heart, if a gaze between two people lingers for more than five seconds, chemicals in the brain start the reaction that leads to physical attraction. I hadn't counted the seconds, but there was certainly something funny going on in my brain. And my palms. And my cheeks.

I spent the rest of the day trying to focus on vines, geology, *terroir*. But all I could see were Gabriel's eyes, shoulders, forearms.

By the time dinner came around, and Philippe and Madeleine had returned from their day of meetings in the city, I'd worked up a passable (if short) list of questions.

But I felt angry with myself for allowing the distraction. I was here to do a job. I needed to be professional. A businesswoman. Not a giggling, moonstruck girl. *You're forty, for God's sake, not fourteen!*

As we sat down to eat, I was pleased to see that Madame Hélène was joining us. An evening with a battleaxe would keep me on my toes, keep me focused, and still my stupid heart.

At eighty-nine, Hélène had managed to retain that elegance that seems to come so naturally, so effortlessly, to so many French women. She carried herself superbly upright, tied her fine silver hair in a neat bun at the nape of her neck, and wore on her breast a short red ribbon from the *Légion d'Honneur* awarded to a father who'd fought with the Resistance. She dabbled on the stock market, drank only the best wine and enjoyed the odd cigar.

The only visible sign of weakness was the stick she carried 'mostly for show.' When she spoke, her eyes sparkled.

'How do you like our little chateau?' She reached for the coffee pot and refilled my cup and her own.

'I like it very much. I'm grateful to you all for having me.'

'If I know Philippe, he will make you earn your supper.'

'That's fine with me. I'm here to work. And to learn.' An image of Gabriel's shoulders leapt into my head and I blinked hard to banish it.

'Tell me about you. Who is Jennifer?'

The mood was relaxed and convivial and, seeing nothing of the battleaxe hinted at by Madeleine the evening before, I opened up. My childhood in Hampshire. My father's own military service in Northern Ireland. My messy breakup with Pete.

My hopes for the future.

'*Qui n'avance pas, recule*, as we say in French.'

I must have looked blank.

'She who does not move forward, moves backwards.'

Was I moving forward?

Well, I was certainly falling under the charm of this place. Adapting to its open spaces, its gentler pace, its warm and welcoming people. All of them.

I was settling in. Life had imposed a series of adjustments on me and here I was again, shedding my skin and, if not moving forward, at least moving.

14

Echoes of Narcissus

The vines had begun to flower and the vineyard needed a lot of attention.

It was all hands on deck to keep the weeds down and let the soil throw all its nutrients into the vines to keep them strong enough to withstand any freak winds or early summer thunderstorms, which, Philippe pointed out, can shake the pollen from the vines and disrupt the delicate process of pollination, causing serious harm to the vintage.

We were all putting in the hours under the hot June sun.

I'm not sure the exertion was exactly showing my complexion in its best light but Philippe and Madeleine seemed to glow more fetchingly under its influence.

And I hardly dared look at Gabriel. His skin was acquiring the colour of melted bronze, which only made him look even more like Adonis, the strikingly beautiful youth legendarily loved by the goddess Aphrodite, who nursed him, dying, in her arms after he was gored by a wild boar.

In my version, he chased the boar away then I dived into his eyes.

Stop it, you silly tart!

I was confident I was hiding my obsession from everyone, if not from myself, but I came to think that Madame Hélène might have rumbled me. She gave me a strange smile whenever I offered to walk Napoléon after dinner, guessing perhaps that I'd likely be heading for the part of the estate where Gabriel had his *dépendance*, the modest stone outbuilding that was his vineyard home.

Being in his company was a useful (and necessary) exercise in self-control and I always turned the conversation to the general and the everyday. But one glorious red and orange evening, I got more personal.

'Do you miss Poland?'

'Of course.' He filled my glass and looked up at the chateau. 'In Poland, not much money. But life is … sweet.' He shrugged.

'In what way?'

'People all live in same house. Husband, wife, parents. Everyone together.' His smile was tinged with sadness. Or was it a mild resentment? I was the new arrival yet I had a spacious apartment in the big house, shared every meal with the family, was treated like an equal. He received the odd invitation to dine at the chateau but, by and large, he lived in this little cottage and fended for himself. I wondered if that rankled.

He disabused me quickly.

'I am lucky. In one way. Here is good. Beautiful house. Nice people. Comfortable. Good money.' He turned his brown eyes on me. 'But is not my family.' His eyes sparkled with tears and I had to use every ounce of self-restraint I possessed not to throw my arms around his gorgeous neck.

On FaceTime later, Will was impressed. Also disappointed.

'In for a penny.'

'He's twenty-eight. I'm virtually old enough to be his mother. That's probably who I remind him of.'

'Bollocks. All sunbleached hair and sunkissed cleavage. I bet he's gagging for you.'

'Shut it.'

'I mean it. How do you know he isn't bottling it up just as much as you are?'

'I'm sure that's not the case.'

'I wouldn't *be* so sure. I'd go for it.'

'I'm not going for anything.'

'But there *is* one pitfall.'

'What?'

'All that pork. And dumplings. Not great for your figure.'

'I don't even *like* pork.'

'But you wouldn't say no to *his* sausage.'

'Goodbye, Will.'

***

We were working as hard as ever, now. And I was learning something new every day. Everything had to be recorded – sugar content, alcohol content, pH level. And the focus was not just the berry clusters. The health of the leaves was just as important.

I made the morning inspection with Philippe.

'A tiny dot can be the first sign of disease. Or stress. Or overwatering.'

'How do you know what the problem is?'

'You develop a feel. Experience.'

I sighed.

'You'll pick it up. This hands-on experience is the best. Better than all the text books.' He smiled. 'But still read the text books.'

I was devouring them. Downy mildew. Powdery mildew. Grey mould. My evenings were full of fungus. My brain hardly switched off. I was feeling the pace.

Relief came in the shape of a surprise message from an old school friend. Natalie had seen my Facebook posts, clocked I was in southwest France, and messaged to ask if I wanted to meet up. She was living in Arcachon, 50 kilometres west of Bordeaux, on the coast.

We'd known each other since primary school and by high school we were best buds. Nat's parents were social climbers and she'd lived in one of the big new detached houses at the posh end of the village. A Kylie Minogue lookalike with a tumbling mane of blonde locks, she was far and away the most popular (and most envied) girl at Brookhill High. Everyone wanted to be Natalie Nicholson's best friend and, at the time, I never quite understood why I was the chosen one. With her Kylie curls and her Levi jeans and Nike tops, and me with my stringy hair and crummy, third-rate gear from Freeman's catalogue (when Mum had enough credit), we made a pretty odd couple.

It had been fifteen years since I'd seen her, and we hadn't parted in the best of circumstances. I hadn't thought about her for a long time.

Looking back on the friendship now, and the reason she'd clung to me for so long, I reckoned it was because of my easygoing nature. She could manipulate me. I'd go along with whatever it was she wanted to do. In most friendships, there are followers and leaders.

I was definitely a follower. *Had been* a follower.

Narcissistic Nat had learned at an early age exactly how to extract whatever she wanted from most people – her friends, her adoring parents and, in her twenties, a string of older men more than happy to shower her with material possessions.

When I was just starting out as a secretary at Intext, and had never been further from home than Farnborough, Nat was disappearing into the sunset with an older man of independent means who was setting up an art school somewhere in Europe.

At dinner, I mentioned my old friendship and the message that had come out of the blue. Madeleine seemed intrigued.

'Why don't you meet her?'

'I'm not sure we'd have anything to say to each other. And she became a bit of a pain towards the end.'

'But that was fifteen years ago. You were both very different people then. Perhaps the friendship will click back on.'

'Perhaps.'

'You won't know until you do it. Go away for a couple of days.'

'Are you sure?'

'Of course. We can manage here.'

***

My account was looking fairly healthy for once – I was still on Cécile's payroll and, with everything laid on at Paulus, spending very little – so I booked myself into a luxury boutique hotel just off the Place Gambetta, a nice, central base for a weekend tourist.

The guy on reception looked like he'd been out of hospitality college for about ten minutes. He greeted me, in English (my sunkissed complexion and sky-blue capri pants were clearly not fooling anyone), handed me my key and wished me a pleasant stay.

I'd been working on my vowel sounds and now was a good time to take them for a spin.

'Merci beaucoup.'

No titter. I was getting better. The first time I'd trotted out the formula, Benoit had buckled at the waist. Again.

'Non non, Jen-nee-fair. *Beau cul* c'est bien autre chose. Oh la!' Doubled up with laughter, he could say no more.

'What's the difference? They sound the same to me.'

Philippe had come to my rescue. 'The slight difference in vowel sound makes a big difference in meaning. *Beaucoup*, with your lips round, like this, means "very much." *Beau cul* means, well ... it means "nice arse."'

I'd arranged to meet Nat for lunch at a restaurant on the Place de la Bourse, the city's swanky main square with its famous reflecting pool, the *miroir d'eau*. On a hot day like this, the water would be a welcome coolant.

I made good use of the complimentary L'Occitane toiletries in the double shower and selected the floaty white dress that would keep my armpits and thighs well aerated in the summer heat. Then it hit me.

I hadn't packed any white knickers.

I slipped the lavender ones back on. No good. The red ones were a non-starter, obvs. Maybe I should just be less British, say bugger it, and go with the black. I tried them. The long cheval mirror in the corner of the room told me this was not a good look.

I thought of Nat and imagined a face and figure unsullied by time and a get-up off the cover of *Vogue*.

There was only one solution.

Basic Instinct had shocked us at the time but that time was 1992. We'd all grown up a lot since then. Become more accepting. And if it was good enough for Sharon Stone, it was good enough for Jennifer Brown. Well, for a couple of hours, anyway.

The bells were ringing as I approached the Cathédrale Saint André and I realised with delight that a wedding was taking place. A vintage white Citroën was parked at the kerb, decked with ribbons, and, at the cathedral door, two lines of young guests had formed an arch with upheld tennis racquets. A sporty couple were getting hitched.

I lingered at the edge of the crowd of well-wishers and drank in the atmosphere.

I remembered how I used to dream of marrying Pete and imagine my dress and the innocent joy of the day. I remembered the last wedding I'd attended and the strange look David Harwood had given me as Jonathan had toasted him and his new bride.

The tennis players emerged – a stunning young woman and, I thought, a rather plain young man – and their guests burst into song, presumably some club anthem. A sixty-something woman in a dove-grey suit – an auntie perhaps – turned to me and smiled. Then the smile died from her lips as the wind caught the back of my white dress and lifted it up to my shoulder blades,

treating the thirty-or-so wedding guests and a few truckloads of
the good citizens of Bordeaux to a ringside view of my brazen
Hampshire buttocks.

By the second *kir royale*, I was beginning to regain my
composure. Nat had messaged to apologise for running late and
I was glad of an extra twenty minutes to gather myself for the
reunion. I was happy just sipping my drink and letting the spray
from the fountains on the square cool my embarrassment.

Then I spotted her, thirty yards away. Same tumbling blonde
hair, same confident walk. I stood and waved and she saw me and
waved back, with apparent delight. I steeled myself for the wave of
self-flagellation that always seemed to wash over me whenever I
bumped into old friends.

But, as Natalie held out her arms to greet me, I could see that
time had been less kind than I'd expected. I was shocked by the
hollow eyes, the gaunt cheeks, the dull skin.

'Look at you, Jennifer Brown! The French climate clearly suits
you. And what a gorgeous dress!'

'Thank you. It's lovely to see you, Natalie.'

'How *are* you? How are you settling into life here?'

'I like it. So far, anyway. It's only been a few weeks. You've been
here years.'

'Fifteen years.'

'You clearly like it, then.'

'It's fine. Yes, it's good.' She looked at my glass. 'Glad you didn't
wait for me. Don't worry. I'll soon catch you up. I'm slow out of
the gate but there's no-one faster coming down the home straight.'
She beckoned to a waiter and ordered champagne.

Over a crab salad lunch, she quizzed me about the last fifteen
years, seemed genuinely sorry to hear about the fallout from my
parting from Pete and convincingly impressed by the things I'd
done since.

But when I asked about her own life, she was reticent. And, an hour and a half later, the champagne and a bottle of sauvignon blanc had been demolished and, of each, I'd had only one glass.

When the coffee was delivered, Nat ordered an armagnac – large – and looked at me.

'No, just coffee for me, thanks.'

The role of sober influence wasn't one I was used to but Nat was sinking lower in the chair and I thought I'd better keep my wits about me. A silver-haired couple at the next table had spent the last twenty minutes looking daggers at the boozy Brits.

After coffee (and brandy), I decided it was best to get Nat on her feet quickly and away from any source of further inebriation. I waved the waiter over and we settled up.

'Right. Why don't you show me the sights of your beautiful city.' I stood up.

'Sure.'

Nat stood with the concentrated care of the drunk feigning sobriety and prepared herself for the task of walking. She took my arm and I took most of her weight.

'It's so good to see you again. It really is. I've missed you.' She turned dewy eyes towards me, all the more hollow-looking for the alcohol they'd soaked up.

'It's good to see you, too.'

'Good friends. The love of a good friend.' I was momentarily unnerved by the turn the conversation was taking. 'That's what I've been missing.'

We stopped on the far side of the square and Nat stared out over the river and breathed deeply. I felt a major confession coming.

'You know it's all a lie?'

'What do you mean?'

'The fabulous expat life I'm supposed to be living with my fabulously rich artist husband.'

'He doesn't exist?'

'Oh, he exists alright. Although most of the time I wish he didn't.'

I must have looked shocked.

'Oh, I don't mean I want him dead or anything. I just wish I'd never … been charmed by him. That's what he is. A charmer. An inveterate charmer. I was his muse for a while. For *quite* a while. I was young and … forgive me … pretty.'

'You were … *are* … pretty. Very.'

'You were always a bad liar, Jennifer Brown.'

'I mean it. I always admired you. Envied you.'

'And now?'

I didn't know what to say.

'Exactly. Time is cruel. To women. Men not so much.'

I thought of old Dashwood-Silk, who only seemed to get better with age.

'We married for love. Genuinely. But we married in haste and with heads full of romantic notions about the artistic life. And Rodney's money gave us the good life for a few years – I'm ashamed to say I relied on it entirely – then, when the art school folded and it became clear that the living to be made from his paintings alone was … meagre, irregular … I think it hit both of us that we'd made a mistake.

She threw a pebble into the Garonne below.

'He moved on to younger, lusher pastures – we're still married but he makes no secret of his dalliances and I no longer pretend I don't know – and I became a woman in early middle age with no discernible talent in any area of life, trapped in a failed marriage, and who doesn't even have her looks to fall back on any more.'

'Don't you want to leave him?'

She turned to me, eyes full of shame. 'I'm not sure I've got the energy. Where would I go?'

'Well, it's not a great solution at our age, but what about your parents?'

'They divorced years ago. Both remarried. And I doubt their new partners would take kindly to a forty-year-old flake turning up on their doorstep.'

She began to sob. 'I've fucked up, Jennifer Brown. The high school queen is now in the gutter.'

Her hollow cheeks were stained with tears. I put my arm round her.

'Come on.'

After a hot shower and a couple of double espressos, and swathed in the rich cotton folds of a hotel bathrobe, Nat was looking a lot more human.

We camped out in my room and reminisced like the schoolgirls we once were – boys we used to fancy, how we never missed an episode of *Friends*, the time we talked someone's brother into renting an 18-certificate horror film from Blockbuster.

'What was it?'

'*The Prophecy*.'

'God, yes. With that guy from *The Deer Hunter*. The mental one.'

'Christopher Walken.'

'That's him. Scared me shitless.'

We guffawed. Then Nat recovered herself and became introspective.

'I always wanted to be you.'

I was completely taken aback. 'But you were so pretty and popular. I was just … invisible.'

'I envied you your family. A sweet mum who baked cakes and let us watch *Neighbours*. Who sat down with us and asked us about our day. Who listened. I wanted that.'

I thought of my mum and my eyes filled with tears. She'd been a great mum. Was I a great daughter? I didn't think so.

We ordered room service and lay on the bed and ate till our stomachs ached and watched crappy French TV and zonked out on the bed and slept.

***

'Bye, darling.' I hugged her tiny frame as her train pulled into Saint Jean station. 'Phone me whenever you want. And come out to the chateau for a visit.'

'I will. Thank you.' She brushed my hair off my forehead. 'You haven't changed, Jennifer Brown. The same kind eyes. The same kind soul. I wish you happiness.'

She kissed my cheek and climbed aboard.

15

Electric Storm

As the summer wore on, temperatures in our Bordeaux vineyard climbed steadily higher and the burgeoning grapes were turning from green to red, signalling it was time for one of the toughest jobs in the vineyard – crop thinning. The task of removing leaves to allow air to flow freely through the vines and dry off the morning dew so it didn't settle long enough to cause trouble was, to use the technical term, a backbreaking bastard. I was now up every morning at dawn and in the vineyard thinning away by 6.30.

But working as a team was rewarding and we enjoyed our breaks in the shade – a morning coffee and one of Sylvie's melt-in-the-mouth croissants, then, in the steamy afternoons, a cooling *diabolo menthe*.

I'd dropped the Boots Factor 30 for an Ambre Solaire 15 and had acquired a golden tan that Gisele Bündchen would covet. I was enjoying the heat of the day.

The heat of the night, not so much.

Sleeping with the windows and shutters open was the only way to keep the room at anything like a sleepable temperature. But an open window in Bordeaux is like ringing the mosquito dinner gong. The busy little buggers keep you awake with the constant drone of their non-stop sorties and their appetite for blood means that, by morning, you look like an extra in a period piece about the Black Death. The pungent perfume that had been Mum's last Christmas gift controlled the blighters a bit but I had to drown the whole room in it and my hot morning shower never quite got rid of the heady aroma of Bet Lynch.

Gabriel was feeling the heat, too.

'If heat early, you know day be tough.' He lifted his heavenly brown eyes up to the clear blue sky. 'Cloud is better for us. Not such good for grapes.'

'No.'

I dragged my eyes away from his enchanting frame and got on with my work. And I truly was enjoying all the hard physical labour.

But it *was* hard. And I relished the prospect of a day free of duties.

My options for leisure pursuits were limited by my lack of transport. Madeleine didn't mind dropping me somewhere if she was going into town, and I'd occasionally asked Benoit for a lift, but being in his presence brought out the gaffemeister in me and he seemed to wear a nervous smile whenever I was around, ready to be tickled by some inadvertently saucy or seedy French malapropism.

A solution to my transport needs presented itself on one of my evening strolls with Napoléon. I stumbled across a stone shed at the back of Gabriel's place (to my chagrin, Gabriel was back in Poland for a long weekend) and discovered, inside, an ancient bicycle that looked like a relic of the Resistance years. When I mentioned it to Philippe, he said nobody had used it since the 70s. But one evening, after we'd all knocked off, he helped me clean it, pump up the tyres, grease the brakes, and drop the seat six inches.

'Are you sure you want to risk it?'

'It looks fine. It'll be good to have some independence.'

***

I hadn't ridden a bike for a decade or so but they say you never forget. And the task of riding a bike is a popular yardstick for absence of difficulty (*Oh, it's as easy as riding a bike*). So, one promising Sunday morning, I set off with a road map, a packed lunch of *saucisson*, olives and goat's cheese, and a strong sense of exhilaration.

My thighs were grateful for the flatness and smoothness of the roads, which were also fairly traffic-free. Those locals who pootled past me gave me a wide berth and a friendly toot as I pedalled beside eight-foot sunflowers and carpets of lavender.

God, France is a beautiful country!

After an hour or so of health-giving exercise, I started to feel peckish and, spotting a shady tree, I hopped off the bike ready to give the *saucisson* a bash. It was then that I heard it – a loud and grating noise of animal complaint.

Across the road, a goat had managed to get its head stuck between the thick wires of a stout fence that separated the road from a field of scrubby pasture. A strip of lush grass on the road side had enticed the goat to chance its neck and now it was regretting the enterprise.

I've never been comfortable around animals of the farmyard variety and goats freak me out with their weird rectangular pupils. It's no wonder the devil dresses up as one in books and films.

On the other hand, here was a sentient being under considerable stress and some sort of action was needed.

I approached it with what I imagined was a soothing manner and, trying not to look at its eyes, placed my hands either side of its head and, with the care of someone easing a landmine out of desert sand, tried to manoeuvre its head slowly sideways, the solution to its problem, I reckoned.

The animal yanked its head out of my hands and bleated at me ferociously.

I looked up and down the road, hoping in vain for a latter-day Gallic James Herriot to materialise. But the road was deserted.

About two hundred yards away, there was an entrance to some sort of property so I hopped back on the bike and set off to get help.

An elderly rustic-looking man, alerted by the booming bark of his monstrous black hound slavering behind the fence that separated it from my throat, answered the door to a small stone cottage.

I managed a 'Bonjour' and a 'Ça va?' and gathered myself to explain my request for help. Luckily, Sylvie had packed goat's cheese as part of my lunch so the word *chèvre* came easily to my lips. Unfortunately, no other useful nouns, verbs or grammatical structures followed, so I simply repeated, broken-record-like, the word *chèvre*. My man was clearly thinking the French equivalent of *And chèvre to you too, darlin'* until, from the dim recesses of my mind, I fished out the word *blessé*. Then I pointed up the road.

He nodded, turned on his heel, then kicked the door closed, leaving me standing alone on his doorstep like a lemon.

I looked left and right at invisible companions and threw them a shrug of puzzlement.

Then the door opened again and the goat's would-be saviour, now armed with a pair of what looked like blacksmith's gloves, stepped out and past me and off up the road.

I trotted behind him and, when we'd reached the bleating demon, I stood by, ready to be of use. The goat whisperer ignored me, clamped his gloved hands over the animal's muzzle, and gave the head a sharp twist as if meaning to break the creature's neck. Upon which, liberated, the beast scampered off to tend to its daily demonic business.

The old boy threw me a scornful look that said *I really don't know why you didn't just do that yourself, you useless tart*, then, wordlessly, strode off back to his house and his dog of death.

Remembering I'd left my bike at the end of his drive, I skulked slowly up the road behind him, retrieved my wartime machine, and cycled off in search of a picnic spot free of goats and grumpy old bastards.

The rest of the day was spent in blissful, sunkissed isolation and I returned to the chateau in time for a refreshing shower and one of Sylvie's delicious chicken *paupiettes* and a green bean salad with caper dressing.

By the time I hit the hay, replete with food and pleasantly aching legs, I didn't care what the mosquitoes got up to. I never heard or felt a thing.

***

As the vines continued to bush out, so did my hair.

Madeleine recommended a salon in Saint Emilion (a settlement with a thin population of two thousand that seemed to sustain no fewer than five *salons de coiffure*, a stylist-to-citizen ratio that probably beats Beverly Hills) so, on my next day off, I cycled into the village, parked the machine at the foot of the Château du Roy, the vast 13th-century castle keep in the centre, and prepared to submit myself for treatment.

I hate going to a different hairdresser. I feel about hairdressers how I feel about doctors. You want one you know and who knows you and your quirks and tendencies. Back home, my bloke Gareth didn't exactly have my hairdressing history on file. But he'd known me for so long he knew what would work and what my face could get away with. So, although a trim was definitely called for, I was nervous about giving my hair up to a stranger.

Then again, this was France. The nation of style, cool, trend. The country that had given us Coco Chanel, Brigitte Bardot and Jean-Paul Gaultier. I was in safe hands. Surely.

I imagined English to be the international language of hairdressing and therefore that my surrogate stylist would have a fairly nifty command of my native tongue. I imagined also that said surrogate would be on the young side and, like the YouTube generation the world over, would be down with the old Anglo-Saxon.

I imagined wrong.

The sour-faced gentleman who stood over the back of my head must have been seventy. He was making a sterling effort to mask his age with hair colourant, a punishing diet (or a heavy Gauloises habit) and a fashion sense that's best described as 'brave'.

But he was no dewdrop.

He may have had a smattering of English for all I know but he projected such a fervent nationalism in the face of my ungallicness that I wouldn't have been surprised if, dropping his leather trousers to reveal tricolour unmentionables, he'd climbed onto the counter and belted out the Marseillaise.

He fired a barrage of bad-tempered questions at me, fingering my hair at arm's length as if handling a bag of something a dog had left behind.

The only single word I caught was 'red.' I shook my head vigorously at what I took to be a suggestion to switch colour from the various shades of blonde I'd been sporting since my schoolfriend Viv had dyed it for me in her bathroom when we were seventeen.

He sneered and set to work with the scissors, at a combative pace. After half an hour of angry snipping, he applied about five litres of mousse then reached for a hairdrier fitted with a diffuser the size of a dustbin lid. An hour later, I was done. Well and truly.

I left a generous tip. Just because you've been shafted, doesn't mean you can't pay over the odds for the experience.

The face that stared back at me in the window of the restaurant opposite was an eighties throwback. Bonnie Tyler and Tina Turner had had a threesome with David Bowie's Goblin King in *Labyrinth* and I was the love child.

'Not *red*, but *raide*,' Madeleine explained. 'Straightened.'

The scales fell from my eyes.

'I imagine your response made him think you wanted it …' – she glanced up at the blonde forest – '… full.'

After a hot shower and half a dozen applications of conditioner, relatively normal service was resumed. During dinner, Napoléon seemed more impatient than usual so, as soon as my plate was cleared, I gave him the nod and we set off for our evening walk.

Storm clouds were gathering and I resolved to make the walk a short one – my hair had seen enough moisture for one day – but we'd only gone a couple of hundred yards when the heavens opened and huge raindrops pounded into the gravel like mortar shells.

The door of the *dépendance* opened and Gabriel stood on the threshold, waving me in, his voice drowned out by thunder.

Napoléon sprinted off towards the open door and I padded across the gravel after him.

Gabriel handed me a towel and watched me rub my hair as he stirred something in a pot.

'What is it you're cooking?' I fingered my hair, feeling for traces of Bonnie Tyler.

'Bigos. National food for Poland.' He dipped a spoon into the pot and held it out towards me. 'Pork, sausage, sauerkraut, apples.'

I reached out to steady the spoon and the touch of his hand sent a surge of electricity through me. I didn't know what to do with that feeling. I looked for a distraction and found one in the shape of a beautiful blue-and-white porcelain plate hanging on the wall.

'What a gorgeous plate!'

'Traditional pattern. From Silesia.' He lifted it off its hook and handed it to me. 'Please. For you.'

'Oh, no. I wasn't hinting. I was just … admiring it.' I handed it back but he was insistent.

'Please. Make me happy to give.' His rich brown eyes held mine.

And then it happened.

Exactly as I'd hoped it would.

16

A Handful

The physical pleasure of my night with Gabriel was accompanied by something much more valuable – a real sense of myself as an attractive woman. I hadn't felt that since my early days with Pete. And Pete had been the reason for me losing it.

My phone buzzed. Nat squealed down the line like an excited eight-year-old who's just won a game of Connect 4.

'I've done it!'

Her elation unsettled me. I imagined Rodney lying at the bottom of the Garonne with a palette knife in his throat.

'I've left him. And it's all thanks to you!'

For a couple of seconds, I didn't know what to say. Should I be proud to have influenced such a brave decision? Or terrified?

'I told him he could shove his festering old art school up his cheating old arsehole. The look on his face was priceless. Which is more than can be said for his lousy rotten paintings!'

'Wow. So … er … what's the plan?'

'Well, I know this a bit of a cheek …'

My heart started to beat a little faster.

'… but I was wondering if I might stay with you. Just for a bit. Get my head round things.'

A bit. Philippe and Madeleine might be okay with a couple of nights. But I wondered what Nat had in mind.

'You've been such an inspiration to me. Such a good friend.'

I couldn't remember what I'd told her about Château Paulus. I remembered inviting her to visit. But had I explained that I lived alongside the family? In *their* home?

On the other end of the line, I heard an announcement over a loudspeaker. Then Nat piped up again.

'Jen! Are you still there?'

'Yeah. Still here. Think I lost you for a second. Where are you?'

'I'm at the train station in Saint Emilion.'

Once again, an image jumped into my head – me on my friend Viv's doorstep, tears running down my face. No warning. I'd just turned up. And she'd asked no questions. Simply taken me in and made things alright.

'Right. Grab a coffee somewhere and I'll call you back.'

Nat's revelation had hit me like a brick in the face. Now I had to think on my feet. My options were limited – empty my savings account and put her up indefinitely in some place in Saint Emilion; book her a flight back to the UK (and God knows what reception from disapproving arm's-length parents); go crawling to Madeleine in the hope that the Sisterhood of the Wronged Woman was a network she'd sign up to.

Madeleine was sympathetic. But she was also pragmatic.

Nat could stay for a couple of weeks. But she'd be expected to pitch in around the house and on the estate. And she'd have to share my apartment.

I had no option but to accept her terms. And neither did Nat.

I found her in a crowded cafe near the cathedral steps, explaining how to make tea to a waiter who looked about three seconds away from smothering her with his apron. I defused the tension with smiles and a hefty order of *marc de champagne* truffles.

Nat looked gaunter than ever and the fragile look in her eyes made my embarrassment with Madeleine melt away. I hugged her diminutive frame. Then, over her shoulder, I saw it.

'I'm hoping it'll be okay for me to bring Dora.' A pair of brown eyes looked up at me from under the table. 'I couldn't just leave her behind with that dreadful man.' Tears bubbled up into her eyes. I pulled her close. But I couldn't remember any previous mention of a dog.

'It's alright. It's going to be alright.'

Nat was gushily grateful to Philippe and Madeleine for the temporary roof over her head and she was on her very best behaviour vis-à-vis drink.

It was accepted that Dora (named after Dora Maar, a French artist best remembered as a muse of Picasso during one of his many trouser-happy periods) would be confined to 'our' apartment and especially keep out from under Sylvie's feet in the kitchen (poor Sylvie already had Napoléon to contend with).

And luckily Dora bonded pretty quickly with Gabriel and she and Napoléon seemed happy to hang out at his place in the evenings, which gave me a good excuse to visit and encourage our fledgling romance to spread its wings.

For the first few days, having Nat around was fun – rather like having the sister I'd yearned for when I was twelve years old – but it was also hard to adjust to sharing my space with someone whose idea of tidiness was marshalling clothes into a single pile and who watched TV on her phone at three in the morning, and I was reminded of a quotation from Benjamin Franklin – 'Guests, like fish, begin to smell after three days.'

But her promise to stay off the booze seemed be holding and, surrounded by a small city of wine, she must have found this a challenge.

I did wonder if she'd secretly fallen off the wagon when, as she was drying her hair one morning, she asked me if I'd seen anything moving around in the room during the night.

'What kind of thing?'

'Never mind.'

Then, after the initial euphoria of her escape from the dreadful Rodney, Nat fell into something of a slough of despond. The mask of self-confidence I'd initially seen during our boozy lunch in the city, and again as I'd collected her from the station, had, I'd come to realise, been kept in place by a constant low (sometimes not so low) level of alcohol in the bloodstream. Stone cold sober, and doubtless in the grip of withdrawal, Nat couldn't stop the mask from slipping and her baseline dropped to depressive with a side order of tetchy.

And it didn't help matters that Nat hadn't exactly bonded with Sylvie, who (understandably) didn't take kindly to my old schoolfriend's assessment of foie gras as 'state-sanctioned animal torture'. Add to that the fact that Nat, resident of these shores for a decade and a half, had such a shamefully poor grasp of French she made me look like a candidate for Secretary General of the UN, which reduced communication with Sylvie to a silent glaring contest peppered with the occasional grunt of displeasure, from Nat whenever Sylvie produced rich dishes dripping with animal flesh and from Sylvie whenever Nat cut the cheese with a table knife.

In the house, I felt like a boxing referee trying to keep each woman in her own corner.

'Why not her family give home? In Poland door is open to family always.' Gabriel tickled the submissive Dora's tummy as the two of us sat under a tree taking a breather from the task of thinning the vines.

'It's not that simple. Nat's parents were divorced years ago. They both have new partners who might not be very … welcoming.'

Gabriel shook his head. The dynamic seemed to make no sense.

'She not happy. You not happy with her. Not good.'

He was right. Not good at all. But there was no immediate solution.

Sensing that all was not well and looking for a way of keeping Nat out of the house for as long as possible, Madeleine gave her a dedicated job.

Château Paulus was one of the Bordeaux destinations offered by Vinous, an organisation running wine experiences for well-heeled clients looking for something off the beaten track. Paulus was one of their most popular spots and July a popular time.

Madeleine did most of the front-of-house stuff – welcome speech, tour of the vineyard, presentation on the process of winemaking – but one thing she didn't do was serve lunch on the terrace. That was Sylvie's domain.

But this summer's groups had swollen from the standard four or five to eight or ten, too hefty for one person to manage the cooking and the serving. Nat and I were drafted in to serve.

I gave Nat a stern lecture.

'Look. I know you have your principles. I respect that. But this is business. And it's going to be *my* business. And Philippe and Madeleine are my hosts, and they've given you a roof over your head, so it's our duty to repay them by helping their business run smoothly. And if that means serving up chunks of animal, then that's what we'll do. Even if those chunks are from animals who might have spent less time than we'd ideally want being kissed and cuddled. Right?'

I gave her my best Cruella De Vil stare.

'Okay.'

The Saturday started well.

As the Vinous minibus (Mercedes, Black, elegant gold lettering) crunched over the gravel in front of the chateau, Nat and I were pinned up and ready for action. Sylvie was busy with her white asparagus starter and with simmering the rich sauce for her *entrecôte à la bordelaise* and I was keeping Nat as far away from her as I could during the time the clients were away on their vineyard tour.

When the eight adventurers hit the terrace a couple of hours later, I could tell from their demeanour that the heat was getting to them. Nevertheless, one retired couple – a woman in a beige jumpsuit and her portly husband in standard merchant banker garb of pink twill trousers and navy blazer – seemed in the mood to party. Husband, 'Geoffrey darling', necked the best part of the carafe in front of them before you could say *Bon appétit*.

By the time Nat and I were bringing out the *entrecôte*, Geoffrey had made the transition from harmless bore to full-on pain in the arse and seemed to be treating the terrace as his personal stage.

'We've been looking at places like this for investment opportunities.' He leaned back and surveyed the chateau as if it were already his personal dominion. 'But you ask people for a peek at their sales forecasts and they take the huff. Bloody frogs! You can't be coy in business. You have to be bloody direct.' He took another big belt of booze.

The other diners, Brits to the core, smiled with polite trepidation, silently wondering how much more direct it was possible to go in the world of Geoffrey darling.

We were soon to find out.

He'd been surveying Nat with the eyes of a man on the hunt (even in her raddled state, she could still turn heads) and when she leant over the table to deliver Sylvie's *canelé* as his dessert, he couldn't resist.

Women have been touched up by tossers since time immemorial. And I'm sure that, at the height of the eighties stock market boom, Geoffrey darling was one of the City's grossest gropers.

But I'm glad to say we now live in different times.

With a handful of Nat's breast, Geoffrey darling looked like a Roman emperor owning what he believed was his to own. Poor Nat was stunned initially into frozen silence. This then quickly dissolved into tearful trembling.

Her saviour came in the unlikely shape of Sylvie, who, having seen the whole sordid incident from her kitchen window, pitched up at the table with all the self-control of a caged wildcat.

The sound of her slap reverberated around the courtyard terrace and sailed out over the vineyard. They probably heard it in Paris.

The chateau management were summoned and an initially combative Geoffrey was quickly cowed by Madeleine's granite demeanour and her threat of charges of sexual assault. A taxi arrived within minutes to remove the pair from the premises.

While the rest of the party recovered their equilibrium, Sylvie sat on the kitchen step with Nat wrapped in her arms, each woman working hard to master her feelings.

***

Feeling like she'd caused the household more than enough upset, Nat, looking somehow stronger and more resilient, took her leave of Château Paulus the following day.

'You've been so wonderful, Jen. And I've been nothing but trouble.'

'Living under each other's feet hasn't been easy for either of us. But I'm genuinely glad I could help. Even though it was only a bit.'

'You'll never know how much you've helped. Seriously. I feel like I'm getting my life back. And it's only because of you. Because you came into my life again.'

'Where will you go?'

'Back to the UK anyway. I'll try to build bridges with my parents. If that doesn't work, something else will.'

'I hope so.'

'I *know* so. That's what you've given me. The certainty that things will turn out wonderful. Well, if not wonderful, at least okay.'

'Stay in touch.'

She smiled. 'You won't get rid of me now.'

I was sad to see her go. But I can't pretend it wasn't good to have the apartment all to myself again.

Then I remembered what Nat had said about seeing 'something' during the night.

17

Through Glass Darkly

With Nat gone, I had more freedom to spend quality time with Gabriel.

I had feared Nat's presence might change things between us – and he might have responded to the feminine charm that, in spite of time's passing, still dripped from her every pore – but I needn't have worried. He'd been immune and seemed to have eyes only for me.

And what lovely eyes they were.

The late July days were as hot as ever and work in the vineyard started earlier each day. The magic hour around dawn was spellbinding and, every morning, I pinched myself as I watched the sun slowly burn through the early morning mist.

But the midday sun was punishing and by early afternoon I was generally running out of steam.

Philippe suggested I move indoors for a few days and asked me if I'd take on the job of batching up some of the chateau's older wines so they could be prepared for dispatch to a handful of private collectors. It sounded like a daunting job but Philippe gave me a couple of spreadsheets that told me everything I needed to know, so that the task was reduced to the mechanical exercise of matching labels to items on a list.

I was enjoying the delicious musty coolness of the stone walls and floors of Paulus's dimly lit underworld when I got Nat's text.

I'm meeting my dad for lunch. I'll let you know how it goes. Just wanted to say thanks again. Take care of yourself (and watch out for ghosts!) x

I've never been one to be spooked by the dark but Nat's little joke unnerved me. I remembered the look in her eyes when she'd mentioned seeing something moving in the apartment.

Then I told myself I was being stupid and that Nat, although unsettled at the time, had clearly shrugged the experience off and was now making light of her earlier reaction. Was perhaps even a little embarrassed by it.

The vault where the older wines were cellared was particularly dark and very dusty. The neat ranks of bottles that lay in its curved recesses looked like they hadn't been disturbed for a good couple of decades. I was apprehensive about handling them.

Perhaps it was the silence of the place, the solitude of the task, the dark unfamiliarity of the space, but I was seized by the desire to get the job finished as soon as possible.

As I crouched on the unforgiving stone floor, peering through the dust at the label on a bottle I'd taken from the bottom shelf, a spider the size of a two-euro piece darted out and ran up my leg.

I jumped like a teenager at a horror flick and the bottle shattered on the stone floor, its contents creating a slowly spreading pool of magenta.

My first thought was to clear up the mess and I set about gathering up the broken glass from under the shelf. Something caught my eye. Words scratched into the cellar wall. Two names and a date. *Sébastien. Émile. 1910.*

My second thought was for the value of the contents I'd chucked about the place.

I handed Philippe the wine-soaked fragment of bottle that held the label, feeling like a naughty schoolgirl in the headmaster's office.

'I'm so sorry.' My eyes started to fill up.

Philippe was utterly charming about it. 'Hey. Relax. It's a small mistake. And it's one less bottle to store.'

'One less to sell. I'm such an idiot!'

'Please. We have a margin for losses. In the field, in the cellar, in transit. This is a very small thing. Believe me.'

In my room before dinner, I Googled the '82 Paulus. 'A stunning vintage with great style.' One UK merchant was selling the stuff for £690 a bottle.

A small thing indeed. I felt my lips tremble again.

Madame Hélène comforted me over dinner. When the others had left the table, I lingered and mentioned the names I'd seen scratched on the cellar wall. She poured two glasses of armagnac and settled into her story.

'My grandfather and his friend were always together. They were children in that special time before the big war. A time of freedom. And they liked to have adventures. To go to places that were forbidden. They were boys. For them, a rule was an invitation to do something bad. To break the rule.'

She took a sip of armagnac.

'So they jumped from the bridge into the Garonne, they smoked cigars they stole from my great grandfather's cupboard, and sometimes they sneaked into the cellar and drank wine. Even in France, this was wrong. Children could have a little wine with a lot of water. But to drink wine *sec*, without water, was dangerous.'

'Of course.' I fiddled with the plaster on my finger.

'One day, they sneaked into the cellar and drank, it seems, a complete bottle. They were ten years old. Only something bad can happen after that.'

'Yes. I imagine so.'

'Well, my grandfather's friend, Emile, climbed onto one of the big barrels. It was a dangerous thing for a young boy to do. Especially a young boy with a head full of wine.'

'What happened?'

'The barrel moved and Emile fell and the barrel rolled onto him. Then more barrels fell down and onto Emile. My great grandfather and his workers tried to help, but it was too late.'

'How awful!'

'Yes. My grandmother told me that he never forgot his friend. On their wedding day, my grandfather told her he sometimes saw Emile walking around the chateau at night, calling his name. My grandmother said the tragedy had made him a little mad. They were married in 1917. Then, like all the other boys, my grandfather went away to be a soldier. He was killed at the Battle of Amiens in 1918, three weeks before my father was born.'

Hélène turned eyes full of tears towards me.

'When I look at my old face in the mirror, I sometimes think about the young boy who was the grandfather I never knew.'

I went to bed with my mind full of the day's events – my clumsiness and its cost, the text from Nat, Madame Hélène's family tragedy.

I woke in the middle of the night feeling like my head had come unscrewed and padded through to the bathroom for a drink of water. My sleeve caught on the handle of the bathroom door and sent me headlong onto the tiled floor.

The clatter woke the entire household and the impact of the fall left me stunned. I sat on the bathroom floor unable to speak.

Madeleine bent down to help me up.

'What on earth happened to you? You look like you've seen a ghost.'

18

Crushed

August was sultry, in the vineyard and in the bedroom.

Around the chateau, I was hardworking and focused – as the vines galloped towards harvest, they needed all our attention – but my evenings were marked by an intimacy and a fire I'd never experienced since Pete. Perhaps not even then.

In front of the others, Gabriel was discretion itself. Both of us were confident no-one had detected the change in our relationship. On the surface, the waters were calm.

Then a pebble was thrown into the pool and ripples began to spread.

Chloë had her mother's flawless skin and her father's athletic physique, displayed to excellent effect in the tight denim shorts and skimpy vest that were her default setting. Philippe and Madeleine's only child had spent the first month of the summer vacation travelling round Europe with friends and now she was home until classes started back at *Sciences Po* in Paris, the top university that is the alma mater of a handful of French presidents and scores of other world luminaries.

The ever-present smartphone and slightly pouty resting face marked her out as a teenager. The hair and the legs and the curves announced her as a powerfully alluring woman.

But she was a pleasant and energetic co-worker and, with excellent English showing only the slightest trace of an accent, she helped me steer a course through the minefield of potential howlers that seemed to characterise my interaction with the French language.

'French is so full of false friends for English speakers.'

'False friends?'

'Words or expressions that sound like equivalents but in fact mean very different things. So, when Sylvie offers you more food but you're full, don't be tempted to say *Je suis pleine.*'

'Why not?'

'Because *Je suis pleine* doesn't mean *I'm full*. It means *I'm drunk. Or I'm pregnant.*'

'My god! Why is French so difficult?'

'English is far worse.'

'English is easy.'

'For you, yes. But imagine how hard it is for a French speaker to know, for example, how to pronounce the string of letters *o.u.g.h.*'

'O. Like in *Though.*'

'Okay. But what about *Through. Ought. Cough. Plough. Rough.*'

I'd never thought of it before. Here I was, being taught about my own language by a beautiful French teenage brainbox.

I might have resented it. But she was charming.

Right up to the moment when, in my last week at the chateau, she witnessed an unguarded Gabriel throw me a look so full of desire it made me blush right down to my cleavage.

After that, although she was charm itself with the rest of the household, around me she became offhand, uncommunicative, hostile even. I tried to ignore the change in her behaviour towards me but, never one who'd been comfortable with conflict, I couldn't deny it was affecting my mood.

One evening, Madame Hélène beckoned me to sit beside her after everyone had left the table. She poured me an armagnac.

'You must forgive my granddaughter. She's had a crush on Gabriel since she was ten years old.' She took a sip of the golden liquid and I followed her lead. 'So it's hard for her, knowing about the two of you.'

I looked at her in stunned silence. She smiled.

'One advantage of being an ancient person is that nothing escapes you. Particularly love.' She lifted the bottle and poured more into both glasses. 'Another advantage is nobody can tell me armagnac is bad for my health. I've lived long enough to disprove them all.'

'Do Philippe and Madeleine know?'

'At this important time of the year, my son and his wife give all their attention to the vines. Your secret is safe with me.'

'But what about Chloë?'

'When Gabriel first came here, he was a teenager himself. The only young person she could relate to. So it's no surprise he became the focus of her attentions.'

She looked wistful.

'First love is so difficult. When I was a teenager, the war took our young men away to fight. The only people who stayed behind were women and children and a handful of men like my father, forced to produce wine for the Germans who occupied our chateaux. I was starved for male attention.'

She smiled at her own naïvety.

'I was pretty and less modest than I should have been, particularly for those times. I made a young doctor the object of my affections. He often came to the chateau when a worker was sick – we had a staff of twelve or fifteen in those days – and I fell for him completely.'

She shook her head at the memory.

'It was only when I declared myself to him – offered myself, really – that I discovered he was almost old enough to be my father.'

She turned sheepish eyes on me.

'He had a wife and *three* children!'

'Goodness. That must have been a shock.'

'I was deeply embarrassed. And so was he. From then on, he refused to come to our chateau – some excuse about having too many patients – but he never told my father the real reason. Then, after the war, I met dear Claude, Philippe's father.'

I went to bed with a head full of troubles. The secret of my relationship with Gabriel was fully out, I'd compromised my professionalism, and I'd made an enemy of the daughter of people who'd welcomed me into their family and been nothing but kind and supportive.

The last few weeks with Gabriel had been … blissful … but, if I'd been worried about how I'd handle the end that was looming – I'd be going back to the UK in a few days – the advent of Chloë had made it clear a clean break was the only option.

As it turned out, that option was forcefully underlined by a further revelation.

Gabriel had always talked fondly about life back in Poland and, as we lay in bed one evening, my hair on his chest, I asked him what his home town was like. I'd never been to Eastern Europe and I had trouble picturing it.

'I have photograph.' He picked up his phone and scrolled through to an album of photos of a pretty town square, brown brick buildings, cobbled pavements, tall spires, fountains.

But one other album had caught my eye.

Its thumbnail photo showed Gabriel in a suit, his arms wrapped round a young woman with tumbling brown hair. A celebration of some sort, presumably. A family wedding. An anniversary. A christening.

He got up to use the bathroom.

Nothing good comes of snooping. I knew that.

But I had a bad feeling about Miss Tumbling Hair.

The album featured a couple of dozen shots of a couple celebrating (judging by the balloons) their thirtieth wedding anniversary. Then came a run of photos of Gabriel and his companion – some cuddles, some dancing, some more intimate embraces.

The beauty (and danger) of the digital image is twofold – its time signature and its zoom capacity.

The timeline was July, about six weeks ago, the long weekend he'd flown back to Poland for. And the zoom afforded me a close-up of an interesting feature – a dazzling diamond and ruby ring on Miss Tumbling Hair's engagement finger.

I was out of the house before he'd had time to flush.

***

Room available in large Victorian house. Wood Green. Quiet area. Good transport links. Fully furnished. Wifi. Shared kitchen and bathroom. Professional person, non smoker. Contact Miranda.

I had the safety net of an open offer of my old room at B&B's but I'd abused their hospitality too much already. Besides, with me around, old Custard's survival would be in serious jeopardy.

So, for the sake of the canary and for my own self-esteem, I emailed Miranda. I got a positive reply within the hour and suddenly my return to the UK seemed real.

I said a fond goodbye to Philippe and Madeleine, and an affectionate farewell to Sylvie. I received the warmest of embraces from Madame Hélène and knew I'd miss her company enormously.

I exchanged a cheerless wave with Chloë.

Of Gabriel, who would have seen the open photo that had prompted my lightning departure, I'd seen nothing since that evening.

Which suited me fine.

Benoit dropped me and my bags at the station. When he kissed me on both cheeks, the tears leapt to my eyes and I had to turn away.

My summer of sun and friendship and fine food and love was over.

19

Definitely Not Fine

My plane nosed through a thick layer of low grey cloud and a minute later the wheels hit the tarmac at Gatwick.

Bordeaux seemed like it had never happened. Saint Emilion a fantasy. The warm air, the ranks of vines rising up to the horizon, the touch of Gabriel's skin, the crushing disappointment of my discovery. I felt a rock in my stomach at the thought of him.

The things we know to be bad for us still have the power to bewitch.

***

Number 27 Arcadia Avenue was typical of the Victorian terraces that populate the London borough of Wood Green.

The front door opened as my finger was an inch from the bell.

'Jennifer! Lovely to meet you!' A warm and very firm handshake. 'I'm sorry to be so inhospitable but I'm making lasagne with twelve spotty adolescents in half an hour and most of them couldn't wipe their own arses so it'll be entertaining at the very least.'

She ushered me quickly into the hallway and pointed up the stairs.

'Your bedroom is the one facing the garden.' She thrust a key into my hand. 'I'll be back around six and we can get to know each other then.'

'Okay.'

She had one foot out of the door. 'The hot tap in the bathroom is *very* hot. And I'm afraid Gordon will snuggle. I hope you don't mind.'

And, with that, this frantic, elfin figure was gone in a whirlwind of scarves and splashy earrings, leaving me to wonder who the hell Gordon the Snuggler was and how he'd respond when I kneed him in the jewels.

I remembered Dirty Dave, the leering live-in boyfriend of my bikerish Intext colleague, Marilyn. In the aftermath of my split from Pete, Marilyn had offered me a room in her house and, desperate though I was, all I could think of was how, at some works do months earlier, Dave had spent the evening with his eyes locked on my cleavage. Then, I'd thanked Marilyn for the offer but had politely declined.

Now I'd be coping with Gordon. The snuggler. What had I got myself into?

Gingerly, I began to explore my new surroundings. This was definitely a woman's domain. Furniture in soft blues and creams. Whitewashed walls. Varnished floors. A shabby chic sideboard. Scented candles.

The kitchen had shelves jam-packed with cookery books – some Delias, a Jamie or two, an ancient Ken Hom from his mop-top days. In the fridge, frantic Miranda had left a bottle of Pinot Grigio with a Post-It saying 'Help Yourself!' and I poured a glass and sat at the kitchen table and listened for Gordon.

After a minute or two of silence, I climbed the stairs, glass in hand, and crossed the threshhold into my room.

It was clean and spacious, with ample room for the double bed. The wardrobe was smallish but it would easily accommodate my clothes. The dressing table had a funky upcycled mirror on it. And Miranda had added a few thoughtful personal touches – fresh alstromerias in a glass jug, some cushions, a handful of books. The room overlooked a small, well-kept garden.

People with a private outdoor space in London feel like the Aga Khan, which is why the parks are always heaving. In Wood Green, I had Alexandra Park along the road and, if I felt like a leg-stretch, Finsbury Park was doable. Even Hampstead Heath if I was in the mood for an expedition. And when I was feeling lazy, a small private space.

Well, a shared space. Shared with Miranda. And Gordon.

I went back downstairs with my wine and, knocking it back and feeling immediately too exhausted to tackle the unpacking, I lay down on the sofa in the bay window, through which welcome afternoon sun was now pouring, and flicked through the previous month's copy of *House Beautiful*.

When I looked at my phone, nearly an hour had passed and a sleek black cat was lying curled up against the inside of my arm. He woke when I did and, with his little motor stirred into action, turned his emerald-green eyes towards me and emitted a soft meow.

I stroked his delicious softness and looked at the silver disc on his collar. Gordon.

I heard a key in the front door. A few moments later, a woman of around seventy appeared at the door to the living room, pulling a shopping trolley full to bursting.

'Miranda told me you'd be arriving today.' She pulled off her navy anorak and red woolly hat. 'I'll put the soup on.'

She fished into the trolley, pulled out two tins of Asda mulligatawny, and headed for the kitchen.

I rubbed my eyes, lifted a quietly protesting Gordon gently onto the floor, and followed her.

'You're bound to be hungry after a long journey. Sit yourself down.' She pulled a breadknife from a drawer and cut two hunks off a brown loaf and popped them into a shallow basket. The phrase *docker's doorsteps* came into my head.

'Do you mind it less than boiling?'

'No.' *And, by the way, who the bloody hell* are *you?*

'You're not supposed to boil soup. Spoils the flavour. Same with all foods, really. Some people think if it's not stripping the skin off the roof of your mouth, it's not hot enough.'

'I'm sure this will be fine. Thank you. But you don't have to feed me.' She ignored my feeble protest and laid two bowls on the table. Then she went back into the kitchen and dragged the shopping trolley through and parked it by her chair. Because it contained gold bullion or state secrets, presumably.

'Not married, then?' She clocked my left hand.

'Afraid not.'

'Boyfriend?'

'Not at the moment.'

'I wish my Miranda would meet a decent man.'

Ah. A dropping penny.

'You're Miranda's mum.'

'Yes. Mary. Sorry. I should have started with that, shouldn't I?'

She plonked herself down, bit off a piece of bread the size of an orange, and started to work her way through it. *They must be all your own teeth.*

She spoke through bread. 'She's made some dreadful choices. My Miranda. And this new one's nothing to shout about either.'

I thought of my own chequered history of relationships as Mad Mary rummaged around in the shopping trolley. She pulled out a battered bible held together with masking tape. It had a couple of dozen pages bookmarked with tiny pink Post-It notes.

She laid her hand on the book and took a deep breath. I put down my spoon and prepared to join in with grace.

Then after a silent ten seconds, she put the bible back in the trolley and fixed me with a fortune-teller's stare.

'Do you have a pain in your shoulder?'

I paused with spoon twixt bowl and mouth.

'No.'

'Hm.' Mary seemed deflated.

'But my mum suffers from arthritis.'

Mary perked up, as if this were the best news she'd had all week. 'That'll be it.'

***

Gordon and I had the house to ourselves again by the time Miranda came through the door. She kicked off her shoes and collapsed onto the sofa.

'How are you settling in?'

'Fine. I really like the house. And thank you for the flowers. And the wine.'

'You're welcome. Any left?'

'I only had one glass.'

'Great.' She jumped up but I waved her back to the sofa. 'You look shattered. Let me.' I poured two glasses, brought them through, and we clinked.

'Welcome.'

'Thank you.'

'Nice to have a wine buddy. I feel like we're going to get on.'

'Yes.'

'And you don't mind Gordon?'

'Oh, no. He's lovely.'

'I wasn't sure you'd be a cat person.'

'I'm more of a dog person, to be honest. But he's gorgeous and lovely. We're friends already.'

Then I mentioned Mary's visit, her kindness with the soup, and the health probe.

'Sorry about my mum. She's as mad as a box of frogs. As you'll have seen.'

'Oh no, she's fine.'

'She's been banned from several of the churches round here.'

'Banned? Why?'

'She keeps wanting to cure people. Thinks she has special healing powers. And not everyone is keen on the laying on of hands.' She took a sip of wine. 'She means well. Sings outside Superdrug every Saturday morning with a bunch of other God-Squadders. So if you're topping up on toiletries, I'd stick with Asda unless you're happy to be collared for a verse or two of *Jesus Wants Me For A Sunbeam*.

'You're not religious yourself, then?'

Miranda shook her head. 'She dragged me along to Sunday School as a kid. But I bolted as soon as I hit puberty. You?'

'No . Not really. I've seen too much … suffering.' I thought of Mum. The cruelty of her condition.

'Blimey! We're getting a bit heavy, aren't we?' Miranda topped up our glasses and changed the subject.

Then, before I knew it, it was ten o'clock, we were on a second bottle, and neither of us had eaten. We ordered pizza and sat up till well after midnight, spilling our life stories.

Miranda had married Patrick straight out of catering college. They'd both had the ambition to run a restaurant and they bought a small cafe in Crouch End, rebranded it as a bistro, developed a menu that brought the punters in, and had a good-going business for four or five years.

Then cracks started to appear in the relationship.

'I wanted kids but Patrick wasn't interested. Kept saying the catering trade was all-consuming. We couldn't do both. Then the business started leaking money and I discovered he was a gambler.'

'A serious problem?'

'More like an illness. Football, horse racing, darts. You name, he'd bet on it. Tried to tell me it wasn't a problem. It was only small amounts. Then he discovered online betting and before I knew it he'd maxed out all our cards and taken out stupid payday loans to pay them off.'

'Goodness.'

'Then the guilt kicked in and he became depressed. Then he recovered but thought he could make it all better if he could just win one big amount. And he spent ages developing this statistical method that was a surefire winner. It was then I knew things would never change and I kicked him out.'

'Well done.'

'It was too late. I lost the business. So now I teach catering to FE college students who, most of them, don't really want to be there but also don't really know what they *do* want. At least I kept the house. I have my accountant to thank for that.'

Miranda went on to tell me about the new man in her life, but that setup was far from perfect, she said.

'Why?'

She looked shamefaced. 'Alan's married. They're on the rocks, he says, and getting a divorce. I'm not holding my breath.' She looked at me. 'Am I a monster? A cow? A homewrecker?'

'You don't seem like one. And if you're prepared to ask the question, I think that shows you're not. Deep down. But I can tell you that being on the wrong end of an affair isn't pleasant.'

And for the next half hour I told her about Pete and the younger model he'd thrown me over for, the woman I'd christened Bloody Bitch Bronwyn.

'That sounds like a very painful period in your life.'

'It was a long time ago. I'm fine now.'

'Fine isn't good enough.' She topped up my glass. 'You know what FINE stands for? Fucked up. Insecure. Neurotic. Emotional.'

'Then I'm not fine. I'm bloody marvellous!'

'That's more like it!'

We clinked glasses again and I sensed that life with Miranda would be an interesting ride.

All the same, two bottles of wine wasn't a nightcap I could sustain for long.

20

Harvey Nicked

Cécile had a call from Harry Sinclair, the former East End barrowboy turned shadowy property magnate and wine connoisseur who was one of the clients I was being groomed to manage.

He was keen to talk wine and Cécile thought it was a good idea to pitch some Château Paulus and, given my personal knowledge of the establishment, an excellent opportunity for me to form a relationship with one of her most important clients. So a trip to Surrey was arranged.

As my taxi from Guildford reached Oxshott, a village that regularly tops the list of Britain's swishest spots, the Range Rover quotient spiked instantly. What few commercial outlets there were seemed like the kinds of places that would operate a dress code. One estate agents' office we passed looked more exclusive than the Groucho Club.

A pair of black-and-gold gates parted silently and the cab nosed its way onto the grounds of Dansford. On either side of the gravel drive, an immaculate garden was laid out in the Italian style – manicured lawns, promenades, fountains, statues, cypress trees, a marble summer house of the sort Don Corleone might retire to in the evening after another long day delivering horses' heads.

It was a good two minutes before we reached the house itself, an elegant mansion you could imagine National Trust spies sniffing round, wondering where to site the café, settling on the twelve-quid entrance fee.

The driver struggled with my wheelie as I tugged the polished brass bell-pull. From behind the ancient oak threshhold, the bell sounded like Big Ben.

The door was opened by a tiny Filipino woman with a sweet smile who escorted me forty yards or so along a wide hallway with a marbled floor and into a light and airy drawing room the size of one of the tennis courts I could see through the huge bay window (*Why would a person need more than* one *tennis court?*).

She gestured to a four-seater sofa. 'I'll tell Mr Sinclair you have arrived.' She smiled warmly and glided off.

I looked around. Ancient oak floorboards highly polished, old oil paintings in ornate gilt frames, walnut cabinets. And, in the corner, a sleek black Steinway grand that Elton John would be happy with. *I don't have much money but boy, if I did, I'd buy a big house where we both could live.*

'It's far too expensive to run.'

I turned round to see Harry Sinclair. El Dorado. The Golden One. One part Cary Grant, three parts Ronnie Biggs. He looked like he'd just helicoptered in from Monte Carlo.

'I was just …'

'The house, I mean. Not the piano. Do you play?'

'Er, no. *Chopsticks* is my limit.'

'Me neither. But Pauline likes it. She's having lessons.' He straightened the sheets on the music stand. 'I'm a bit OCD.'

'Your house is gorgeous.'

'Thank you. It's comfortable but it's too big, really. Good for parties, though.'

I imagined the kind of party where errant business associates might be taken outside for a 'chat.'

'Yes.'

'Tell me about your time in Bordeaux.'

He gestured to the sofa and I took my seat beside him and talked about Château Paulus, its heritage, the personal care the owners took over the vines, the decades of experience, the attention to detail. Harry was an interested and attentive listener and I found myself easing into the role of knowledgeable client manager. He asked a handful of questions and seemed satisfied and a little impressed by my answers.

I opened my wheelie case and produced five bottles for tasting – two white, three red – and managed to uncork each one without explosions then pour them without spilling any onto the prime Persian under our feet.

As Harry was swilling a 2010 Cabernet-Merlot blend that I was telling him would age particularly well, 2010 being a belting vintage, a woman wearing half of Hatton Garden's combined stock marched into the room. Miss Luscious Legs 1974.

She waved a card angrily. 'I've told them not to leave deliveries on the drive.'

Harry turned indulgent eyes towards her.

'Sorry, love. I'll sort it.'

'They say they're ringing the bell but they can't be. That's the third time this month. It's bloody Prada, for Christ's sake!'

Then she noticed me. 'Sorry. Excuse me for interrupting.'

'It's no problem. I'm sorry you're having that bother.'

'I shouldn't get worked up. It's only a little thing. But what if it rains?'

I wasn't sure I'd write off Prada as 'a little thing.'

'Of course. They should be waiting until the door is answered.'

Harry watched this female back-and-forth with a twinkle of amusement.

'I know. But everybody's rush rush rush, aren't they? Targets. Schedules. But where's the customer service?'

I could see that, around 1974, Pauline would have been pretty convincing as a Farah Fawcett lookalike. Decades later, she was still a very attractive woman. Some of the freshness was clearly chemically enhanced – there was that telltale look of permanent alertness round the eyes – but I told myself if I looked half as good in twenty years, I'd settle for it.

And I liked her ballsy style.

Harry's mobile buzzed and he excused himself.

'I was saying to your husband how much I like your house.'

'Too far out in the sticks for me, if I'm honest. I miss the shops. I mean, I can hardly pop to Harvey Nicks for a quick browse, can I? And driving into town is a bloody nightmare. Pardon my French.'

'Yes. A car in the city is a good way to get your blood pressure up, isn't it?' Pauline looked at the glasses on the table and I lifted the 2010. 'Can I pour you a glass?'

'No ta. I only drink champagne. Half the calories.' She patted her tiny belly.

Harry reappeared. 'I won't be long, love. Jennifer and I just have a bit of business to see to then I'll come through.'

Pauline took her cue and stood up. 'Nice to meet you.'

'You, too. I hope you get the delivery thing sorted.'

I chatted for another half hour about the Saint Emilion offerings and Harry listened and nodded and swilled and, by the time my taxi had arrived, I'd secured, by means of a generous discount on the cellar door, a substantial increase to the already hefty amount of business he was putting our way.

I'd also secured an invitation to a charity event he was organising at his golf club. Excellent networking, he said.

So that's what I was now. A networker.

21

Handbags and Glad Rags

Pauline was right. One advantage of living in London is proximity to shops. The charity fundraiser was an excuse to treat myself and, on the salary Cécile was paying me, plus generous bonuses of the sort I'd just bagged after my meeting with Harry, I could afford to be a little indulgent.

Now the calendar had nudged into November, London's retail outlets were gearing up for Christmas and you could feel the stirrings of festive panic in the hordes of shoppers scouring the windows for early seasonal bargains.

I strolled along Piccadilly not with any serious plan to buy anything but rather to drink in the exclusivity – The Ritz, Burlington Arcade, the discreet premises of BAFTA – before heading up to Oxford Street and my favourite department store.

The iconic Corinthian columns at the entrance to Selfridges reminded me a little of those at Dansford. Inside the store, Christmas music was in the air and a man in his forties was revelling in his teenage daughter's distress as he jigged his way up the escalator to the strains of Wizzard.

In Ladies' Fashion, I blinkered myself from the delights of Burberry and Armani and headed through to the affordable sections. A teenage girl with bright blue eyes and an Essex twang brought me half a dozen dresses in a twelve and helped me settle on a strapless number in midnight blue, teaming it with a delicate silk shawl edged with tiny crystals.

Restrained but with a dash of glam.

Feeling relaxed and rather chuffed with myself, I celebrated my find with a ten-pound glass of wine and a plate of *amuse-bouches* in a glass-fronted art deco bistro off Portman Street.

I took out my phone, flicked through half a dozen emails and discovered nothing urgent, scrolled through half a dozen screens of Facebook news feed and saw nothing remotely interesting, then mooned over my album of summer photos from Château Paulus.

I didn't notice anything was wrong until I thought about a second glass of wine and reached for a handbag that wasn't there.

I looked under the table. In the Selfridges bag. In the ladies. I asked at the bar and the young Polish woman who'd taken my order asked the lad who was waiting tables if he'd seen it. But I knew the truth already.

The Polish woman made me a coffee while I phoned the bank, sweating on hold for five minutes and wondering how many thirty-pound contactless purchases the average handbag thief makes per minute.

When I finally got through and explained the situation, the bank guy stopped all my cards on the spot and the total losses amounted to £187, a little over what I'd paid for the dress. Could have been worse. It just meant I'd be going to Harry's charity do in a dress that had cost, effectively, three hundred and fifty quid.

A Google search told me there was a police station on Savile Row (*Really?!*) so I trekked back down to Piccadilly. In the rain.

I was given an incident number.

'Selfie sticks. That's one thing they're using to spy on people in crowded places.'

'I'll bear that in mind.'

'The chances of recovering the bag are minimal, to be honest. I take it you've called the bank?'

'Yes. The bastards took a couple of hundred pounds but the cards are all stopped now.'

'You've got off lightly. I know it doesn't feel like it.'

'No.'

***

Miranda tried to be upbeat. 'At least you weren't hurt. And they never got your new dress. Which is lovely, by the way.' She tilted the brandy bottle towards my coffee mug but I put my hand over it.

'No, thanks. I think I'm just going to head upstairs.'

'Have you changed your online passwords? Just in case?'

'I've done the main ones. I'll do the rest in the morning.'

I padded up to my room feeling stupid, deflated and a good bit lighter in the purse.

22

A Bid Too Far

Harry Sinclair's golf club, on the outskirts of Guildford, had the same vibe as his Oakshott mansion – exclusivity and wealth with a sprinkling of flash.

As I stepped out of the taxi, I felt the silky midnight blue was making the right impression and I had only a faint residual pang of dismay over what it had cost me to get it. I smoothed the dress, admiring the polished fingernails that had been glittered to match the crystals on the shawl.

I handed my invitation to a giant of a man in black wearing an earpiece, which all seemed a bit *Lock Stock and Two Smoking Barrels*. Without a word and with no discernible facial expression, he pointed me through to the main reception. I headed to the ladies to touch up my lipstick and give myself a quick spray of Jo Malone.

Looking not bad, Jennifer Brown. Now for some networking.

The room was a sea of dinner suits and sequin-studded dresses (which put me in mind of the Christmas decorations in Selfridges). I spotted Harry at the bar, suave in his dinner suit and deep in conversation with a huddle of other suits. A tall young man with a pointy nose and a tray of champagne smiled at me and I took a flute and thanked him.

I was wondering what the seating arrangements were when I spotted Pauline waving over to me and I walked over to say hello.

'You're on our table, love. Sit yourself down. Oh, you've got a drink. Good. Cheers.' We clinked. 'I love your dress.'

'Thank you. You look lovely.'

She ignored my compliment. 'Harry's fair taken with you. That's why you're sitting here. You'll get a few looks but bollocks to them.'

I wondered why the looks. Would there be speculation as to my … relationship with Harry?

Then another woman touched Pauline's arm and she turned away. I scanned the room.

This was a very glamorous affair indeed and a fair proportion of the guests looked entirely at home in the luxury surroundings. But I spotted a handful of younger men who looked as if wearing a dinner suit was a novel experience and a couple of guys who looked like they normally spent their evenings lying on a park bench. Or shinning down someone's drainpipe with a bagful of ill-gotten gains.

Pauline's friend walked away and she turned back to me.

'It's a good turnout.'

'Yes. Erm, so is this a fundraiser?'

'Yes. Unchained.'

I guess I looked blank.

'Harry's charity. It gives support to ex-offenders. Getting them back on their feet, finding them a flat and a job and stuff. And helping with appeals. When they're stitched up by the police. That sort of thing.'

'Right.'

'Like, see that bloke with the grey beard?'

She pointed to one of the guys talking to Harry at the bar.

'He's just out after a long stretch. Fitted up for a jewellery job. His wife's had all the locks changed and her lawyers have taken the house. So Harry's helping to sort things out for him.'

Grey Beard was telling a story and, at the punchline, Harry and the others guys threw their heads back and laughed. Whatever needed 'sorting out' in his life, it didn't look like it was bothering him much.

And I wondered what form Harry's 'sorting out' might take. I started to feel scared for a woman I'd never even met.

A face I'd seen a thousand times on TV walked past, under a hairstyle that looked like it'd taken a good few hours to assemble.

'Isn't that …?'

'Yeah. There's a few people here off the telly. Harry's got lots of friends in high places.'

And some in fairly low places, I'm sure.

I was suddenly aware of a fleece of curly white hair belonging to a middle-aged man with a belly that hung over his trousers like a mailbag. One of the mailbags from the Great Train Robbery. His eyes were fixed on me. Pauline followed my eyeline.

'Sean McQuire. He manages a couple of nightclubs up north. Lecherous old bugger.'

Sean the Sheep sashayed over and held out a chubby hand. There was something of the serial killer in his eyes.

'You must be the charming wine lady Harry's been telling me about.'

'Jennifer Brown. 'Sean took my hand and, before I could retract it, lifted it to his fat lips.

'Pleasure to meet you, lovely Jennifer Brown. Let's share a glass of something later.'

He smiled his serial killer smile and slid away.

The band struck up an intro and a man in a white tux with a microphone announced that more champagne was being delivered to the tables, which brought a roar of approval from the room.

Pauline shook her head. I wondered why.

'Is Harry paying for that?'

She smiled. 'He's not daft. He knows if they're pissed they'll splash the cash.'

The compere in the white tux warmed the room with a few jokes while everyone took their seats, then a young *X Factor* finalist in a skimpy dress came on and belted out something by Adele, before we were all invited to take up our personal iPads and prepare to place our bids on 'a stunning array of items offered for sale for a very worthy cause.' Bids declared would flash up on a twenty-foot screen.

I was definitely on the fence as to the worthiness of the cause but I was here as Harry's guest and there were certainly networking opportunities to be had. But I'd have to tread carefully.

The first item under the hammer was a weekend for two at a five-star hotel in the Cotswolds whose kitchen was run by a two-Michelin-starred chef. I'd bought his book a couple of years ago when I was teaching myself to be a cook and housekeeper and now he was sitting twelve feet away from me at the next table, looking about ten years older than the photograph on the book's cover.

I briefly wondered if it was the right time to tell him his beef bourguignon recipe had effectively got me the job, then I quickly decided it wasn't.

A woman in a tiara bagged the Cotswold weekend with a final bid of twenty-two grand.

Next up was a crate of '77 Mouton Rothschild donated by someone Pauline referred to as Speed Merchant Charlie. I reckoned he must sell a lot of cars to afford such a generous donation. I'd seen the '77 on some websites at four hundred quid a bottle. Then Pauline revealed that what Charlie sold wasn't the experience of speed. It was *actual* speed. Amphetamine.

Who *were* these people?

I noticed Sean the Sheep was bidding. He saw me notice and winked over at me. I remembered his comment about sharing a glass of something and felt a bead of cold sweat run down my back.

As soon as a rival bid flashed up on the screen, Sean fired in with an overbid. I willed someone to make the game too rich for him but nobody did and, with a fist pump that looked as out of place on a fat middle-aged man as his whitened teeth did, he smiled across at me and winked again.

Pauline saw the look on my face.

'Don't worry. I'll piss on his bonfire.'

'What do you mean?'

'There something coming up later I know he's dead keen on.'

She whispered in my ear as the compere announced a break while dinner was served.

All through the meal – lobster cocktail, chicken valentino, some gorgeously moist layer cake with pecans and brandy – I smiled to myself every time Sean the Sheep glanced over in my direction.

As the coffees and liqueurs came out, the compere took the stage again and the auction resumed.

'This next item has been kindly donated by Mason Moretti of Piccadilly.' He gestured towards an oil painting in an ornate frame. The kind of thing I'd seen a dozen of in Harry's drawing room. This was a 19th-century landscape. A view of a bit of the Yorkshire Dales that was, it seems, close to Sean's heart. Trees. Fields. Sheep.

'Let's start at ten thousand.'

Sean the Sheep battered away at his iPad and the bid flashed up on the screen. Pauline turned to me and smiled. She fired in a bid of fifteen.

I looked across at Sean and he looked momentarily knocked off balance. Then, every red-blooded sinew in his macho makeup tightening at the prospect of a good fight, he punched in a bid of twenty.

By the time Harry returned to the table from some 'meeting' on the terrace, we were up to seventy-five grand and he threw his wife a *What the fuck?!* stare. She winked and punched in eighty.

Sean was licking his lips, alive with the thrill of the chase. He lifted his fat finger and delivered what he was sure would be the killer blow – one hundred thousand pounds.

There was a gasp in the room and all eyes turned on Pauline.

The dramatic quality of Pauline's performance of desolation could not have been bettered by Dame Judi herself. I almost believed her. She laid her iPad on the table and shook her head.

Sean punched the air in celebration. The TV star with the fancy hair came over to our table to commiserate and Pauline kept up the dejected routine womanfully.

She turned to me and whispered again.

'I'd say the painting's worth about five grand. Tops. The dozy bastard has paid twenty times its real value. Ha! Blokes. When they start swinging their dicks around, you can get them to do anything.'

Sean the Sheep was sidling over to our table and Pauline sprang up to head him off at the pass.

The slimeball was all smiles. He put a fat hand on her waist in a manner that reeked of proprietorial sleaze. Then Pauline leaned in and said something that killed the smile on his face in an instant. He looked over her shoulder at me. Then he turned on his heel and slunk back to his table.

Pauline chuckled as she sat down beside me.

'What did you say to him?'

'I made up a little story. If anyone asks, you were banged up for GBH. An ex-boyfriend who got on the wrong side of you and your Stanley knife.'

'I stabbed someone?'

'Well, put it this way ...' She lifted her champagne. '... you've still got his bollocks in your freezer.'

23

Christmas Spirit

Business at Artisan Wines was booming and, with the festive season approaching, it was only going to get boominger.

I'd settled in nicely to my sales and management role and Cécile seemed delighted with the way things were going at my end. I was adding value, it seemed.

And I was enjoying my role of mother hen to Kellie – we just seemed to get each other. So when she was tasked with organising the office Christmas meal, I felt I knew her well enough to point out that Wetherspoons was probably not the kind of thing Cécile would think suited the company vibe.

Kellie was frustrated. 'I just don't know what people want. And *people* probably don't know what people want. And I know whatever I do, someone's going to pull their face about it.'

She looked close to tears and I remembered well the minefield of tastes and egos you had to negotiate as the 'admin girl'. I put my arm round her.

'Look. Just find somewhere that looks interesting and a bit … different. Nothing you can find on the high street. And don't bloody stress about it.'

***

The place we all pitched up at two weeks later had the same style of décor as that cave Indiana Jones finds himself in just before he runs away from the big ball – raffia screens, tribal masks, fertility idols with engorged genitalia.

And the menu had taken its inspiration from the bush tucker challenge on *I'm A Celebrity*. Starters included such delicacies as deep-fried crickets and python carpaccio. Among the desserts I spotted chocolate-covered scorpions.

I glanced along the table at Kellie, who raised her eyebrows defiantly. *Well, you did want something you can't find on the high street.*

Cécile claimed to find the place 'delightfully cutting edge' and congratulated Kellie on her excellent research and 'bold choice'. And with that public seal of approval from the boss, we tackled the meal without demur.

I tried to think I was being 'bold' as I cracked my way through crispy leaf-cutter ant (like a rather firm popcorn) and broaching the honey-glazed mealworms did make me feel more than a bit Xenia Warrior Princess. All in all, a good evening. It was agreed Kellie had done a good job.

And nobody died.

***

When I'd popped down to Portsmouth to see Mum, I'd told Leon I'd be there on Christmas Day. He'd told me they'd been invited to spend Christmas Day at the Lindale Centre, where Mum was now going for daycare sessions on Tuesdays. There'd be a four-course Christmas lunch, games, and music from (for reasons not entirely clear to me) an Elvis impersonator. Mum was looking forward to it.

So we'd arranged for me to visit on Boxing Day.

Which left me free to help Miranda prepare and serve Christmas lunch to the homeless people to whom the college had been throwing open its cafeteria doors ever since Miranda had persuaded the people upstairs it was an appropriate thing for a community college to be doing.

When I trotted down to the living room on Christmas morning to exchange presents with Miranda, I found her comatose on the couch, her face streaked with mascara. There was an open bottle of rhubarb-infused gin on the coffee table, with about two tablespoons left in it.

I didn't know what had inspired this descent, but Miranda was clearly too far down the well to be pulled back up in time to do anything with turkeys and sprouts.

So I showered, grabbed a coffee, fed Gordon a tin of tuna fillets, left Miranda's present under the tree (a voucher for a gin flight at The Wade in Shoreditch, a prospect that, in her current state, would doubtless send her sprinting to the toilet bowl), left a flask of strong coffee and a note on the coffee table and set off for the college.

Once more unto the domestic breach, Jennifer Brown.

***

By the time the doors were opened, the veg was steaming nicely, the potatoes browning, and the turkeys filling the cafeteria air with their delicious aroma. If you limit yourself to one turkey a year, you can enjoy its savoury, crispy loveliness and forgive the way the breast meat is always a little dry even if you baste the bugger every thirty seconds. And I'd be counteracting that dryness with a corking gravy I'd knocked up with a touch of armagnac (a nod to Sylvie).

I was organised enough in the kitchen to be able to flop down beside the diners halfway through the main course and spend a bit of time getting to know them.

Don had lost his wife to leukaemia a week before her fiftieth birthday and the sheer tragic injustice of that trauma had sent him over the edge and into the arms of alcohol. Fifteen years on and he'd lost his health, his job, his house.

Steve, who looked about forty but was just twenty-six, had lived on the streets for the last eight months, trying and failing to find a job after a short term in prison for fraud (I made a mental note to speak to Harry about him). Jan had fled a violent and controlling partner who'd stolen her identity and tied her into such a knot of trouble it made me nervous just to think about it. But she still had the strength to feel compassion for others.

I must have looked exhausted because Jan refused to let me lift another finger.

'We'll sort the desserts. You put your feet up.'

'I can't let you do that.'

'You can't stop us. It's twelve against one.'

I smiled and, like a warrior queen marshalling her troops, Jan steered Don, Steve and a handful of others into the kitchen to heat up the individual puddings Miranda had piled into the fridge the day before her private ginfest.

Half an hour later, a ghastly-looking and sheepish Miranda rocked into the kitchen, with Mad Mary in tow, just as I was wielding the CO2 extinguisher.

'Don's never used a microwave. He didn't know you had to take the foil off. I'm really sorry. I should never have let them help.'

Miranda was unfazed. 'Don't worry. The students set these things on fire about twice a month. The college is used to it.'

She put her arm round me. 'I'm sorry for being such a bloody washout.'

'What happened?'

'I got a text from Alan. Ten to midnight on Christmas Eve. He and his wife have decided to give it another go.'

'I'm sorry.'

'I'm sorry I ever believed in him. I think *that's* what got to me. How bloody stupid and naïve I've been.'

'You've been a trusting person. That's a good thing. Don't let this … bastard change that.'

She gripped my hand.

'Thank you for coming into my life, Jennifer Brown. You are good for me.'

'We're good for each other.'

24

Angels and Demons

January was icy cold and Miranda was still struggling to recover from her Alan misadventure.

But she'd made a conscious effort to ease back on the booze (I was also giving Dry January a bash), had given away all her rhubarb gin, tipped half a bottle of brandy down the sink and taken three bootfuls of bottles to the recycling centre.

At Cécile's instigation, I was expanding my wine knowledge with a blind tasting course run on Wednesday evenings by a retired sommelier who complimented me on my discerning taste buds.

'Women are genetically superior to men in the palate.'

'As in so much else,' I joshed.

He smiled. 'Indeed. But yours is particularly sharp.'

We'd been travelling the world in wine and I'd been the only one in the class to spot that the softer, less acidic Pinot Noir was not from Burgundy but from Oregon.

Not bad for a girl from the sticks who, six months ago, didn't know her arse from her Aligoté.

His kind words put a spring in my step.

***

As did the air of romance in the office.

Kellie had reached the stage where ripped and permatanned TOWIE types were no longer doing it for her. She'd made it known she wanted someone with a bit of character and seemed to have set her cap at Lee. Whenever a man and a woman step up the banter to the point of mutual ridicule, you can be pretty sure the fire is burning. Kellie and Lee were each giving as good as they got and I knew it would only be a matter of time before their tendrils intertwined.

The sparkle in their eyes as they flung abuse at each other filled my heart with joy.

Then that joy was dashed on the rocks.

***

When your phone rings in the middle of the night, unless you have relatives in Australia or you've buggered up your alarm, it usually means something's wrong.

Mum had suffered a mini stroke. That's what the doctors in A&E had told Leon. She was sitting up in bed drinking tea and complaining about the lack of real sugar (they only had sweeteners), so she was basically fine. Nevertheless, I told him I'd get the train to Hampshire the following morning.

They'd moved her up to a ward by the time I arrived. I found her sitting in a chair next to the bed, clutching the Care Bear that had been my favourite toy when I was eight. Leon said she'd wanted to bring it with her.

Her blue-grey eyes were so like the ones I saw every morning in the mirror. But the spark that had been growing dimmer in recent years had now all but disappeared.

The consultant came to see me.

'The blood supply to the brain has been blocked, briefly. There's been some damage, which will result in confusion and memory loss.'

'She's been a little confused for some time. And her short-term memory is already quite … patchy.'

'Well, you'll see a worsening in both respects.'

The social worker chipped in.

'We're not sure that home care is appropriate for your mum any longer. We know that she's had very good full-time care in the home up to now ...' I glanced at Leon, who looked tearful. '... but, in our view, she'll need access to professional nursing care for everyday living.'

'I understand.'

'You have Power of Attorney. Is that right?'

'Yes.'

'Then the decision as to where your mum is placed rests with you.'

All the old demons played their guilty tune inside my head. I tried to reason with myself – I couldn't have given her any better care than Leon had done these past two years so why was I beating myself up about not having been there for her?

Because that's what women do. We're the first ones we put the boot into.

But I told myself we were where we were, and my duty was to find the right care for her from now on. The whirlpool of emotions in my head would have to be suppressed while I dealt with the practical tasks, but I knew I'd find that difficult. I couldn't shake the image of her sweet smile at the kitchen window whenever I used to visit. And I remembered what Natalie had said about her. What she'd thought of my mum when we were kids.

A sweet woman who sat down with us and asked us about our day. Who listened. I wanted a mum like that.

My mum's job, as she'd always seen it, was simply to be there and to give love. Whether I was winning or losing, and even when I was being stupid and clearly in the wrong. I hadn't always repaid that kindness and devotion, particularly in recent years. But now I had the chance to do the right thing for the remainder of her life.

Cécile was as wonderfully understanding as I knew she'd be. I was to take off as much time as I needed to make the arrangements I needed to make and not give work a second thought.

I told Miranda I'd be away for a few weeks at least. Mum's house would be my temporary home while I sorted out her care.

I said an emotional goodbye to Leon.

'What now?'

'I'm going back to Birmingham.'

I handed him an envelope.

'What's this?'

'She's been putting the money you wouldn't take for looking after her into a savings account. She'd written your name on the bank book, so it's money she wanted you to have.'

He opened the envelope and looked at the cheque. 'It's a huge amount. I can't accept it.'

'You have no choice. I have special powers, remember. I'm a superhero. Power of Attorney Woman.' He teared up and, as the tears leapt to my own eyes, I hugged him close.

'I don't know how to thank you.'

'Hey. You don't get to say that. That's *my* line.'

***

So I began, during office hours, the task of combing through Care Inspectorate reports on all the homes in the district, drawing up a list of definites and maybes and definitely nots and making appointments to visit.

And, in the evenings, sitting with an elderly mother who now hardly recognised me at all. There were little, occasional windows of normality – a light bulb temporarily switched on, a sentence or two of lucidity – and the odd moment of humour when Mum, boundaries now dissolved, would blurt out something she'd never have dreamt of saying before, as when she once told a young doctor examining her that he was the first man in thirty years to see inside her knickers.

But the bulk of our time together was spent in the thick grey fog that the cruel disease ushers in.

The nurses and doctors were an unfailingly patient army of kind-hearted souls who steered my mum through the indignities of daily life as an elderly person with dementia. And, if Mum wasn't always tuned in to their conversations, I found them comforting and occasionally entertaining during the long evenings I spent at her bedside.

One young nurse, a heartbreakingly pretty Polish girl called Anna, seemed particularly fond of my mum.

'She's very gentle. Very easy. Some of the patients! Ah!' and she raised her eyes heavenwards.

'Aggressive?'

'Yes. Aggressive. And the men, very saucy.'

'Oh dear.'

'One man, I won't say which one, tells me, "Anna, you are the only nurse I allow to wash me."'

I bet he allows it, I thought, looking at her gorgeous eyes, mermaid hair and shapely figure.

'But I always check him first. To make sure everything is … flat. If it's not, I bring a cloth with ice water. Then all is good.'

On my list of care homes, I was making more crosses than ticks and I was beginning to lose all hope of finding a place I'd be happy to entrust with the care of my mother.

I phoned Will – his outrageous voice always cheered me up and, buried within all the smutty repartee, there was sometimes a nugget of genuine widsom.

'Do you think you're being too choosy?'

'Well, I think I *should* be choosy. It's my *mum* we're talking about.'

'I know. But you might be making choices for the wrong reasons.'

'What do you mean?'

'When we had to do this for my nan, my mum spoke to a friend of hers who worked in a care home. She told my mum, Don't go into a place and look at the state of the carpets and the curtains and the pictures on the wall. If they've got that crappy 70s picture of that Spanish woman in the residents' lounge, that shouldn't be a dealbreaker. Look at the *care*. Watch how the carers behave. Do the residents look clean? Do they seem happy? Is the place clean? It doesn't have to be like something out of *Ideal Home*. It's not a furniture showroom. It just has to be a clean and happy place that's comfortable enough.'

***

With Will's mum's friend's advice firmly planted in the noddle, I pitched up at Roselands.

Twenty years ago, Roselands had been a popular country hotel, one of the poshest places in Portsmouth. I'd taken mum there for afternoon tea once and she'd told me that, if she ever won the pools, she'd book herself in for a whole month.

The crushing irony of the situation swirled around in my head as the manager, Marvin Gray, ushered me into an armchair in his office in a building for which the phrase *faded grandeur* might have been coined.

'We specialise in caring for dementia patients. Our mission is to get the best out of each person every day. I think we do that pretty well. But don't take my word for it. Speak to people here. I'll give you the tour. Then I'll leave you alone for a while and you can chat to residents and staff. Get a feel for the place. *You* are the one who knows your mum the best and *you* have to be satisfied she'll be happy here.'

I was impressed.

I sat in the light and spacious residents' lounge (no 70s Spanish lady but fairly garish and amateurish landscapes I definitely wouldn't have on my walls – *not relevant, Jennifer Brown*) and observed.

After several minutes, a woman in her fifties with kind eyes and a blue tabard sat down on the sofa next to me.

'What do you think?'

'It seems like a really nice place.' I was watching three old women, huddled round an old photo album, giggling with a male carer. 'People seem happy.'

'That's what we aim for. Happy, comfortable, clean. In that order. We don't drag people out of bed and push them into the shower if they feel like a lie-in. And if they want breakfast before they've had a wash, that's what they get. We're here to make *their* lives good, not *our* lives easy.'

'A great philosophy.' I sighed.

'Mum or dad?'

'Mum.' The tears rose to my eyes.

'It's hard. And you want to be sure you choose a good place. I've worked in four or five over the years. This is the best. By a long way.'

'The manager seems to have the right idea.'

She smiled. 'He's a good man. And a very good manager. But ...'

'What?'

'He's a bit of a performer. Thinks of himself as a singer. But between you and me ...'

'He's not Frank Sinatra?'

'He's more Frank Spencer.'

I laughed. She stood up. 'I'd better get back to work. I'm Irene, by the way.'

'Jennifer.'

'Well, Jennifer, I hope I see you again.'

I felt like I'd found it. The place where my mum would spend what was left of her life. The feeling was relief mixed with intense sadness.

As I walked down the steps, my phone buzzed. A text from Veronica, the woman who'd taken over from me as Estate

Manager at Thornhill Hall. Whose rather frosty resting face had got us off to a bad start but who'd soon opened up and become someone I now considered a friend. I kept up with her and with Rosemary, Thornhill's astonishingly talented but very understated chief cook, whose scones were one of the many reasons I'd loved my time at Thornhill.

I hadn't heard from her or from Veronica in a while. I wondered what was wrong.

'Nothing. Just checking in. Wondering if you're coming to see us anytime soon. Camilla's always talking about you. I'm sure she'd love to see you.'

I promised to look at my diary and plan a weekend trip soon.

25

Discovery

Mum moved into Roselands on the first Sunday of February. I spent the day settling her into her room and installing and arranging her most treasured personal possessions around her – the carriage clock that had sat on the mantelpiece and always lost a few minutes on the hour; the jewellery box from her dressing table that played Beethoven's *Für Elise*; the porcelain doll that had sat on a chair in her bedroom and whose eyes were as blankly staring as Mum's.

Although I'd been living alone in Mum's little house for a few weeks, it seemed somehow quieter and emptier now that I knew for sure she wouldn't be coming back.

The wall clock in the hall had stopped and I was strangely reluctant to wind it up.

In the days that followed, I began the monumental task of sorting out the house's contents. Most of the furniture would go to charity, barring a small carved oak table I'd always admired and she'd told me I could have 'when I go'.

A few of the more valuable possessions – a Wedgwood bowl, a few bits of silver, an oil painting Dad had bought at an auction – I'd hand in to Mrs Jennings, Mum's neighbour and close friend for the last thirty years.

It was all a bit ... weird. Like settling the estate of someone who's died.

But Mum had taken all the things that meant something to her, and there was not really space in her room at Roselands for terribly much more, and the house would have to be sold to pay for her care. I could foot the bills myself for a few months, but that was all. It was another time for pragmatism.

After one long day spent bagging up old clothes Mum should have thrown out years ago, I walked into the village to buy the wine that would be my reward for a day spent wrestling with ghosts and emotions.

I pulled my scarf tighter round my neck as I turned the corner onto Moss Lane. There, sitting in the layby opposite the shop, was a very familiar vehicle. A young man I recognised jumped out of the passenger side and I heard the driver's voice.

'And don't forget my ciggies!'

Some things never change. Pete was still living in the village. Still driving his treasured Land Rover. Still getting Darren to run around after him.

I pulled my furry hood around my face and took a few steps closer. There he was, chatting on his mobile, smoothing his shirt, fixing his hair in the rearview mirror. Probably on his way to price a landscaping job. Some woman who wanted a patio laid.

I stood behind Darren in the queue at the checkout and when he turned to leave I thought I saw a glimmer of recognition in his eyes as he brushed past me. But when I stepped back onto the street, the Land Rover was gone.

I stood on the pavement and laughed out loud to myself. At how freaked out Pete would have been at the possibility of bumping into me. At how different I was to the crazy, crushed flower he imagined me to be. At how good life was now compared to the desperate enterprise it had seemed a relatively short time ago.

At how I'd moved on.

I was drying myself after a long soak in Mum's bath when Miranda called. She sounded upbeat.

'You'll never guess who showed up at my door last night?'

'He didn't!'

'Saying he'd made a terrible mistake. Saying things weren't working out with his wife. Begging me to take him back.'

'You didn't agree?'

'I invited him in.'

'Oh, Miranda!'

'Wait. I invited him in. Listened to him. Patiently. Opened some wine. Brought him a plate of a 'delicious new paté' I wanted him to try. I've told you what a foodie he is. How he loves to give his opinion.'

'Yes.'

'Well, he fawned all over me for half an hour, and I let him, and I told him I'd think about it. Which I won't – don't worry.'

'Good. Bloody good.'

'Then, casual as you like, I asked him about the paté. And he put on his connoisseur face, took another bite, and prepared to contemplate its flavour.'

I wondered why she'd been feeding him some fancy paté and hadn't just smashed the wine bottle over his head.

'And he went, "Yeah. Really nice. Earthy. A little bit fishy." Then I showed him the door.'

'So what's the deal with the paté? Why would you waste some fancy new stuff on that wanker?'

'Because it wasn't fancy new stuff. It wasn't even paté.'

'What was it?'

'Gordon's cat food.'

***

The following day, I was flicking through a bundle of old newspapers Mum had saved in the sideboard by the TV. One from January 1972 featured a report on Bloody Sunday and the fourteen people killed in Northern Ireland when troops had opened fire on demonstrators. I thought of Dad and his time serving in Northern Ireland and I wondered what atrocities he might have witnessed. Or, worse, what transgressions he might have committed.

Another from December 1986 had a review of the Christmas Day episode of *Eastenders* when Dirty Den served divorce papers on Angie. Mum had always loved the soap.

I resolved to take these two newspapers with me on my next visit to Roselands, to see if they would draw her out.

Under the pile of newspapers was a wooden box full of old photographs and I sat on Mum's sage-green carpet and spread around me snapshots from my life – a caravan holiday in Devon, my first pet rabbit, a terrible end-of-year school photo of me with a homemade haircut – and some photos from times before I was born.

I came across one photograph of my father that I remembered seeing before. Dad dressed in military uniform with a young boy sitting on his knee. I'd assumed the boy was some second cousin – Dad had dozens of cousins – but Mum had been cagey and a little snappish on the one occasion I'd asked her about it.

Then the doorbell rang and Mum's neighbour, Mrs Jennings, came in to ask how things were going and to offer help. She lowered herself onto the carpet beside me and picked up several of the photos. I picked up the one of my dad with the little boy and she looked at it over my shoulder.

'He was a handsome devil, your dad.'

'Yes. He was.'

'She had quite a time with him in the early days.'

'I remember him being … bad-tempered … after he came back from Northern Ireland.'

'Yes. It was a difficult time for them. For other reasons, too, of course.'

'What other reasons?'

Mrs Jennings looked at the photograph then back at me. It dawned on her that I didn't know what she was talking about. She became flustered.

'Never mind. I'm speaking out of turn.'

'Just tell me.'

'It's not my … place.'

'Mrs Jennings. Everyone else is dead or … senile. Nobody else can tell me.'

She took a deep breath.

'Your mum always said how hard it was in the early years when your dad was in the army. Being apart, I mean. For them, absence *didn't* make the heart grow fonder. And for a while they were … apart.'

'They split up?'

She nodded. 'Yes.'

'Why?'

'Your father was a charming man. Not very good at fidelity.' She took the photograph from my hand. 'The little boy was your father's … indiscretion. Then your dad came home, he and your mum made up, and the … matter … was never spoken of again.'

My heart was pumping fast.

Mrs Jennings went into the kitchen and put the kettle on. I followed her. She turned to me with a teaspoon in her hand.

'I'm sorry, dear. I thought, by now, she must have told you.'

'No, she's never said anything. She's never told me I have a half brother.'

26

Speed Dating and Canoodling

With Mum settled in nicely at Roselands and most of the associated admin under control – the house was largely cleared but not yet on the market – I was back at Miranda's and getting back into the swing of work again.

After the frantic activity of the last few weeks, I began to feel that my evenings were a little sterile. I was still doing the wine-tasting course on Wednesdays, but that fell squarely into the category of busman's holiday.

As I watched a particularly depressing episode of *Eastenders* – Stacey considering suicide for the umpteenth time and Phil sticking one on Ian Beale – I was feeling more and more dissatisfied with what was passing for my social life.

Then Miranda came into my room, ostensibly to moan about Mad Mary giving her bronze buddha to the Clic Sargent shop by the tube station without asking, under the unilateral policy of 'ridding the house of idolatry'. But when she sat down on my bed, there was clearly something else on her mind.

'I've been thinking, Jen.'

'Yes.'

'We're both pathetically single.'

'Well, single. Glumly single, maybe. But not pathetically.'

'So I've taken some action.'

'I'm not going on a blind date.'

'Not *a* date. *Eight* dates.'

'What?'

'Armando's, next to the cinema. Thursday. Speed dating.'

'I don't think so. Sitting opposite some stamp collector who lives with his mum, wearing a stupid badge. No chance.'

***

I sipped a passable sauvignon blanc and adjusted my name badge. Two tables away, Miranda raised her glass and smiled. I gave her my best *You bloody well owe me one for this* stare then adjusted the little pad and pencil on the table in front of me and waited for an evening of squirmworthy embarrassment to begin.

Most of the guys fell firmly into the harmless but uninspiring category and the chat was the kind of awkward smalltalk you might exchange with someone while waiting for your flu jab or, if you were Suzi Quatro, giving an interview to *Jackie* magazine – Have you done this before? What's your favourite takeaway meal? If you could invite anyone who's dead to dinner, who would it be? By that last one, I was three sav blancs to the wind and giving very little of a shit and the full-throated answer I gave – *I'd invite my dead dad so I could ask him why he bloody well cheated on my mother!* – made the poor bloke on the other side of the table look at me like I'd been let out for the weekend.

A couple of days later, Miranda and I got the emails through telling us our matches.

I had two, which, considering I'd only ticked two, was a pretty impressive stat. I was chuffed.

Miranda got eight.

'You ticked every box?'

'Modern love is a numbers game. I won't sleep with *all* of them. Obviously.'

'So. Who first?'

'Gary. Seriously fit. Cute arse. 'She turned her iPad towards me.

'He looks alright. Bit macho, maybe.'

'What about you? That Ian seemed right up your street. Into outdoor pursuits and stuff. You like all that countryside crap, don't you?'

'To be honest, I just ticked the box for the sake of it. None of them made much of an impression on me.'

'You've got to get out there, Jen. And this is how it's done these days. I don't want to end up like my mother – feeling people up like some kind of low-budget shaman.'

After a couple of days of hemming and hawing, I emailed Ian and we arranged to meet at Pangbourne at the weekend. It was a bit of a trek from London but, after a few weeks of concrete and glass and tube trains, I was ready for open spaces relatively empty of people. And Pangbourne is a gorgeous little village on the Thames. We could go for a stroll by the river, stop off somewhere scenic for a spot of lunch, perhaps visit Kenneth Grahame's house.

Ian picked me up at the station. In what looked like cycling shorts.

That's when my first warning light went on.

The second started flashing when we got to his car and I noticed a large inflatable thingummy strapped to the roof. It looked like a longer skinnier cousin of the paddling pool my mum used to fill from the garden hose.

'There's a stretch of the river I thought you might like to explore.'

I looked down at my floaty turquoise dress and strappy white sandals. Then I looked back at Ian, hoping to see a lightbulb go on over his head and hear an alternative plan spring forth from his mouth.

But Ian was clearly the kind of guy who regarded a plan as a tablet-of-stone kind of thing.

Warning light number three.

'Don't worry, Sweet Cheeks. I've got a wet suit in the boot that will *probably* fit you.'

Sweet Cheeks. Warning light number four. The whole dashboard.

I waddled out of the car park toilets feeling like a cross between a sea lion and a packet of Uncle Ben's microwave rice. *Why are you doing this, Jennifer Brown?*

Ian had lowered his craft onto the river and was doing knee bends on the bank, like something out of a public information film from 1967.

I imagined we'd just climb in and start paddling. I was wrong. First, there was a little lecture.

'We're looking for long slow strokes.' *Are we now?* 'There's always the temptation in the novice to stab at the water with the paddle.'

This novice (the assumption was correct but it still nettled me) *knows exactly where she'd like to stab you. And it wouldn't be with a bloody paddle.*

I was determined not to disgrace myself in front of this cocky, macho little shit but I had to work hard to keep pace with him. Like so many men in the company of women, Ian felt the need to demonstrate physical prowess by pushing himself to the limit of peacock knackerdom. Steve Redgrave would have struggled to match his stroke rate.

On my side of the inflatable prison, I was determined not to give in and, although my arms were in serious danger of detaching from my torso, I was holding my own.

Then Ian eased up as we reached a sort of fork in the river marked by a sign with a very grand-looking crest. He turned to me.

'This is where it gets interesting.'

He steered the inflatable onto the narrower of the fork's two prongs and the stretch of water that lay ahead looked entirely different from the mighty Thames we'd just powered down. As the canoe nosed onto it, I was overtaken by an almost magical sense of calm. A moorhen with six little chicks paddled along beside us as the boat cut silently through the emerald-green surface.

Ian turned to smile at me. 'Gorgeous, isn't it?'

I was beginning to think I'd misjudged my companion when a stentorian voice broke the serenity of the scene.

'WHAT THE BLOODY HELL DO YOU THINK YOU'RE DOING?'

A hundred yards ahead of us, an elderly gentleman in a tweed jacket had dropped his fishing rod on the bank and was waving his fist at us. Another half dozen men of similar cut of jib were swarming towards The Shouter and one of them, making good use of his chest-high waders, marched into the water carrying some sort of pole.

The Shouter resumed shouting.

'YOU WILL REMOVE YOURSELF FROM THIS WATER, SIR, OR YOU WILL REGRET IT!'

I flashed a panicked stare at Ian. 'Is this private land?'

He didn't answer me. Instead, he got to his feet (which seriously compromised the stability of the canoe) and launched a tirade of his own.

'OH REALLY? TRY AND FUCKING MAKE ME, COLONEL!'

The twin emotions of mortification and rage were struggling for supremacy in my breast. Rage prevailed.

'Ian. Sit down, for God's sake! We're clearly in the wrong here!'

'Bloody posh privileged bastards! Think they own the bloody world!'

By now, Waders Man had reached us. Ian was still in the mood to fight.

'Don't you dare touch this boat!'

Waders Man ignored him and hooked the end of his pole onto a ring at the front of the canoe and began to pull, which sent Ian, now red-faced with apoplexy, tumbling backwards into my lap.

'You bastard!'

Waders Man continued to pull us towards the bank, the force of the pull thwarting each attempt by Ian to get himself upright.

At the bank, The Shouter pulled himself up to his full height.

'You are guilty, sir, of unjustifiable interference with land which is in the immediate and exclusive possession of another.'

Ian stepped out of the canoe onto the bank. 'Fuck off, Colonel Mustard.'

I pitched in, anger blazing from my eyes. 'I'm very sorry. I wasn't informed that the afternoon's activity involved a spot of casual trespassing.'

Ian turned to remonstrate with me. 'Don't apologise to these Oxbridge twats! They think the fucking world belongs to them!'

'Stop talking, Ian. I'm warning you.' I stood up in the canoe, my right fist preparing to connect with his jaw.

A second later I was in the water.

When I spluttered to the surface, Ian was already twenty yards away, marching up the river bank, and Waders Man was stabbing at what was left of the canoe with his boat hook, putting it well and truly beyond repair.

The Shouter, his blood pressure now under control, became charm itself. He gave me his hand and helped me out of the water and onto dry land. All my anger had been washed away.

'I really had no idea.'

'Not your fault, my dear. Now, let's get you warm and dry.'

I was ushered into a sort of pavilion where a woman in her sixties with long grey hair and a jolly hockeysticks demeanour took me into a locker room, helped me peel off the wet suit, dried my hair and clothes and ,without asking, poured me a brandy about the size of a cup of tea.

'My husband's very protective of his little club. The members pay a hefty annual fee for the pleasure of fishing on this little stretch uninterrupted. Seems crazy to me. But you know what boys are like.'

***

Back at Arcadia Avenue, I told my tale of woe. Miranda's first date with Gorgeous Gary hadn't exactly lived up to expectations either.

'We had a couple of drinks in a really nice pub and it was going really well. There was chemistry there, you know. So when he suggested going back to his place and snuggling on the couch, that was fine with me.'

'But snuggling was code for sex?'

'No. Snuggling was code for rugby.'

'What?'

'Telly on. Beer popped. Wasps versus Harlequins.'

'You're joking?'

'That's not the worst part.'

'Go on.'

'He keeps a Quality Street tin on the couch beside him.'

'Handy.'

'It would be if he kept chocolates in it.'

'What *does* he keep in it?'

'His mother's ashes.'

27

Capes and Kaftans

May arrived in all her glory and I started to look forward to endless summer days and heady nights. It made me think of the bittersweet heat of Bordeaux.

Pink blossom covered the trees in Arcadia Avenue and, cocking a snook at the old proverb about the perils of getting hitched in late spring, a wedding invitation dropped onto the doormat. Handwritten on recycled paper and bearing an injunction on the back to RSVP using the same envelope, I knew immediately who it was from.

My old landlady Helen and her hippy boyfriend Paul were among the sweetest and most committed people I knew. Most of us think we're doing our bit to put the brakes on climate change by washing out yogurt pots, recycling newspapers and keeping a pocket shopping bag in our handbag. Helen and Paul are the real deal. They're not your average couple and I knew this would not be your average wedding. There would be no John Lewis list. There'd likely be a scheme involving goats in Zambia. And Helen and Paul's honeymoon would be spent delivering them.

The invitation came with a short essay on the perils of globalisation, the outdated patriarchies of the Christian church and the traditional wedding, and an insight into their pagan vision for the day. The guest list, included, was modest and restricted to close family and twenty-odd friends, including a handful of close colleagues from Intext. And, although now an ex-colleague, I featured in their number.

Thus it was that I found myself, a few weeks later, limping along the A303 on an ancient sixteen-seater minibus, wearing a shapeless dress in ecru organic cotton and feeling like a milkmaid from a Thomas Hardy novel.

As our guest chariot grunted and creaked its rusty way towards the sacred site of Stonehenge, I noticed that, although the day had started off bright and sunny, it had now taken a decided turn towards the tempestuous. I imagined my headgear scampering over Salisbury Plain.

As the thirty-or-so guests assembled in the shadow of the famous site's stone pillars, I felt a hand on my shoulder and I turned round to face another milkmaid, an attractive brunette with an oddly familiar face. She held my gaze for a couple of seconds, then she spoke. In Will's voice.

I wrapped my arms around him. 'You look amazing.'

'Well, I wasn't going to let you girls have all the fun!'

Over his shoulder I clocked the HRTs. Hilary, Rose and Trisha waved over to me with genuine delight and I waved back. I looked at Will.

'How has it gone down at work?'

'It's not a look I sport in the office. But I've tried it on the odd evening out. Those three have been bloody marvellous, to be honest. I'm their new project. Non-stop advice on hair and make-up and clothes.' He pointed to the strappy size 10s on his feet. 'They've hooked me up with a site called *Footwear Fetish*. I didn't ask.'

His lip suddenly looked a bit wobbly again. 'I was so worried about telling you.'

'You dozy bugger! It's *me*! What did you think I was going to say?'

'I know it's a bit … weird.'

'Look. First question. Are you happy?'

'Yes.'

'Then the first question is also the last question.'

He hugged me close and kissed me on the cheek.

Helen looked like a gorgeous forest nymph in a dress she'd clearly made herself from fabric offcuts. Paul had his ratty ponytail tied in a black bow and (the only nod to traditional formality) was dressed in a black suit that looked like the previous owner might have been Isambard Kingdom Brunel. Before and between them stood a woman with a kind of high priestess look about her, her long red cape embellished by a gold medallion straight out of *Harry Potter*.

The celebrant invited us to join hands and form a circle. There was a blessing of the space by the ringing of bells and the banging of drums. Then we all looked on as the bride and groom pledged themselves to each other and, very touchingly, entwined each other's hands with coloured ribbons. 'Merry meet' and 'Blessed be' took the place of 'Hallelujah' and 'Amen' and the ceremony concluded when the couple stepped over a broom to loud applause.

Then we trekked half a mile down the hill to a barn-like structure where the wedding feast was to be served. A ceremonial fire (to cleanse the area of negative energies and ward off evil spirits) had been lit unsettlingly close to the wooden structure and was presided over by a teenage youth with an arsonist's twinkle in his eye. I wished the wind would die down.

But the vegan meal was tastier than my sceptic's palate had expected and, in spite of the absence of alcohol, the knees-up that followed could be justly described as rollicking.

I found a quiet spot for a postmortem with Will.

'It's gone okay. I feel less self-conscious than I thought.'

'Good for you.'

'I've always known I wanted to explore this side of me. In public.'

'Then you're doing the right thing.'

'I just wish I'd had the courage to explore it sooner.'

'You're a late bloomer. Like me.'

I was aware of a stirring among the HRTs and then I saw the stimulus – Jonathan swept into the barn, looking every inch the handsome prince, and his fan club fluttered friskily to his side. He indulged them suavely for a few minutes, during which time Will nipped away to powder his nose (I didn't ask).

Then Jonathan glided over to offer his congratulations to the bride and groom, discreetly handing over a substantial personal donation to their chosen cause (not goats in Zambia, as it turned out, but a sanitation project in Tanzania), before seeking me out and looking me up and down.

'Nice dress. I prefer it to your floral number at David's wedding.'

'Don't remind me.'

'So, how was France?'

'Interesting. Enjoyable.'

'I'm hoping you'll give me the benefit of your new-found wisdom.'

'Well, I think "wisdom" is stretching it, but I can point you towards some very good drinking and some very sound investment.' *Hark at you, Jennifer Brown!*

'Sounds wonderful.' He seemed fidgety. 'Can I call you to arrange lunch or something?'

'You're going?'

He looked sheepish. 'This isn't really …'

'You've only just got here.'

'It's the whole tree-hugging thing …' His blue eyes twinkled. 'Now, *you* I *could* hug.'

He leaned in and pecked me on the cheek, then, like a celebrity on the clock, he was gone.

My lasting image of the day will be of Handy Dick, the Intext sleazebag, sidling slimily over to a crossdressed Will he clearly hadn't recognised and getting a rather stiffer response than the one he'd bargained for.

***

I was glad to get back into my office gear, although soaring temperatures were making the morning commute a sticky experience, coupled with the fact that London was now packed solid with tourists all working their way round the famous landmarks that had become everyday sights for me.

And, like the weather, things were hotting up on the work front.

Impressed by the way I'd been managing the account of urbane wide-boy property merchant Harry Sinclair, Cécile thought it was time for me to make the acquaintance of the second of the 'high net worth individuals' who were to be my personal clients.

Sheikh Saeed bin Sohal had recently taken over a chain of hotels in Europe and we already had the contract to supply them wine, but Cécile wanted to ensure relations were kept in top gear. Added to which the Sheikh himself was keen to develop a personal cellar. I explained my surprise to Cécile.

'I thought Muslims didn't drink. Isn't alcohol forbidden?'

'It depends on your viewpoint, it seems. There are some Islamic scholars who claim there's nothing in the Quran that outlaws the drinking of alcohol. Actual drunkenness is frowned upon by everyone in the Muslim world, it seems, but drinking alcohol for pleasure is okay. According to some. In moderation.'

Sheikh Saeed (as I was to call him) was in London for the first time and excited to be here. He wanted to see everything. Cécile asked me how I'd feel about spending a few days in his company as his sort of personal tour guide. It would be an excellent business opportunity, she said. A chance to cement and perhaps enhance the relationship.

I said that was fine by me. The PA in me was used to dealing with male bigwigs, although this wig was bigger than any I'd dealt with before.

The title *sheikh* is a confusing one for Westerners – it's applied to members of royal families (people we'd call princes or even kings) and it's also applied to people who are merely (although this is a big deal, too) heads of tribes, as well as being a kind of religious title in some Muslim cultures.

My guy, it seems, was the 'head of a tribe' kind. He'd been the head of a fairly cash-poor but land-rich tribe in coastal Oman. Then the Sultan decided he needed land to build a new marina to house a couple of his superyachts and the purchase had made Saeed's people billionaires overnight.

And now Sheikh Saeed was spreading his wings.

Muslim culture can be awkward to negotiate for a woman, and I also had to factor Arab culture into that negotiation. My research told me I'd probably be alright as long as I didn't cross my legs or show the soles of my feet (the ultimate insult, it seems).

As I stepped into the elegant dining room of Knightsbridge's Beauchamp Hotel, a tall man with a bushy black beard stood to greet me, wearing the traditional white robe I associated with Arab leaders.

'Hello, Miss Jennifer.'

'Pleased to meet you, Sheikh Saeed.'

He pulled a chair out for me. 'Please.'

'Thank you. How are you enjoying London.'

'I like.' His beard made him look, at first glance, older than his forty years but his skin and eyes were fresh and young-looking. His English seemed to be a work in progress, though.

'Forgive me.' He smiled. 'English very poor.'

'I think it's probably much better than my Arabic.'

'Yes. Perhaps. But I learn from you, I hope.'

'I'll try to be a good teacher.'

'Thank you.'

I liked him immediately. He seemed modest, polite and interested. We talked for a good ten minutes before we were bothered by a waiter (bringing water) and I learned he had two wives and nine children and was passionate about English football, although he was a little disappointed when I explained Manchester United was not a club from London.

Food arrived without being ordered and was followed by an unctuous manager with the scent of wealth in his nostrils. He ignored me and spoke to my distinguished guest.

'If you will allow me, Your Highness, I will bring you the very best that British cuisine has to offer.'

Sheikh Saeed inclined his head graciously and I snatched up the leather-bound menu, scanned the prices at the rich end of each column, and started to do some rather panicky mental arithmetic. My company credit card had a fairly generous limit, and Cécile was far from a skinflint, but this place was eyewateringly pricey and the manager, not realising 'His Highness' wouldn't be footing the bill, seemed determined to push my card to its limit. I didn't want to make a scene or, worse, cause my guest offence, so I feigned composure as the delicacies just kept on coming.

We'd got through, by my reckoning, about half my credit limit when the food supply finally stopped. Sheikh Saeed had been so enthusiastic about the new taste experiences that the manager moved on to experimenting with liqueurs – cherry brandy was followed by amaretto and armagnac and, finally, a glass of 1977 vintage port at sixty quid a pop.

To everything, Sheikh Saeed's response was the same.

'I like.'

I politely declined a lift from the sheikh's driver and, in the taxi on the way home, I called Cécile. She was relaxed about the monumental restaurant bill and delighted that I'd made such a good impression on the new client. His assistant had already called her to pass on his thanks and to say how much he'd enjoyed my company.

The following day was earmarked for sightseeing.

His driver picked me up at the office and we whizzed round all the main attractions, which Sheikh Saeed seemed happy to experience from the car – Buckingham Palace, Marble Arch, the Palace of Westminster.

But one thing he wanted to experience in the flesh, as it were, was the London Eye.

I sometimes feel a bit iffy standing on a chair to change a lightbulb. And, when I was eight, I'd blacked out when Dad had coaxed me to the top of the helter skelter on Southsea Pier.

And now this.

One hundred and thirty-five metres. That's four hundred and forty-two feet in old money. About half the Eiffel Tower.

In a little glass box.

I'd booked premium tickets, to impress my sheikh, so we were whisked to the front of the queue, along with a couple of twenty-something Japanese hipsters, and ushered into our private capsule for the Champagne Experience.

Sheikh Saeed accepted the fizz and sipped it with restraint as he marvelled at the panoramic view of the fine city. I stood with my back to the glass and necked a flute to steady my nerves.

At the top of the wheel, I was two and a half glasses in and feeling like someone had unscrewed my head and replaced it with a cabbage. I wanted to get off.

The Japanese bloke was standing on his hands with his back to the glass while his companion took a couple of dozen photos of him on her iPhone. Looking at a man with feet where his head should be wasn't doing wonders for my vertigo so I looked at my shoes and breathed and prayed I wouldn't faint or wet my knickers.

Whenever I screwed up the courage to look up, I was relieved to see Saeed drinking in the view and paying me no attention at all.

I hoped he wouldn't get a taste for heights and suggest a trip to the Shard.

In the few days that followed, the Shard was just about the only thing we *didn't* see – we shopped at Harrods, took in the delights of the V&A and the Natural History Museum, trailed round Madame Tussaud's (where my sheikh was keen to be photographed beside Kim Kardashian), had afternoon tea at the Ritz, and enjoyed a lunch cruise down the Thames to Hampton Court Palace.

After our several days of opulence, I began to feel that Saeed was struggling with his role of nabob-about-town. We'd talked only a little about wine, and he was evidently happy to trust my judgment when it came to recommendations for his personal cellar (he'd given Cécile a gargantuan budget and was basically leaving us to it). The focus of the trip for him was soaking up British culture.

'I like to see normal people.'

So I steered him onto a number 18 bus and we rode all the way from Euston to Wembley Stadium. He seemed delighted to see young mums with buggies and West Indian pensioners with bags of shopping.

And he was gracious when the bus was invaded by a horde of teenage schoolchildren who, spotting him, crowded round and excitedly asked him for selfies. I heard one of them say the words zombie juice, which piqued my interest. When I Googled the phrase, my phone threw up a dozen photos of a thirty-year-old rapper from Brooklyn with that strange moniker and a remarkable facial resemblance to my dignified guest.

The sheikh's mislabelled face was destined to do the rounds on Instagram and Snapchat.

He seemed a little sad when our allotted sightseeing days were over.

'Please to come Oman. My house is waiting for you.'

I wasn't sure what, if anything, was behind this kind invitation and I wondered if I'd caused offence by *not* inviting him to *my* home. I wondered if his comments about seeing 'normal people', and his evident delight at getting a glimpse of everyday life, had in fact been a hint.

I'd said it before I could stop myself. 'And you must come to *my* house.'

His eyes lit up. 'I like very much.'

Miranda seemed initially horror-struck.

'An actual sheikh? In my little hovel?'

'He's not really a sheikh. Well, he *is*. But he doesn't act like one.'

'But you've been dining at the Ritz and the bloody Beauchamp.'

'I know. But I think all that makes him a bit … uncomfortable. I think the best bit for him has been our ride on the number 18 bus. He wants to hang out with ordinary folks.'

This seemed to calm Miranda's nerves.

'Well then, what about a barbecue? Some real cockney hospitality.'

'Ideal.'

Which is how it came to pass that a sheikh from Oman found himself standing on the small but freshly manicured lawn at number 27 Arcadia Avenue (Miranda had actually trimmed the edges with kitchen scissors), chatting to our neighbour Pat, and holding one of Miranda's best Doulton china plates and tucking into a burger ('real beef cow') and three or four of Miranda's delicious salads.

'He seems lovely.'

'He's the nicest billionaire I know.' I looked around. 'Where's Mary?'

'I haven't told her. I didn't want her whipping out her bible and causing a major international incident. He seems to be a big hit with Pat.'

Our neighbour, a big Arsenal fan, was talking football through mouthfuls of Miranda's orange and avocado salad. Saeed was listening and nodding but not saying much. Even if Saeed had been a more confident speaker of English, Pat wasn't the ideal language partner. She barely took a breath.

Pat turned to the barbecue and speared a couple of sausages and loaded them onto her already-creaking plate.

She said something to Saeed and I turned to Miranda in a panic. 'What kind of sausages are they?'

'Prime organic pork. From Henderson in the High Street. Why?' Then it dawned on her. 'Oh, shit!'

I dashed across to save Saeed from a serious religious infraction and steered him towards the philadelphus in Miranda's mixed border, inviting him to smell the heady aroma of its showy white blooms.

Standing by his car at the kerb in the fading light, he thanked me for 'again very nice day'. He nodded to his driver and the young man passed him a small gift-wrapped box, which the sheikh, in turn, passed to me.

It was a beautiful gold bracelet I'd admired in Harrods a few days earlier. I was deeply touched by his thoughtfulness and had to work very hard to control the urge to hug him.

He saw that my eyes were glistening and he smiled at the knowledge that the gift had hit the mark. He inclined his head slowly, climbed into the car, and sped away.

28

Not-So-Special Agent

Cécile was delighted with the way I'd cemented the relationship with Saeed, and Harry's account was healthier than ever, it seemed. My efforts were paying dividends and she was effusive in her praise.

'It's only what I expected. From someone as talented and charming as you.'

Professionally, I was riding on the crest of a wave. I felt confident.

In the realm of my personal life, however, my confidence was still bruised from my riverbank encounter with the obnoxious Ian. I hadn't (ahem) dipped my toe in the water since then.

Kellie was upbeat.

'Finding blokes has never been easier. Just get yourself on Tinder.'

'Isn't that the "Fancy a shag tonight?" site?'

'It used to be. Now it's just your standard dating site. And everyone's on it these days.'

'Including your dad?'

'Everyone *apart from* my dad.'

So I downloaded the app and, in my lunch break, knocked up what I thought was a cute bio, then took a tentative peak at the men in my age range (35-45) and my geographical range (20 miles). I felt optimistic.

I shouldn't have been.

Carl, whizz kid in the City, was a match. Apparently. I spent a dispiriting half hour in a Fenchurch Street wine bar listening to him brag about the number of women he'd dated before making a run for it while he was in the gents.

Nigel was a fitness instructor. Cute smile. We exchanged a few messages and made a lunch date. Then, two days before the date, as I stood in the queue to pay for my pastrami and rocket on sourdough, my phone pinged and there it was – a picture of his pecker.

I blocked his number.

And, in the online dating game, I threw in the towel.

***

It'd been a good few weeks since Helen's wedding and I was keen to see how Will was getting on. I nipped down to Southsea for the weekend.

We strolled along the front in blazing sunshine. Will was in shorts and a T-shirt. No wig.

'Do you think you're too picky?'

'I don't think so. I just want normal. I don't want a brawler, a braggart or a bonehead who sends me dick pics. Is that asking too much?'

'Shouldn't be, should it?'

'Where are all the normal blokes? At home with their normal wives and their two-point-three normal kids?'

'Or pulling on a dress and falsies and calling themselves Deirdre.'

A chance to catch up with Will wasn't my only reason for being on the coast. I'd arranged to meet an estate agent at Mum's house, which I'd finally cleared completely of contents and which I was now eager to put on the market so that the income from the sale could offset Mum's costs at Roselands.

Fifty minutes after the appointment time, when I was on the point of phoning a taxi to the station, I heard a screech of brakes and looked up to see a Volvo estate perched on the pavement. The driver leapt out and slammed the car door so hard it's a wonder the handle didn't come off in his hand.

Derek Divine of Divine Homes looked to be in his early fifties. His thinning brown hair was parted neatly at one side and combed over to mask an area of barren upland.

He swept into the house like he owned it. With no apology for the grossly late arrival, and with a very perfunctory introduction, he strolled off with his clipboard, tutting and clucking.

He'd only been in the place ten seconds and I wanted to throttle him.

'Is this the kitchen?'

What was your first clue? The cooker? The worktops? The wall-to-wall cupboards?

'Yes.'

'Hmm. In need of upgrading.'

'I'm not proposing to offer the house as ready to walk into. My mother is 85. It goes without saying that whoever buys it will probably want to do some work.'

'Quite a lot of work.' He ran his chewed and grubby fingernails along the worktop where my mum used to stand and mix her cakes.

He strode through to the living room.

'It's very cosy, isn't it?' That was backhanded estate-agent-speak for *small*.

'Knocked through to the dining room, it would be twenty-seven feet by thirteen. I wouldn't call that cosy.'

'Lot of work, though. Knocking down walls.'

'As I've said, I'm expecting the buyer to be a person prepared to do some work.'

'They'll have to be.'

I took a breath.

There are times when you have to draw a line in the sand. When you have to say, in the face of shit, *I'm not putting up with this*. You arrive at a crossroads and you have to choose the right way. Not the easy way.

I looked Derek Divine squarely in the eye. 'You seem like an intelligent man.'

He smirked.

'So I'm sure you'll be able to find the front door.'

His smirk fell away. I didn't blink. For three seconds, he wasn't sure how to process what was happening. Still I didn't blink.

Then Derek Divine turned on his heel and took his combover out of the house. Desperate to save a little face, he slammed Mum's front door behind him. I sat down at the kitchen table in my childhood home and waited for my blood pressure to normalise.

On the train back to London, I got a call from Will, asking how it had gone with the estate agent. I told him.

'What a twat! And what a ballbreaker you are!'

'What can I say? Some balls just need breaking.'

'So, no sale.'

'Not even the first step *towards* a sale.'

'I may be able to help you there.'

And he told me about Kavi's brother and his fiancée, looking to get on the property ladder with a doer-upper. He asked me if I'd be happy for him to show them round and I said that would be perfect and he could get a key from Mrs Jennings next door.

Three days later, they saw it.

And put in an offer five thousand over my lower limit.

29

My Weekend is a Bust

Letting go of Mum's house was an emotional leap it had been hard to take. For forty years, the house had been my safe haven. As summer shaded into autumn, I felt strangely adrift.

I must have seemed distracted at work. Over coffee, Cécile, ever the solicitous friend, had picked up a change in my mood. I told her about the house and my irrational reaction to the sale.

'I think you're being hard on yourself. It's entirely rational. It's like losing a part of you. I know people say we shouldn't be attached to things, but a house is a big thing. And a childhood home is where a lot of your life has happened. Most of it, perhaps. It's a very big thing indeed.'

'I'm sorry. It's just hit me harder than I thought.'

'You need a distraction. What are you doing this weekend?'

'What do you have in mind?'

She'd received an invitation to spend the weekend at Arlington Manor, the palatial country pile near Bath that was the home of Lord Stapleton, the distinguished nobleman with the cut-glass vowels I'd heard occasionally on TV in speeches made from the red benches in parliament's upper house. Her Ladyship was a friend of Cécile's via someone else and the nobles were having an open house. Cécile had been told she could bring a friend.

'Sounds great.'

'It's a "dress for dinner" kind of place. Plus there'll be outdoorsy stuff.'
'I'll cobble something together.'

That evening, I flicked through Tatler online and tried to get a handle on what the moneyed country set was sporting this season.

'For an autumnal weekend away, you can't go wrong with a lovely cashmere roll neck and Dubarry Birch Jacket. A Madison Fedora tops off the outfit superbly well.'

Nice. Except I'd need Victoria Beckham's figure AND bank balance.

I flicked through my wardrobe and plumped for a lilac Joules V-neck and my dark navy chinos from Jigsaw. The old Barbour jacket from my Thornhill Hall days might score me some brownie points with the horsey set at Arlington.

I was used to rubbing shoulders with a certain level of gentry but Arlington would probably be a couple of notches up from my usual, so I googled etiquette and got a short list of dos and don'ts for guests invited 'down' to the country, of which the highlights were:

DO leave at least ten pounds in your room for the daily. Even if it's clear your hostess will pocket the money.

DON'T make a lot of noise if you do find yourself having sex. Guests who've hunted in vain don't want their noses rubbing in it.

On the M4 speeding towards Bath in Cécile's spacious Jaguar XJ, I settled into gorgeous mink leather and flicked through a few emails on my phone and tried not to think I'd be spending the weekend in one of those bedroom farces where hairy-arsed dukes chase the maids in and out of bedchambers.

It was two hours to Bath but a two-hour drive was no hardship in this level of comfort.

Sooner than I expected, we hit the honey-coloured outskirts of the fine Georgian city. Jane Austen territory. I wondered if the bonneted wordsmith had ever visited the house we were gliding towards. I wondered if she'd have approved of the black strapless number I'd be wearing to dinner.

We pulled off the main road and drove for about a mile alongside a high wall of ancient brick before sweeping through a grand arched entrance flanked by lodges and into wide parkland dotted with ancient oaks. A hundred yards away, near a lake, I spotted a herd of deer, their sentinel a magnificent stag with regal antlers.

A couple of minutes later, the parkland gave way to vast lawns rising gently up to one of the grandest country houses I'd ever seen. If the *Gosford Park* location scouts ever need a new pile for their exteriors, Arlington would do the job very nicely.

It looked like the kind of joint that it takes a small army to keep up, a place with a guest book that includes ambassadors, governors, maharajas, caliphs, sultans, princes, and an emperor or two.

Lord Stapleton was waiting to greet us in the Great Hall, with his wife, 'Penny'. Lady Penelope was about five-eleven and had that lush ash-blonde hair that people with breeding and wealth pull off so effortlessly. As she stepped towards me, I wondered if I should curtsy, but Cécile went straight in for the standard handshake. Penny took her hand and also leaned in for a single air kiss on the cheek. She took my hand with genuine warmth (no airbrush for me – too soon) and asked about our journey.

'Fine, thank you.' *What do I call you? Your Ladyship? My Lady? Lady Penelope?*

A couple of butlers glided past carrying our bags.

'Good. You'll be ready for some refreshment, I expect.'

His Lordship stepped forward and shook my hand rather stiffly. 'Andrew.'

'Pleased to meet you. I'm Jennifer.'

He gestured towards a doorway. 'Please.'

I glanced at Cécile and she gave me a relaxed smiled and we walked with Lady Penelope into a large, light drawing room where a couple of liveried maids were laying out afternoon tea.

The small talk bubbled along for a few minutes, then the other weekend guests rocked up. Cécile and I were, it seemed, the only non-couple. The eight of us made a very mixed bunch indeed.

Freddie Falkingham (a later Google search threw up the nickname 'Filthy Freddie') was a property dealer. When I mentioned my time in Bordeaux, he talked about the 'several chateaux' he'd 'acquired in Gascony and the Loire valley', which conjured up an affluent landowner image sharply at odds with his bullish, high-street-bookie demeanour. His French wife, Simone, cut a very demure figure by comparison and they made a strikingly odd couple indeed. The diamonds swinging from her ears I took (rather unkindly, perhaps) to be the main attraction for her in this thick-necked, red-faced ogre of a man.

Miles and his wife Lucinda looked typically Chelsea. He was something in finance by the sound of it. By the svelte looks of it, they both spent half the week in the gym and the other half in a tanning salon. Or on a beach in Antigua.

The American tones belonged to Danny de Marco, introduced by 'Andrew' as a film producer, a label that always makes me see a small fat bald man with a cigar who says the word *goddamn* a lot. Danny, by contrast, looked like he'd just won second prize in a middle-aged skateboard competition.

His partner, Rhona, was from Glasgow and had a curious mid-Atlantic accent that put me in mind of Lanarkshire-girl-turned-Las-Vegas-superstar, Sheena Easton. She sounded like an artist of some sort – she talked about 'collections' and 'shows' and 'installations' – although it didn't sound like there was any painting involved. I wondered if her get-up today was some sort of living artwork. She wore a kind of dressing-gown affair and a leopardskin turban, like a twenty-first-century Norma Desmond. It looked ridiculous to me, but nobody else batted an eyelid.

I listened more than I spoke, tried to relax, remembered not to curtsy and generally found the hour or so pretty exhausting. I was glad of the chance to finally close a door behind me and fling myself on onto a king-size damask-covered bed and relax for a while before girding my loins for another few hours of minefield conversation over dinner.

A couple of hours later, I was back on the clock, standing nervously at the window of another oak-panelled room sipping champagne and wondering where the hell Cécile was (she was serving as a sort of combination lifebuoy/comfort-blanket).

'Andrew' came over to engage me in conversation, doubtless sensing my unease and seeking nobly to make me feel more at home.

I remembered my mum's words of wisdom when I'd been preparing for my interview at Intext, a lifetime ago. *Just be yourself. People respect that.*

'How is your room?'

'Oh, it's lovely, thank you. It's very kind of you to invite me.'

'We're delighted to have you. Any friend of Cécile's is very welcome.'

I looked around at the room. A fire crackling in an ornate, French-looking fireplace. A cluster of family photos in silver frames on an ancient piano. Old portraits in oil, eight feet tall.

'Have you always lived here?'

'Yes. I'm very lucky. The house was gifted to my family in the seventeenth century by William the Third. A reward for helping him to rout the Catholics, I'm afraid.' He gave me a smile that looked apologetic. I wondered if I looked Catholic to him.

'I see. Well, it's a beautiful house.'

'It is. A little draughty in the winter. And a beast of a place to heat. We're confined to a few apartments for half the year. But good in the summer. And ideal for gatherings of friends.'

'Yes.'

Cécile appeared at my elbow and a wave of relief washed over me.

At the dining table (ten yards long, oak, candelabra at each end), I had the skater-boy film producer to my left and the perma-tanned hedge funder to my right. Danny chatted largely to Lady Penelope, to *his* left, about the latest film he was making – something to do with superheroes which sounded dreadful and not, I imagined, Her Ladyship's cup of darjeeling – which left me making polite conversation with City Boy. Or rather listening to him drone on about the accumulation of wealth being a vicious circle.

'The more you acquire, the more you find yourself *needing* to acquire. We seem born into this world to be sent to school to get an education so we can then earn enough money to send *our* children to school. And so the cycle continues.'

'How many children do you have?'

He grimaced. 'Six.'

The arrival of beef Wellington caused a lull in everyone's conversation and, as waiters poured a dark crimson wine into our glasses, Lady Penelope leaned across Danny and addressed me directly.

'I'll be interested to hear your assessment of the wine, Jennifer. It's not often we have an expert at our table.'

I started to sweat. I looked at Cécile. She gave me a look that said *Relax. You can do this.*

'Oh, I'm not sure I qualify as an expert.'

Lady Penelope wasn't letting me off the hook. 'Nevertheless, we'll appreciate your insights.'

All eyes were on me.

I tried to look relaxed. I remembered what the tutor had said on my Wednesday-night wine course about my palate being 'particularly sharp.'

I lifted the glass and swirled and remembered all the hours spent in the kitchen at B&B's, practising the swirl with water. I thought of Lee and imagined him complimenting the flick of my wrist.

I looked at the wine's thick long legs. I got my nose into the glass and breathed in its oak and its blackcurrant and the unmistakeable hint of incense.

I prepared to pronounce.

'A very nicely aged wine. Early eighties, I'd say. Pauillac. I'd plump for Pichon Longueville Baron.'

Lady Penelope looked impressed. 'Gosh. You clearly know your stuff. It *is* a Pichon Longueville but it's Comtesse de Lalande.'

'Ah. Well, like I said. I'm not really an expert. I thought I'd detected a slightly heavier Merlot presence than you normally get in the Lalande. But I was wrong.'

His Lordship looked at his wife. 'Actually, darling, the Lalande is finished. This *is* in fact the last few bottles from that rogue case of Baron.' He looked at me. 'How marvellous, Jennifer!'

Cécile beamed over at me.

I looked across at Lady Penelope. She pasted on a polite smile. 'Yes. Very impressive indeed. A testament to Cécile's excellent training.'

Cécile waved away the compliment. 'Absolutely not. Jennifer has a very discerning and educated palate. It's a special gift and it's entirely her own.'

Lady Penelope's smile was not entirely convincing. 'Yes. Special indeed.'

Oh, dear. I'd unwittingly done the unforgivable and caused the hostess to lose face at her own dinner table.

After liqueurs and single malts in front of the fire, I made my excuses and bade the company an early goodnight. Rhona, too, decided to head upstairs. On our way up, she revealed she wasn't entirely at ease either.

'I find all this grandeur a bit of a turn-off. I grew up on a sprawling council estate just outside Glasgow. Danny and I have plenty of money but I'm still happier with a bacon roll from a van than I am at this kind of gig.'

'The trouble for me is the world of my job is largely the world of rich people. I've got to learn to be comfortable in this kind of setting.'

'You seem to have learned pretty well. You look the part.'

'Well, it's not how I feel. It's not really me, either.'

'I guess we'll never be true toffs, will we? Good night, Jennifer.'

'Night.'

I slept like a log (a combination of wine, Grand Marnier and emotional exhaustion) and was late down to breakfast.

Most of the guests had settled on their activities for the day. The hedge funders went off to play tennis, doubtless to banish the effects of the excesses of the night before. Danny would be on Skype for most of the day with investors in LA and had been given a study to work from. Filthy Freddie and Self-Effacing Simone had taken a rowing boat out on the lake. And, through the dining-room window, I saw Lady Penelope and Cécile, in full hacking gear, standing beside two magnificent-looking steeds held by a couple of stable lads. Cécile turned and I waved and she waved back.

I trotted outside to greet them both.

'I'm so sorry to have overslept. I guess the country air is more potent than my London-girl lungs are now used to.'

Lady Penelope smiled. She seemed to have forgotten the awkwardness around the dinner table.

'Yes. A change of air often disturbs the body clock, doesn't it?'

Cécile grimaced. 'I wish I'd slept as well as you. I forgot to put my phone on silent and a text from New Zealand pinged in at around three and I've been wide awake ever since.'

'Oh, I'm sorry.'

'It's fine. A canter round the estate will do me good.'

Then, for a brief couple of seconds, Lady Penelope's cultivated mask slipped. 'I'm sorry we didn't wait.' She looked me up and down. 'I assumed you didn't ride.'

That was unmistakeable shorthand for *I doubt equestrian pursuits fell within the purview of your state education and council-house upbringing.* I was clearly *not* forgiven.

'No, you go on, please. I haven't ridden in a while (an image came into my head of a donkey on Brighton Beach and me bobbing along painfully on its back, aged six). 'I'm happy to amuse myself.'

'Andrew may be up for a game of tennis.' She mounted her steed. Cécile popped up onto hers with the poise of one for whom getting on a horse is as natural as climbing into a bath.

'Okay. Thank you.' I didn't fancy a knock-up with His Lordship. Even at twenty-odd years my senior, I imagined him as a bit of a demon on the court. Added to which, years of watching Wimbledon champions at close range from the royal box had probably done his game no harm at all. 'I'll see if I can find him.'

Then the two ladies trotted off, elegant peas in a genteel pod.

When I turned back to the house, I saw Rhona, in puce dungarees and with her hair tied up in a denim scarf, a get-up that gave her the look of a Soviet-era poster girl. She was sitting on the stone steps, her head buried in a huge sketchbook, her hand buzzing over its surface.

I started to walk over. She looked up.

'Stop!' I froze. 'Sorry. Could you just …' She held her hand up like a traffic policeman, looked up at me, took me in, and went back to her sketchbook. '… stand like that for a few seconds.'

The role of artist's model was new to me. She glanced up a few times, hand flitting over the paper.

'So, you're drawing *me*?'

'Your breasts are just … perfect… for my next project.'

I glanced down at my puppies. 'Really? What is it?'

'A twelve-foot expressionist sculpture in mirror fragments and fibreglass. It'll be a permanent installation in the atrium of a new arts centre in Coventry.'

'A sculpture?'

She looked up. 'Yeah. Lady Godiva.'

30

A Staggering Blow

The first biting wind of winter cut through my raincoat as I stepped out of Old Street tube station. My phone buzzed and it was Marvin, the manager at Roselands, Mum's care home.

Mum had suffered another, bigger stroke. She was now much weaker and unable to speak.

***

A few hours later, I was sitting by her hospital bed, holding her limp and papery hand, staring at her closed eyes, listening to the bubbling bleep of the heart monitor.

A short male doctor with a gentle manner and an accent from sub-Saharan Africa explained to me that Mum's heart had been considerably weakened by the 'episode' and that 'extreme fatigue and lack of communication' were going to be the norm from now on.

'She will be like this most days now.'

'How long …?' I couldn't finish the sentence.

'It's impossible to say. But I have spoken with your mother's care manager and we're confident that her care needs can be met at the nursing home, if that's what you think she would prefer.'

'What *are* her care needs?' I thought I knew the word he was going to use.

'We are really talking about palliative care, now. Your mother will have a trained specialist nurse who will be available on a round-the-clock basis. It's a system we call Hospice at Home.'

Mum mumbled something and I gripped her hand and felt tears run down my cheeks.

'Although she may appear to be very unresponsive, she may still hear a lot of what you say to her. It's important to keep talking. Hearing is … the last thing to go.'

So my fragile little mum was transferred, with great care and sensitivity, back to Roselands.

I called Cécile, who told me to forget about work. I called Miranda, who cried down the phone, and I told her I'd be away for a while. I called Will, and he cried down the phone, too, and told me to call him any time, day or night, if I needed someone to talk to. Finally, I called an estate agent, who found me a tiny holiday cottage ('with a wood-burning stove') about four miles from Roselands that the owners rented out on a weekly basis.

***

I started a routine of days spent sitting by Mum's bed and reading to her from the books she'd given me and had loved reading to me decades before. And, at night, I made myself comfortable in the armchair in her room and slept fitfully.

After three days, I was shattered.

The palliative nurse, a woman in her sixties called Sue, had a word with me.

'Trust me when I tell you that there could be no change in your mum's condition for a few weeks. And you can't go on sleeping in a chair.'

'I'm terrified of leaving her. I want to be here …'

'I know. And you *will* be. We'll make sure of that. Go home.'

So the new routine was established – 9 till 6 at Roselands, evenings at the cottage, phone by my side, trying to get out of my head with emails and reruns of *Ab Fab* on UKTV Gold.

Weeks went by with no change and, before I knew it, it was Christmas morning. A thin layer of snow covered the short path that separated the little cottage from the street. A rare White Christmas. My mum's favourite thing in the world.

I thought back to all the Christmas dinners she'd prepared in the kitchen of the house that Kavi's brother now owned, all the new recipes she'd been unafraid to try – stuffing the turkey with lemons one year, to great acclaim; serving the sprouts in a blue-cheese sauce another year, to a universal thumbs-down.

I'd have given almost anything for another of those Christmases with her, fishing for bits of foil in the Christmas pudding and settling down beside her to watch the *Morecambe and Wise Christmas Special*.

Over at Roselands, I sprayed a little of the perfume I'd bought her on her cheek and her papery neck and she didn't flinch.

After a couple of hours by her bedside, reading from The *Railway Children*, I left her and joined the others in the lounge for the afternoon's entertainment, a medley of Christmas favourites performed by Marvin and a female carer who sang in the New Forest Rock Choir.

Then Marvin and the staff handed out presents. This remarkable man had gone to the trouble (and, I discovered, the personal expense) to find something that was appropriate for each individual.

One man who'd been a carpenter all his working life was given a box of gorgeous old tools with polished wooden handles. Marvin had picked them up at an auction.

Another resident, a woman who'd been a stalwart of Hampshire RSPB for over fifty years and whose eyesight was now virtually non-existent, was gifted *The Definitive Audio Guide to Birds in Britain* on CDs.

For Mum, he'd bought an electric diffuser and half a dozen bottles of oils infused with spices that would fill Mum's room with the aromas of baking – cinnamon, nutmeg, star anise, ginger, vanilla, cloves.

I felt like kissing him. So I did.

As I settled down for the evening at the cottage, I got a text from Jonathan. He wished me a Merry Christmas and also asked me for a favour. He wanted to surprise Steph on New Year's Eve with a 'commitment ring'. Would I be free in the next week to accompany him to the jeweller's and help him choose?

We made an arrangement I was clear might have to be broken at short notice.

Boxing Day at Roselands passed unremarkably and, in the evening, I was tucking into a family-size bag of mature cheddar and onion crisps and struggling to follow the plot of an episode of *Vera* that involved a murder in a boatyard, when the doorbell rang.

'SURPRISE!'

Will and Kavi stood on my doorstep armed with three Sainsbury's bags. I was gobsmacked. Will pushed past me.

'Let us in, then. My balls are frozen solid!'

In my fleecy dressing gown and slippers and with my sofa hair, I stood and gawped at him.

Will looked me up and down. 'Been shopping at Primate again?'

I struggled to put a sentence together. 'How …?'

'Look. I know things have been rough. But everyone needs a bit of pampering at Christmas. You go and put some clothes on and leave the rest to us.' He smiled at Kavi. 'We'll sort you out.' He pulled a bottle of fizz out of one of the bags and began to pull the foil off.

When I came down ten minutes later, the pair of them had set the table, poured nibbles into bowls and had a vegan nut roast and some sort of aubergine and courgette side dish in the oven.

'You might have found a place with a decent cooker. Bloody electric. Can't stand it.'

'Well, if I'd known it would have to match up to your exacting standards …'

'You can't control electric. It's either on or off.'

It went off. As did all the lights.

Will went outside and looked up the street. 'Every house is out.'

We looked at each other in the gloom. I went and fished a pack of scented Christmas candles out of the cupboard and we soon had a bit of light on the scene, together with aromas not unlike the ones Mum's diffuser was creating back at Roselands. Kavi got the woodburner going, as much for a bit of extra light as for heat.

Will opened the oven door. The nut roast and ratatouille-ish number were looking cold and dark and uncooked, but my lovely friend was upbeat.

'At least we've got breadsticks to soak up the wine.'

He filled our glasses and we sat on the floor in the glow from the logs crackling in the stove.

This was the longest time I'd spent in Kavi's company. He had soft eyes and a warm smile and seemed very reserved. I coaxed some conversation out of him and he talked about his home in Kerala, about his family back there, and about the move to the UK to study and how difficult he'd found it settling here. He struck me as a very delicate individual and I was just wondering what the hell he was doing with the outrageous Will when a loud knock at the door made the three of us jump.

'It's probably an engineer from Southern Electric.' I got up and walked over and opened the door.

'He's trying to kill me!'

A woman in her twenties I'd never seen in my life pushed past me into the living room.

'Phone the police! Please!'

I closed the door. 'Calm down. *Who's* trying to kill you?' *And, by the way, who the bloody hell* are *you?*

She wiped tears away with her fingers. 'Charlie! My boyfriend!'

Will gave me a look that said *She's a lunatic*. I shrugged, helpless. 'I'm sure it's not that bad.'

'You don't know him. He always gets like this when I talk to other blokes.'

Will rolled his eyes and I glared at him to keep a lid on his disapproval. 'I'm sure you two can sort this out calmly.'

I'd only just got the words out when there was another thunderous knock at the door.

'Tanya! I know you're in there! Open this fucking door!'

Will stood up. 'This is ridiculous!' Kavi also got to his feet and Tanya dashed over and stood behind him.

'Don't let him in!'

I was beginning to feel that, on top of a power cut and a half-cooked nut roast, this farce was taking the biscuit.

'Look. I'm going to open the door so the two of you can sort your problems out.'

I'd only got the door open six inches when Charlie, built like a prop forward for the Southsea Nomads, barged in and scoured the room for the woman who'd tested his manhood.

As he stepped towards her, Kavi was on him like a ninja, driving the heel of his hand into Charlie's square jaw with such force that the mountain of a man staggered backwards and out onto my front step.

Before Will and I had time to process what was going on, a screaming Tanya had rushed to her boyfriend's side and was cradling his dazed head. Suitably cowed and repentant, Charlie pulled himself to his feet, upon which Tanya showered his huge head with kisses and the dysfunctional pair staggered off, doubtless for a night of drunken makeup sex that would see them through till the next time Tanya had the temerity to speak to another man.

I closed the door on them, looked at Will and Kavi, and blinked.

'Did that really just happen?' Will looked at Kavi. 'Where did you learn to do *that*?'

'I did four years of taekwondo at university.'

'You macho hunk. I had no idea.'

Kavi smiled. 'Well, they do call it *Boxing* Day.'

31

A Pact. Then a Fact.

'No, it's fine. I need something to take my mind off …
everything else.'

At the door to Franklin's, Winchester's premier jeweller, Jonathan put his arm round me. 'You're incapable of not being selfless.'

'That's a triple negative. I don't know if it's a compliment or not.'

'I only *ever* pay you compliments.'

'So, what exactly *is* a commitment ring?'

'It's a symbol of my … affection.'

I narrowed my eyes. 'Affection? So it's an *affection* ring.'

'Why do women make things so complicated?'

'It's *men* who complicate things. You either love her or you don't. Or you don't know. Which is it?'

'I'm deferring my answer.'

'By buying a ring?'

'Yes.'

'Is that wise?'

He smiled his matinee idol smile. 'When have I *ever* been wise?'

The assistant practically rubbed his hands when Jonathan asked to see a tray of diamond rings with cosmic prices. As he laid the tray on the marble counter, I could see the cogs whirring in his brain as he calculated the commission and weighed up his options for a last-minute winter break.

He had the smarmy delivery that was the trademark of the presenters on the shopping channels Mum used to watch.

'Our most exclusive range, sir.'

Jonathan pointed to a huge rock. 'I quite like that one.'

'Wonderful choice, sir.' In his head, the assistant was swapping the long weekend in Paris for a Caribbean cruise. 'You have excellent taste, sir.'

I thought I'd better chip in before the needle broke on the *sir*-ometer.

'I think that's more of an engagement ring.'

The assistant glowered at me. And mentally unpacked his *Berlitz Guide to Bermuda*. 'The ring wears quite flexibly, I'd suggest, sir.'

Jonathan was still keen. He hadn't even looked at the price. A cool twelve and a half grand. An extravagant best friend for any girl.

'Would you slip it on, Jen? So I can see how it looks.' The assistant smiled and lifted the rock and the platinum ring it was perched on from the tray, repacking his guide and throwing in a fedora for good measure.

He took my hand fawningly in his own and tried to slip the ring onto my engagement finger. The band was a little too small for my sausage and balked at the knuckle. It may have been the pure pleasure of being, however temporarily, associated with such a gorgeous gewgaw but, against my better judgment, I managed to force it past the knuckle and into its intended place.

Jonathan's face lit up. 'It looks stunning. Perfect. I'll take it.'

The beaming assistant waved us towards a leather couch then produced, either by retrieving it from a hidden fridge under the counter or being handed it by unseen oompa-loompas stationed in some underground vault, a bottle of prosecco in a wine cooler. He took two flutes from a cabinet behind him, filled them, and slithered over to hand them to us.

He smiled his oily smile. 'Congratulations on a very wise purchase.'

I turned an acerbic eye on Jonathan. 'See. You *can* be wise.'

I sipped the prosecco. It tasted like something you might clean your oven with.

The assistant beamed. 'Shall I gift wrap the ring, sir?'

'I'd be grateful. Thank you.' He looked at me and I put down my glass of plonk and tugged at the ring.

It didn't budge.

I felt a bead of sweat on my upper lip.

'Erm … I can't get it off.'

Jonathan smiled at what he thought was my little joke. 'Well, I'm always saying we'd make the perfect couple.'

The sweat had spread to my armpits. 'I'm serious.'

A cloud of concern began to gather on Jonathan's brow. The assistant looked like he might need a change of underwear.

'It does happen. The studio is very warm today.'

Studio? Where are we? Pinewood? It's a bloody shop!

He gestured towards the wine cooler. 'Perhaps madam could try …'

I stared at him for three seconds. I looked at Jonathan, who shrugged. Then I dipped my hand in the wine cooler and we waited. And waited.

Nobody actually whistled but we were all wanting to.

When you're watching a clock while sitting with your hand in a wine bucket, sixty seconds is a very long time.

The assistant scurried off. He came back with a towel and handed it to me. I dried my reluctant fingers and gripped the ring again.

Nothing.

It felt like it was welded on.

The assistant looked like he was about to throw up. Not only had he unpacked his case but the *Symphony of the Seas* had hit a rock and was listing badly.

Jonathan, ever the gallant knight, climbed onto his Arab charger. 'It's no problem. Let me pay for the ring now and we'll work out a solution later.'

Solution? Like what? Surgery?

The ship miraculously righted herself, the assistant's blood pressure dropped a couple of dozen notches, and the oily little man threw his fedora back into the case.

'Excellent, sir. Thank you.'

Jonathan looked relaxed. 'It went *on*. It'll come *off* sooner or later.'

Back at the cottage, I made my dinner with one hand, the other appendage encumbered by a freezer bag filled with ice and wrapped in a tea towel. I slept with my hand sandwiched between two ice-filled 'hot-water' bottles.

In the morning, I took a cold shower.

A couple of minutes before 9 am on New Year's Eve, and with the help of three-quarters of a bottle of Fairy Liquid, the beautiful little bastard was finally detached from my body.

I texted Jonathan and got a reply within seconds.

'Great. I'll drive over.'

An hour later, I heard a growling engine and through the cottage window saw his white Morgan Roadster pull up outside.

Steph the Stick Insect was in the passenger seat.

When I opened the door, Jonathan had one arm around Steph and the other wrapped around a large hardback book, *The Complete Bordeaux*. He handed it to me.

'Here's that book you wanted to borrow.' He stared at me conspiratorially. Steph smiled a Hollywood smile. 'Hi.'

'Hello. Nice to see you again.'

'You, too. I think it's very impressive. But you should really get some downtime.'

Jonathan looked at my puzzled face and filled in the blanks. 'I've been telling Steph how you never switch off. Even in the holidays. Always doing your research. Expanding your knowledge.' He nodded at the book.

I picked up the ball and ran with it.

'Right … Yes … Well, you know what it's like. I just want to do a good job.'

Steph, a good fifteen years my junior, laid a maternal hand on my shoulder. 'Seriously, though. Try to slow down. You'll burn yourself out.'

I'll burn your eyes out if you don't move your hand.

'Yes. I'll try.'

Steph glanced round the room. 'What a lovely cottage!'

'Yes, it's been a nice base for a few weeks. There's a pretty little garden at the back, if you want to take a look. Just through the kitchen.' I stood back.

Jonathan looked conspiratorial again. He turned to Steph. 'Oh, you love horticulture, don't you, darling?'

Steph lit up, ready to have any interest bestowed on her if it sounded a bit brainy. 'Absolutely.' She strode past me and headed for the back door.

Jonathan whipped out the ring box and I plucked the ring from my bag and handed it over. He popped it in the box, snapped it shut and thrust it into his pocket.

He kissed me on the cheek and stayed close enough to whisper. 'Thank you for always saving me.'

Steph breezed back into the room. 'It's absolutely gorgeous. I love that spiky tree with the red berries.'

'The holly. Yes. It's lovely, isn't it?'

'Oh, that's *holly*? I didn't know it grew on trees.'

Jonathan gave me a glance that fell somewhere between amusement and pain. 'Well, we're heading up to Salisbury for lunch. Can we drop you at the care home?'

'That's very kind, but I've already booked a taxi,' I lied. 'Besides, you lovebirds don't want me cramping your style.'

Steph threaded her arm through Jonathan's and he patted her hand. 'Well, we'll be off then.'

'Yes. Thanks again for the book.'

His eyes expressed the warmth and affection of all our long years of friendship. 'No problem. Happy New Year when it comes.'

'Yes. Happy New Year.'

***

Mum died two days later.

I had a call from Marvin, who met me in reception and walked with me to Mum's room. Sue was holding her hand. She stood and moved away to let me in. 'Not long now.'

I sat by Mum's side. I held her hand and stroked her head and kissed her cheek. I told her what a wonderful mum she'd always been and how much I loved her and how much I owed her. I told her that my world had been a warm and loving place because of her. I told her I was sorry for all the times I hadn't been there for her.

And then she breathed her last breath and I felt like someone had hit me in the chest with a hammer.

The days that followed passed in a blur. A confusion of feelings and memories and the absurdity of admin that accompanies death.

At Mum's graveside, the frost cracked under my feet and those of the handful of other mourners – Mrs Jennings, Will, Bob and Brenda, Marvin, a bereft-looking Leon.

I struggled through the words in Mary Elizabeth Frye's famous poem and my voice cracked when I got to the line *I am the diamond glints on snow* and Will put his arm round me and held me up.

The beautiful, gentle lady who was my mum had gone.

32

New Year, New Zealand

For the first few weeks of January, I felt like I couldn't get out of second gear. The air was like soup, the ground like quicksand.

Kellie put her arm round me.

'You need a break.'

'I've hardly *been* here.'

'You're not at your best, though. Which is entirely natural, given everything that's happened to you. Get away for a few days. You know Cécile will sign off on that.'

'I feel like a wimp. I just need to pull myself together.'

'You need a rest.'

The uncomfortable truth was, after settling Mum's account at Roselands, I was left with a substantial sum of money. I'd been intending to squirrel all of it away in an ISA I'd been meaning to swap for something with a better interest rate. But there was nothing stopping me from keeping back a small amount for a treat – a short break somewhere peaceful. Get my head together.

I looked online at short-haul winter sun deals but the usual portfolio of offerings – the Canaries, Corfu, Madeira – didn't light my fire. So I started to look closer to home – I wasn't really fussed about sun, I decided, as long as the place was pretty and relaxing. I found a couple of cottages in the Lakes that ticked all my boxes and one of them wasn't far from Hill Top, the house Beatrix Potter bought with the royalities from her first half dozen books, tales I'd devoured as a child and had read to Mum only a couple of weeks ago.

Then a chat with Cécile changed my plans.

Sheikh Saeed had acquired a chain of hotels in Germany, Switzerland and Austria. And Cécile wanted to ensure we acquired the contract to supply them.

'So I need to be in Europe, to do that deal. So I can't go to New Zealand. So I'd like you to go in my place.'

'But I thought the New Zealand connection was done and dusted.'

'It is. Pretty much. But I'm not signing anything final until I've seen their operations first-hand.'

'But you wouldn't be seeing them first-hand. You'd be getting everything second-hand. From me.'

'That's more than good enough.'

I winced, but she was adamant. 'Look. It's all booked. Flights, accommodation, internal travel. A full schedule of appointments. Cancelling would be an admin nightmare.'

'I'm not sure I'm up to it.'

'If you weren't up to it, I wouldn't be asking.'

Business Class on an Emirates Airbus A380 is rather comfortable.

Champagne from my own personal minibar. Complimentary canapés. Twelve yards away, a semicircular cocktail bar if I needed to stretch my legs.

I was feeling better already.

Most of my fellow passengers were either business types or well-heeled silver-haired couples with time and money on their hands. But the guy in the little private pod across the aisle from me was different.

We got chatting at the bar (Gimlet for me, Manhattan for him). Steve was a Bruce Willis lookalike, an American ex-marine on his way to Afghanistan. Our flight was taking the pair of us as far as Dubai.

'Afghanistan's a pretty unusual destination.'

'I'm Head of Security for an oil company there.'

'That sounds scary.'

'You'd be surprised how safe it is over there now. Probably safer than New York City or London.'

I thought back to my stolen handbag. I doubted incidents like that would be on Steve's radar.

'There must have been hairy moments, though.'

'One or two. But I did a few tours in Afghanistan a while back. It sort of prepares you for hairy.'

'Yes. I'll bet.'

'What about you?'

'I'm in wine. As it were.'

'Sounds great.'

'It isn't bad, actually. Our company, in London, is developing a relationship with a bunch of producers in New Zealand. That's where I'm heading.'

'New Zealand sounds like fun. If you're ever looking for security guys …' He fished into his pocket and pulled out a business card. '… give me a call.'

Since getting my own batch of 500 business cards from Cécile, I'd handed out maybe a dozen or so. But now was a good time to add to the modest tally. I pulled one from the little leather case in my handbag. *Artisan Wines. Jennifer Brown. Client Manager.*

Steve looked at the card then up at me. His smile was warm. 'Well, it's lovely to meet you, Jennifer Brown.'

We clinked.

At Dubai airport, I had half an hour to linger in the duty free shops. Temptations were easy to resist and included a wine shop offering Château Cheval Blanc, a Saint Emilion joint I'd passed dozens of times during my summer in Bordeaux, at the equivalent of eight hundred quid for a 2014, a lovely vintage, admittedly, but one we were buying at the cellar door for forty.

My flight to Auckland was unremarkable save for a spot of turbulence near Papua New Guinea that caused a few couples to hold hands and one young flight attendant to sprint to the galley with his hand over his mouth.

I drank champagne, dozed off during *The Notebook* and had intimate dreams about a Ryan Gosling who, at intervals, morphed into Steve the Afghanistan-bound ex-marine.

It was mid-morning in Auckland and, despite the cosseting comfort of Business Class, I still felt like a baboon had been sleeping on my face. I wanted a shower.

What I *didn't* want was the Spanish Inquisition delivered by an unsmiling twenty-something Kiwi with epaulettes.

'Any comestibles?'

'Sorry?'

'Food items. Sandwiches, biscuits, fruit, nuts, honey, fresh meat, fresh fish …'

'No.' *Fresh fish?!*

'Any plant products? Seeds, cuttings, cones, herbal medicines, items made of straw, rattan, coconut fibre, bamboo …'

'No.'

'Any animals or animal products. Feathers, eggs, shells, ivory, whalebone, coral …'

'Coral? I'm from England.'

She looked at my suitcase. 'The animal keyring. Could you remove it, please.'

For some years, I'd been in the habit of distinguishing my anonymous black suitcase by means of a miniature purple gonk on a keyring attached to one of the case's zips.

'You're not serious?'

The border guard standing across from me had never been seriouser in her short life.

'Biosecurity is a serious matter.'

'It's a stupid little plastic toy with nylon hair.'

She wasn't backing down. I didn't have the energy to argue. I pulled the gonk off the zip and passed it to her. She took it in her gloved hand and dropped it rather too ceremoniously into a large black bin by her side.'

'Enjoy your stay in New Zealand.'

My shower was further delayed at the car hire desk. Kellie had overlooked the need to change the name on the booking from Cécile's to mine. Making the transfer at the desk itself, rather than online, involved a level of bureaucracy comparable to the signing of the Treaty of Versailles.

When I finally got to my hotel, nearly three hours after landing, the need for a shower had been superseded by the need to close my eyes.

I lay on the bed and slept for eleven hours.

33

I Mean Business

I quite like a road trip.

But this was work, I reminded myself. When I thought of the responsibility Cécile had placed on my shoulders, I started to sweat and turned the aircon up a notch.

I'd be meeting different sorts of people. Some were straightforward producers, like Philippe and Madeleine. They owned the place, grew the grapes, produced the wine, bottled it, and sold it.

But I'd also be meetings agents and merchants, a far murkier bunch. Murky in the sense that I wasn't exactly sure what they did. At what point in the process did they get involved? And what cut were they taking for themselves before the finished wine was sold to us?

I pointed the car towards Rotorua and headed south on Highway 1.

After half an hour or so of the kind of industrial sprawl familiar to city-dwellers everywhere, I hit first rolling farmland then, after an hour, the green hilly Hobbit country Peter Jackson had filled our screens with in *Lord of the Rings*.

The roads were pleasantly empty – a handful of rusty SUVs and a logging truck the size of an ocean liner were the only things I'd come across.

I fired up the radio. Coast 105.4 was playing John Denver's *Country Roads*, a vision of relaxed motoring that properly belonged a couple of thousand miles east of me but fitted my mood just fine.

Jennifer Brown was on the move again.

An hour or so later, I started to get jumpy about petrol. So when a shack with pumps rolled into view, I pulled in. A guy in his fifties with a Grateful Dead T-shirt came out of the shack and strolled over.

'Gidday, mate. How ya goin?'

'Fine, thanks.'

'Bit out in the wop wop's here, aren'tcha?'

'Sorry?'

'Middle of nowhere.'

'Right.' I looked around. They say the horizon is seven miles away. Here, there was no other edifice, or sign of life, in any direction. 'Yes. Peaceful.'

'One word for it.'

I smiled. 'And hot.'

He looked at my jeans. 'Why don't you chuck on your stubbies and head for the beach?'

'My what?'

'Shorts.'

'Right. That would be nice. But I'm working.'

'Bugger.'

'Yes.'

He finished filling the tank. The flap over the petrol cap wouldn't stay shut. He looked up at me and smiled. 'I'll get some Durex.'

I scanned the empty horizon nervously and was about to leap into the car and scream away without paying when the man I'd mistaken for a sex fiend re-emerged with a roll of sticky tape, tore off a length, stuck it over the cap and handed me the roll.

'It'll come off eventually. You'd better take this.'

It was clearly going to take me a while to get used to Kiwi slang.

I reached Nielsen's Winery by early evening. Its curved white walls and black slate roofs were a modern interpretation of the more traditional Maori buildings I'd seen on the road. The winery's outbuildings had an architect-designed look about them and the crisply landscaped gardens also suggested this was an establishment on which no expense had been spared.

I announced myself in the cool and spacious reception area and an elegant young woman with a blonde ponytail escorted me across a cobbled courtyard to a smart chalet on the edge of a vineyard that stretched up to the low wooded hills of the Kaweka Forest.

The fridge was well stocked with the winery's produce and I thoughtfully sampled them on my little patio, making notes for Cécile and for my meeting the following day and watching the blood-orange sun set over the Te Mata Peak.

Greg was Nielsen's oenologist. His latest project was a Chardonnay-Sauvignon blend that was winning a lot of medals in Kiwi country but wasn't making inroads in a European market dominated by varietal wines.

'People think of heavy oak when they think Chardonnay. And Sauvignon produces the crisp grapefruity varietals that Marlborough does really well. And there's this view that never the twain shall meet.'

'I tried your blend last night. It's gorgeous.'

'They've been using this marriage in Italy for decades, and in Napa for a while. But most of Europe's hung up on varietals. Which is good in a way – people are becoming educated in flavour. But that shouldn't stop us experimenting.'

'Especially when the results of your experiments taste so good.'

'Thank you.'

'I think our clients will like to feel they're ahead of the curve. I can see that supermarkets might be hard to convince but, generally speaking, our clients like a craft product and they're happy to pay for it. If the product also has the feel of exclusivity about it, they're happy to pay a lot more. I think we can do business.'

Nielsen's had been a great first appointment. I had another four on North Island – three wineries (two thumbs-ups and definite thumbs-down) and a *négociant* who treated me to an expensive restaurant overlooking a flashy marina and told me a story I'd heard before, about how New Zealand winemakers had got round European trade embargoes by smuggling rootstocks in their wellington boots.

I told him about my experience with the gonk a few days before and said his nation's vintners had been lucky not to come across my sour-faced sentinel.

I took the Picton ferry across to South Island and spent three days kicking about small wineries in Marlborough a fraction of the size of the operations run by the likes of Cloudy Bay and Brancott Estate – good enough wines but not our sector of the market.

After eight days spent swilling and spitting and studying, my taste buds and my brainbox were running out of steam.

I typed up my reams of notes into a ten-page report and emailed my findings and recommendations to Cécile. At what was 4.35 in the morning for her, she fired back a reply.

'Wonderful. You're a very safe pair of hands. Now enjoy yourself.'

I'd booked, on the company's account, an Airbnb on the golden sands of the Abel Tasman National Park.

I couldn't wait.

34

A New Zealand Fleece

Sweat was running down the back of my neck as I rang the bell.
I looked around. This white clapboard cottage overlooked a short, deserted stretch of sand the colour of golden caster sugar. The water was bright turquoise. I wanted to be floating in it.

No answer.

I checked the itinerary on my phone. 3pm arrival. My watch showed 3.04. I rang again.

Nothing.

I tried the contact number on the booking and got voicemail. I left a message then found a spot of shade on the sandy grass at the side of the cottage.

An hour later, my host arrived.

'Could you move your car? You've parked in my spot.'

'Sorry?'

'The shady spot by the tree. That's mine. It'll be like an oven in the morning if I leave it there.'

'You leave your car here overnight?'

My unmannerly host glared at me. 'Where else would I leave it except outside my house?'

He opened the door and strode inside. I looked at the booking details on the app on my phone. I've stayed in Airbnb places all over Europe and only ever go for places that specify 'entire house' or 'entire apartment'. Sure enough, under the section headed The Space, it said 'entire house'. I was confused.

I wheeled my case over the threshold. Mistake.

'Lift it, please. Wheels scratch the floorboards.'

Hm. Wonder if I can buy a cheap tent and camp on the beach.

'So, a couple of house rules. No suitcases on the bed. And no windows open – the sandflies round here are bastards.'

I think I know where they get it from.

'This is your room.'

'I think there's been a mistake. I've booked the entire house.'

The man who hadn't introduced himself but certainly wasn't the smiling Susan from the property's homepage stopped and turned to look at me. In his eyes, there was a hint of Hannibal Lecter.

'The house is never rented out. Just a room.'

I showed him the booking on the app. 'Look. Here. On the app. Property type: entire house. That's what I've booked. That's what I've paid for. And, by the way, the agreed arrival time was three o'clock.' In my eyes, a hint of Cruella De Vil.

Hannibal smiled. 'You're European, aren't you?'

'I'm English.' Hannibal smiled again and gave a little snort. English was clearly worse still.

'If you're not happy, you'll have to take it up with your … app people.' He said the word *app* like it was a liberal leftie conspiracy responsible for bringing the right-thinking redneck world to its knees.

'I'm not happy.'

'Then take it up with your app people. I have a room available, as agreed …'

'It wasn't agreed by me.'

'… as agreed. You don't have to take it.'

'No. I don't.'

'But I have to warn you, you won't find anything else round here at such short notice.'

'Frankly, I'd rather sleep in the car.'

I turned on my heel and, dragging the case as heavily as I could across his precious floor, took my leave.

I drove a couple of miles down the coast and parked up outside a cute little shack not so much a stone's throw from the beach as a short underarm lob. Judging by the clientele of sunkissed twenty-something blokes in T-shirts, the place was a popular hangout for surfers.

I needed a drink. A brown-haired girl with a tanned midriff came out to take my order.

'Hi. Do you have wine, or is it only beer?'

She smiled at my assumption. 'We have wine.'

'Great. What whites do you have by the glass?'

My pretty and pleasant interlocutor rhymed off a list of grape varieties that would make most Shoreditch wine bars green with envy, including a Picpoul-Clairette blend I'd never heard of. I ordered one.

Its crisp and beefy lemony gorgeousness sipped here, the turquoise water inches from my feet, was just the antidote I needed to the brashness of my earlier encounter. I phoned Airbnb customer services and, after a long recital of the details of my booking (which they couldn't find), they suggested I'd been the victim of some kind of phony, cloned site. When I suggested going back to have it out with the guy, the Airbnb woman said he'd have done a runner seconds after I'd left.

So I'd been fleeced out of 550 New Zealand dollars, about 300 pounds.

A couple of young surfer guys on the next table overheard the whole conversation and one of them shouted over to commiserate.

'We're not all criminals, honest.'

'Oh, I know. I've been made very welcome, generally.' I looked out over the bay. 'Not surfing today?'

'No chance. Looks alright now but there's a storm coming. Hope you find somewhere.' The pair of them necked their beers, stood up and waved as they strolled away.

I was having to shade my eyes from the glare of the sunlight on the sea and found it hard to believe there'd be a storm in the next couple of *months*, let alone *hours*.

Sixty minutes later, under a gunmetal sky and in the teeth of a downpour that the wipers couldn't cope with, my hire car was sliding off a side road running with mud, somewhere near the town of Takaka.

I tried not to panic as the vehicle came slowly and gently to rest against the trunk of a very exotic tree at the edge of what looked like a farm. The wind was now whipping small branches and other debris through the air and onto the windscreen. The car was rocking under its force.

Outside it looked like a Discovery Channel special on extreme weather. But inside I felt under siege.

I threw the door open and headed for what I took to be the farmhouse. A tree ahead of me was bent double by the wind. My canvas shoes, soaked within seconds, hit something soft and my body crumpled and hit the mud.

I pulled myself up and set my sights again on the building ahead, still a hundred yards away. I fell a further twice before finally reaching the stone structure and pounding on the door with both hands.

The letterbox flew open.

'Whatever it is you're selling, I'm not buying. Bugger off!'

I screamed above the wind. 'I'M NOT SELLING *ANYTHING*! MY CAR HIT A TREE!'

Silence.

'PLEASE!'

The door opened.

He must have been six feet five. He was wearing rust red overalls. A grey ponytail hung down from a green baseball cap.

And he was carrying a shotgun.

He looked at my sodden shoes. My muddy trousers. The blonde hair plastered to my face.

'You'd best come in.'

I stepped out of the rain and the wind and into the nineteenth century.

The bare stone walls were covered in hunting trophies – the heads of deer, some large and some very small, jostled with stuffed duck, geese and several samples of a strange little furry creature I wasn't familiar with that looked like a gremlin.

As I looked at the ancient furniture, several dogs of varying sizes and uncertain breeds came to sniff my sodden legs. I flinched when one of them, something crossed with an Irish wolfhound by the look of it, sniffed in the vicinity of my pockets.

'They'll be right. Relax.'

I didn't dare move. I didn't want to wind up being this guy's next trophy.

'The long drop is through there.' He pointed to a door that looked like it was made of old railway sleepers.

'The what?'

'The toilet. So you can get out of your wet clothes.'

'Erm …'

'I can find you something. If you don't mind … country gear.'

He propped the shotgun up in a corner and walked over to a huge oak linen press that looked like it had been in the family for a couple of centuries, the kind of thing that would fetch three grand in a Chelsea auction house. Inside the cupboard, there were neat stacks of clothes, towels and other linens. He pulled out a towel the size of a tablecloth and handed it to me. Then, selecting carefully, he produced a pair of bright blue dungarees and a green T-shirt and held them out. I took them. He looked bashful.

'I don't have … anything for … under.'

'Under is okay, I think.'

'Right. I'll make coffee.'

In the corner of the room, a sturdy farmhouse table supported an industrial-looking stove.

The man gave me an awkward smile. 'Cooper.'

'Jennifer.' I held out a muddy hand and he shook it once, gently. He nodded towards the 'long drop' and that was my cue.

Stripped to my dryish undies and with my sodden clothes in a pile on the floor, I stood next to a basic but scrupulously clean wooden lavatory and slipped into the clothes Cooper had given me. They were a good fit. I wondered who they belonged to.

I rejoined what was the house's only other room, clutching my wet gear. Cooper held out his hand.

'Here. I'll take those.'

I handed the wet and muddy clothes to him and he walked over to the corner of the room that served as a kitchen and plunged my clothes into a basin of steaming water. He turned to me and nodded towards a battered leather armchair covered in a sheepskin, next to a log fire that was just beginning to blaze. An enamel pot with a wooden handle was sitting on a low table next to a porcelain mug.

'Grab a seat and some coffee.'

He plunged his hands into the basin of water and began to knead my clothes with a practised hand.

I poured myself some coffee and watched him wash my clothes. After twenty seconds of silence, I spoke.

'The storm caught me by surprise.'

'They do that round here.' Cooper transferred the soapy clothes to a second basin of water and began kneading again.

'This is very kind of you. Looking after me like this.'

He looked up. 'All good. How's the coffee?'

'Delicious.'

'Sweet. Pass me them pegs, will you?'

I heard 'pigs' for a second, then, following his eyes, saw a pile of plastic yellow clothes pegs on a wooden chair. I got up and handed them to him. He draped my jeans and blouse over a spindly wooden frame, applied the pegs, and placed the frame in front of the fire.

He went back to the cupboard and pulled out a small pair of sandals and handed them to me. 'Here. Try these jandals. Be about your size.'

I slipped them on. Good fit.

He lifted my sodden canvas shoes and plunged them into the first basin and rubbed them lightly with what looked like a nailbrush. After a minute, he fished them out, clean, and rinsed them in the second basin. When he pulled them out again, they looked like new. He laid them in front of the fire.

'Couple of hours. Make yourself comfortable.'

I don't know if it was the softness of the sheepskin, the toastiness of the interior, or the comforting sense of being looked after, but I dozed off almost as soon as I sat back in the chair.

When I woke up, the sky was blue through the window and Cooper was laying two steaming bowls on the table.

'Come and knock the bastard off.'

I took that as an invitation to join him for food.

'I'm sorry for sleeping. That was rude.'

'Not even.'

I was suddenly ravenous. I tucked into the bowl's contents, a kind of soup thick with vegetables and chunks of a meat I didn't recognise. I looked at the animals decorating the walls and realised the field of possibility was pretty wide. The concoction was faintly spicy and absolutely delicious.

He read my mind. 'Possum. Little bird-eating bastards. Scavengers. The trick is to catch them clean, then feed them corn for a few days. Clean them out. Then they're ready for the pot.' He nodded at the gremlin-like creature on the wall. 'Not pretty. But tasty enough.'

'No. And yes.'

We ate in silence. Then an ancient oak wall clock broke the silence when it chimed five.

The log fire was dying but the sun was doing a good job of warming the room and Cooper let it die. On the chunky mantelpiece stood a framed black-and-white photo of a man in full Highland regalia clutching a set of bagpipes.

Cooper followed my eyes. 'My grandfather. Came out here after the First World War. A rough ride. Ten kids.'

At the mention of children, I thought I saw his eyes moisten.

'Goodness. Must have been a hard life.'

'A bloody mare.'

He stood up, which roused the dogs, and went over to the drying frame. He felt my clothes and shoes.

'Stuff's good to go.'

'Right.' I stood and he handed me the clean dry gear and I went through to the 'long drop'.

When I emerged, Cooper had donned a kind of tartan cape and was standing by the door. The dogs looked eager.

'Like to meet the folks?'

I wondered how far a trek it would be to his parents' house – there was no other building for miles – but I couldn't refuse this kind man anything after all he'd done for me.

I looked again at his cape, then at the photo on the fireplace. It was the same garment. This was a man for whom family was a strong bond.

'Sure.'

He smiled and opened the door. Sensing freedom and fresh air, the dogs bowled through the doorway ahead of him.

On the main road, I noticed my hire car was upright and properly parked, not slumped against the tree where I'd left it.

Cooper circled the house to a flight of stone steps set into a hillock. The dogs ran off into a little wooded area at the foot of the steps and he didn't call them back.

The top of the hillock was flat, like a little plateau. There was a neat, well-tended garden surrounded by a wooden fence, newly painted. Inside the garden were half a dozen small headstones, some wearing the signs of decades of exposure to weather, a couple clearly much later additions.

'Mum left us last year.'

'I'm sorry.'

'She had fair hair, like you.'

I put a hand on his arm and he laid his hand on mine for a second then withdrew it quickly, reached under his cape and pulled out the chanter from a set of bagpipes and raised it to his lips.

As *Amazing Grace* took flight into the New Zealand sky, I stood next to a man I hadn't known a few hours before and would never see again, tears running down my cheeks.

***

A couple of hours later, I was a million miles away, back in the world of marble, chrome and air conditioning.

I made a boutique hotel in Nelson my base for a couple of days, soaked up some sun and some wine, paddled in Tasman Bay, and flicked lazily through Julie Arkell's *Complete Guide to New World Wines*.

Before I knew it, I was handing back the hire car, catching the short flight from Nelson to Auckland, then settling myself once again into business class.

My New Zealand interlude was over.

35

Look Back, But Not in Anger

After the sunshine and endless skies of New Zealand, London looked grey and cramped and Dickensian. And, once again, a smattering of snow was testing the transport system to its limits. In the taxi queue at Wood Green tube station, I felt like cracking the litre of gin 'with 28 botanicals' that I'd hauled back from the airport as a gift for Miranda.

Back at work, Cécile could hardly contain her admiration for the way I'd handled business in New Zealand. She'd cleared her diary so we could have a catch-up lunch at Le Gavroche.

'New World sales are already up seven percent. That's in just under two weeks. You're adding real value to the company. All the time.'

'I'm really pleased. Also a little amazed. I don't really feel like I'm doing anything special.'

She squeezed my hand and looked into my eyes. 'That's the beauty of working with you. You don't realise how good you are.' It felt like a moment. I didn't know what to say.

'Honestly. I'm just … being myself. Most of the time, I'm terrified I'm mucking things up.'

She smiled. 'We're *all* like that. We're *all* acting. It's just that some of us are better at acting than others.'

'You always look so relaxed. So in control. I just want to be more like you but I'm worried I'll never get there.'

'Don't. Don't worry. And don't ever get there.'

'Why?'

'Because being you – being Jennifer Brown – is …' Her eyes were glistening now. '… is the best thing to be. The best thing anyone could be.'

I felt a lump in my throat. 'That's such a wonderful thing to say.'

'Well. It's true.' She regained herself. 'So there!' She took a sip of wine. 'And when you get back to the office next week, you can dive right back in.'

'Next week?'

'Take a break.'

'I've just been to New Zealand.'

'That was work.'

'Not all of it.'

'Take a proper break. Besides, having you in the office all the time, working your magic, is making the others look bad.'

Hours later, I was whizzing down the A3 in a hire car, passing through the snowy lower reaches of Surrey that, but for the flatness, could have been Switzerland. I fiddled with the radio and got Whitney Houston belting out *When You Believe*, which made me reflect on what Cécile had said. She'd described a person that didn't sound like me. A person I still, in spite of the successes I could see on paper, struggled to believe in. I could see the path my life had taken since my breakup with Pete and my departure from Intext – Cook and Housekeeper to a randy old fisherman (I'd had to box clever for that one), Estate Manager at the crumbling and financially dormant Thornhill Hall (I'd transformed it into a thriving concern with a solid portfolio of ongoing business), and now, apparently, successful Client Manager with a leading independent high-end wine merchant.

I knew all that. But, underneath it all, I was still *me*. Still the Jennifer Brown who, in the past, had mucked up Jonathan's memos at Intext and who'd mistaken Spanish Sharon's cannabis crop for parsley. The Jennifer Brown who, not that long ago, had exploded a bottle of Cécile's priciest stuff all over the restaurant floor of a top Mayfair hotel. The Jennifer Brown who still pretty much closed her eyes and crossed her fingers and hoped for the best. Who didn't know where it was all leading.

Does it have to lead somewhere? I don't know. It's nice to have a plan. I had a good job with people I liked and who seemed to like me. And I was living in a nice enough flat in a nice enough bit of a nice enough city with a landlady I counted as a friend.

But was this the culmination of my plan? I hadn't really *had* a plan, so I wasn't really sure. And if this wasn't the plan, what the hell *was*?

I didn't know the answer to that one either.

The hire car pulled into my old home town and I steered it towards my childhood street, the heart strings pulling me to take a glimpse at Mum's old house.

I parked over the road. The net curtains in the living-room window had been replaced by smart wooden venetian blinds and the old brown door was evidently lying in a skip somewhere, its replacement a shiny new woodgrain composite in duck egg blue. I smiled at the memory of a promise Dad had made to Mum to replace the front door, circa 1995. Now the house had what had been promised.

Just then, the shiny door opened and a young Asian couple came out – Kavi's brother and his gorgeous (and very heavily pregnant) fiancée. She looked about ten minutes away from labour. Mum would have been thrilled to know her house would once again be a happy home to a young family. Through moist eyes, I watched Kavi's brother help his fiancée shoehorn herself into the passenger seat. Then they were gone.

After my little trip down memory lane, next on my agenda was a lunch date with Will, who'd managed, three minutes after getting my text, to wangle the afternoon off. Whatever Will wanted, Will wangled. He was an arch wangler.

When I breezed into Herman's on the Southsea front, Will (in relatively sober slimfit lavender chinos and outrageous cerise floral shirt-cum-blouse, no wig) had already ordered wine and had sunk at least one large glass.

'Oi! *I'm* the wine expert. You should have waited for the benefit of my wisdom before tackling the wine list.'

'Oh, sit down and shut up! Just because you have tits, you think you know it all. I mean, they are *marvellous* tits, but still ...'

I looked down at my balcony. 'You're right. They *are* marvellous.'

'Well, there's nothing wrong with *your* self-confidence, is there!'

I looked Will in the eyes. 'Actually, I think there's been something wrong with it for quite some time. I'm trying to change that.'

Will could see he'd touched a nerve and his caustic mask dropped away and he leaned in and hugged me.

'I hope you know that most things I say are complete bollocks. I hope you know I think you're the most ...' His voice was breaking. '... the loveliest person I know. Simple as that. Completely without comparison. I adore you. My life would be ... poor ... without you in it.'

At this point, the pair of us were in tears. And, as this beautiful little speech had been delivered in front of a nineteen-year-old waitress with a pad and paper in her hand, *she* was in tears, too.

Will looked up at her, then back at me. 'See what you've done. You and your loveliness. You've made this poor girl's mascara run all down her face. Right. Let's eat.'

After seafood bisque and lemony Moroccan tuna kebabs, we were on the mint tea when Will dropped a little pebble into the pond to see how my ripples would spread.

'Has Jonathan been in touch?'

'Not lately. Why? Everything okay at Intext?'

'Oh, work's fine. No, it's a personal thing.'

'He's getting married? To Steph the Stick Insect?'

'God no! I don't think that'll *ever* happen. With Steph or anyone else. He's too much of a … what's the technical term? … shag bandit … to ever settle down. I just thought he might have been in touch to let you know about David.'

Plop.

I tried not to ripple. Tried to keep the colour from rising to my cheeks.

'Which David?'

Will spluttered into his napkin. 'You are so shit at dissimulation.'

I chuckled. And blushed. 'I haven't heard anything about David. What's the gossip? Sarah's pregnant, presumably.'

'She might be. I don't know. But I *do* know it won't be to David.'

'What? Why?' My balcony was blushing now. And I could hear my heart pounding in my ears.

'Because they are no longer together. Haven't been for several months. Didn't make it to the one-year milestone, as a matter of fact.'

I felt a curious mix of sadness and something else I couldn't put my finger on. 'That's really sad. She seemed lovely. Really nice, actually. As well as gorgeous. And he seemed so happy on his wedding day.' I had a flashback to the curious glance David had given me during Jonathan's best man's speech. 'They seemed like the ideal couple. What happened?'

'I don't know. Something, clearly. Anyway, they're no longer together.'

'Goodness. I hope he's okay.'

'You could always call him. Offer comfort. You and your balcony.'

'Shut up.'

'Maybe he'll text you.'

'Get the bill. You're paying.'

I did get a text. But it wasn't from David. It was from Nat. She'd seen a selfie of me and Will in Herman's (Will was, as well as a toilet-mouthed smut monster, an Instagram junkie) and, now installed in a flat in Winchester and working part-time in an art gallery, Nat had been busy making new contacts and dusting off old ones.

'Saw your photo. How long are you in Hampshire? It would be great to meet up.'

'I'm here until the weekend.'

'That's fabulous. You'll be able to come to the reunion.'

'Reunion?'

'Brookhill High. I got an email from Dean Andrews. Our whole year's going. It'll be great fun!'

Great fun wasn't on my mind as I gave my hair a last run-through. An unmarried woman of around two-score years tends, in my experience, to attract one of three labels – lesbian, librarian, or lush. My job for the evening was to rip these three labels up and sell myself as the successful and well-balanced singleton I felt myself to be. Felt it if I tried hard. Really hard.

Nat's taxi pulled up and the driver peeped his horn. When I climbed in, I was surprised at the transformation in Nat. The scrawny bag of wine-sodden bones I'd waved off at Saint Emilion station had bounced back and looked much more like her old Kylie self – more meat on the bones, more colour in the cheeks, more sparkle in the eyes.

I was delighted to see her looking so well and she hugged me warmly.

In the taxi, we swapped dating site horror stories and, when I told her about my tale on the riverbank with the idiotic Ian, she laughed so much her lipstick went up her nose and she had to start again.

The old seventies Brookhill building, with its Soviet-toilet-block styling, had been replaced by a shiny glass and stone edifice fronted by a wide paved esplanade planted with small trees and raised beds with lush shrubs.

It looked a high school in Barcelona.

Nat had a twinkle in her eye I hadn't seen since we were seventeen – the look of a desirable woman about to unleash herself on an expectant crowd of adoring men. I heard Bette Davis's immortal line in my head – *Fancy your seatbelts. It's going to be a bumpy night.*

We crossed a kind of atrium (which I guessed roughly occupied the space of the old reception area where, twenty-five years before, sour-faced admin staff would frisk us for Walkmans and order us to remove hoop earrings and studs) and strolled into the main hall where a small sea of people were already mixing and where a teenage DJ was belting out tunes his mum had listened to in the 90s.

Men with expanding waistbands and retreating hairlines were hugging each other and slapping shoulders. Women in a variety of sartorial styles were shrieking with delight and pointing. I didn't see a single person I recognised.

The bar seemed like a good move so I nudged my companion and we sauntered over, Nat scanning the crowd eagerly, me weighing up my gin options.

A man in his seventies with thick white hair and a walking stick was working his way through a pint of something the colour of Bovril and, decoding his features beneath the years, I placed him as Mr Skidmore, my old Chemistry teacher. The walking stick had a hearing aid for a companion.

I'd thought of him as a desperately old man back then, when in reality he'd probably been not much older than I was now.

He looked terminally bored. After ninety seconds in the place, I was already bored, too. I thought we might make good buddies.

'Hello, Mr Skidmore.'

After only a second and a half of searching in the dark, the lights went on. 'Jennifer Brown!'

'Yes! And I'm sorry.'

'What on earth for?'

'For being so useless at Chemistry. I think I was probably the worst pupil you ever had.'

'Oh, you were very far from it, I can assure you.'

'Really? Did anyone else *suck* the lime water instead of blowing it to make it turn milky? Or set a bench on fire with a bunsen burner?'

'Only about twice a week. And they did it with much less charm than you. It's lovely to see you. What are you doing now?'

'I'm in the wine business.'

'How interesting! Making or selling?'

'Selling. To people with so much money that wine is not so much a pleasure as an investment.'

'How sad. For them, I mean. To have at their disposal the delicious results of perhaps the most interesting of chemical experiments and to forgo that pleasure for the sake of something as boring as money. They strike me as – forgive my French – arseholes.'

I guffawed with wide-eyed delight at this storming of the social barricade that separates pupils from their teachers.

'Your glass is nearly empty, Mr Skidmore. Let me get you another.'

'*I* shall buy *you* a drink, Jennifer. And you shall call me Peter.'

'You're very kind. Peter.' I turned to introduce Nat but she was ten yards away, chatting to a man in his forties I couldn't immediately place.

'What would you like? With your expertise, will you risk the wine?'

The lad behind the bar poured me a large Chardonnay and I settled in for a chat with a lovely man whose desk I used to burn.

'And how about you? Retired now?'

'Yes. Almost ten years.'

'Does it suit you?'

'It did. For a while.'

'Not now?'

He hesitated. 'Things didn't really go according to plan.'

'I'm sorry.'

'Someone once said, If you want to make God laugh, tell him your plans. Well, our plans seemed fairly modest. Although our children thought we were crazy.'

'Why?'

'Helen and I visited California as a joint fiftieth treat for both of us – long time ago now, of course – and we fell in love with the place. The beaches, the warmth, the gorgeous scenery. And we made a pact, on the beach at Carmel, that, when we retired, we'd sell the house, buy a stylish old camper van, and live out our retirement cruising up and down the Pacific Highway. Perhaps nipping over the border into Mexico if the mood took us. Up into Oregon, maybe. Anywhere that took us away from the world of mortgages and council tax payments and Jeremy Bloody Kyle.'

'Were your children unhappy about you selling up? Moving away? I can understand them being worried.'

'No, they were – nervously – fairly supportive. Claimed to be, anyway. Claimed they didn't mind us using up what would have been their inheritance to fund a lifestyle they openly but good-humouredly referred to as 'bonkers.' We even had the van sorted. An old VW T1 – you know, the classic camper with the split windscreen. Sid Withers – you remember him? Metalwork – he and I spent three or four months stripping and rebuilding the engine and doing up the bodywork and tweaking the interior so we'd got everything just the way we needed it. It was ready for life.'

He sipped his beer.

'But Helen wasn't. She'd been feeling lousy for months. Stomach pains. Hadn't told anyone. Least of all me, whose stupid boyish head had been consumed by gearboxes and crankshafts and all that nonsense. She thought – hoped – the pain would all blow over. Then, when it got so bad she couldn't hide it anymore, of course it was too late. Five weeks. That's all we had. Took the van as far as the Peak District. Which was nice. But it wasn't the plan. None of it was the plan.'

I couldn't speak.

The injustice of the tragedy robbed me of words.

'After she'd gone, I sold the van. Couldn't look at it. Bought a one-bedroom flat in Lee. Near the Titchfield Nature Reserve. There's water. But it's not the Pacific.'

I put my arm round the shoulder of my old Chemistry teacher. 'I'm so sorry.'

I felt a tug at my elbow and looked round to see Nat, face lit up. She pulled me towards the buffet.

'You'll never guess who I've been chatting to?'

I shrugged.

'Scott Chandler!'

Scott had been every girl's heartthrob. He'd had the nickname 'Carter' for his uncanny resemblance to Nick Carter, the teenage pop idol from Backstreet Boys with the blonde curtains hairstyle and the cheeky grin. Of course, we all fancied Scott like mad. And when he'd sent me a Facebook friend request about ten years after we'd all gone our separate ways, I'd been cock-a-hoop – that was in my pre-Pete period – and I'd wondered if there might be the chance of something developing between us. He was still a fine-looking man.

But two minutes on his Facebook page made it clear his sexual preference was for other fine-looking men.

We reached the buffet and Nat was hardly taking a breath as she piled onto her plate items from the 'ironic' buffet – turkey drummers, smiley potato faces, chips.

'He's still gorgeous. Better now he hasn't got that daft haircut. He gave me a big lingering hug and told me how gorgeous I looked. And smelled.'

I gave her a quizzical look. 'Yes. He was always a really nice guy.'

'And look at his mate! He's almost as stunning as Scott. How about the two of us getting ourselves a bit of that?'

'Erm …'

'Oh, come on!'

Without waiting for me, she dropped the plate and sashayed over to the area of the room that was serving as a dance floor.

A voice at my shoulder piped up. 'Mind if I join you?'

I swung round to find myself face to face with a James McAvoy lookalike. 'I see you're still in touch with Nat.'

I rummaged through my memory files but found nothing.

'Her Kylie routine was never really my cup of tea, to be honest.'

I felt I needed to defend my friend. 'She was very popular. And she's very nice. Now. I mean … she was *then*. But she's … grown up. We all have. 'I was racking my brain. Nothing.

'Yes. *You* haven't changed, though. Got a picture in the attic?' He smiled sweetly. The sweet smile gave him away.

'Josh!'

'Yes. Have I changed that much?' He patted a belly that was modest indeed for a man of his age. The shy, tousled young boy had blossomed into a shy, tousled and unquestionably handsome man.

'No. Actually, you really haven't.'

'I'd have picked you out of any lineup.'

I smiled. In 1995, Josh Turner had followed me round the school like a puppy. He was just about the only boy in our year who was impervious to Natalie's charms. He must have asked me out a hundred times. He'd once placed a hula hoop ring on my finger and declared his intention to marry me. And when I'd revealed I had (for reasons embarrassingly unclear to me now) a crush on footballer Paul Gascoigne, Josh had gone out and got his hair bleached. But something had gone wrong with the dye and the resulting vibrant shade of orange had earned him the nickname Jaffa for a couple of months, during which time I imagine he'd hated me.

'I've often thought about you. Wondered what you were doing. What sort of life you had.' His eyes were intense.

'I've been fine. Ups and downs. Mostly ups. And life's good.' I looked over his shoulder and glimpsed Nat gyrating provocatively in front of a politely bopping Scott. 'And how about you, Josh?'

'I'm alright. Professional life's good. Personal life has its challenges.'

'I'm sorry.'

'It's always more complicated when kids are involved. Do you have kids?'

It took me a second to answer. 'No.' And I thought, *That's my label. No kids. Pigeonholed by things I didn't do.*

'You're lucky. I mean, I love my kids – they're everything – but when … things … go wrong in a relationship, they make things … harder to sort out.'

'Nice to have them as grown-up friends, though. I imagine.'

'Mine are at the teenage stage. Most teenagers are pretty horrible, aren't they. And divorce doesn't improve their mood.'

'Well, I hope they come out okay at the other end. And realise what a good bloke their dad is.'

'Thanks.' He took a breath. 'Do you still live round here?'

'No. I live in London. I came back for a few days to visit an old work colleague. Then Nat got in touch about tonight. I'd never have known otherwise.'

'Right. Well, I'm going to head off, I think. But …' He took a card out of his pocket and handed it to me. '… if you're ever down again, and you fancy a coffee or … something … just give me a shout.'

I leaned up and kissed him on the cheek. 'Thanks, Josh. I will. Take care.'

He smiled and walked away.

Nat was still writhing on the dance floor when I spotted the Goth Girls. In 1995, they'd strutted around Brookhill High like they owned it, all black lipstick, Dracula eyeliner, and wardrobe from Siouxsie Sioux meets Morticia Addams.

Over twenty years on, they all looked more like Uncle Fester.

For a period of a year or more, they'd made my life a misery. Taunts. Chinese burns. At least one head-flushing.

And, years later, they'd had their five minutes of fame. I remember my mum phoning me and reading out an article from *The Portsmouth News* about a trio of women who'd been done for shoplifting in the Co-op.

The three of them sidled over to me like snakes. Snakes who'd swallowed a couple of goats. I couldn't remember the ringleader's name but the hateful sneer hadn't changed.

'Jennifer Brown. Poshed up a bit, haven't you.' She looked me up and down. 'Your little friend Kylie says you're in the wine business. Very middle class.'

'It's okay. I hear you're in the Community Service business. How's that working out for you?' I held her gaze. The sneer faded. She blinked. I didn't.

A feeble snort was all she could manage before turning on her heels and taking her sorry sidekicks with her.

On the dance floor, Nat was leaning in as Scott was whispering in her ear. I watched with trepidation as Nat's smile died and Scott gestured to the handsome man by his side.

Nat kept her cool admirably in the face of what was clearly, for her, an embarrassing revelation. Then she headed for the bar. I followed her with my eyes and noticed that Mr Skidmore had gone. I scanned the room but could see him nowhere.

I walked over to join Nat, who was necking a highball glass of something clear with ice.

'I'm such an idiot.'

'I tried to tell you, but you were off like a shot.'

'Will I ever grow up, Jen? Will I ever stop looking for … I don't know … admiration. Is that what it is? Is that what I need? Why? Why do I need to be admired by other people?'

'I think we all do. Maybe not admired. Liked, though.'

She turned to look at me. 'What's your secret?'

'I haven't got one.'

'How do you do it, then? How do you … be … so likeable?'

'I don't know that I am. But if I am, I'm not setting out to be. Deliberately. I'm not trying.'

'Maybe that's your secret. Not trying.'

'I *have* tried, though. I've tried to like *myself*. For a while … quite a long time … that wasn't easy. It's getting easier. And I've had a lot of help. From friends. Who say and do nice things.'

Nat cuddled into me and put her head on my shoulder. Over her head I saw, striding into the atrium, our old PE teacher. He still had the streaked blonde Pat Cash hair, still wore the skinny Mick Jagger jeans, still (at pushing 60) clearly fancied himself the object of teen-girl admiration.

I whispered to Nat. 'Christ. Look out. It's Wanker Wilkins.'

Nat looked horrified. 'Don't make eye contact. Keep walking.'

He strode past us and into the main hall.

'I thought you liked him, Little Miss Captain of the hockey team, netball team, badminton team …'

Nat looked sheepish. 'There was a reason for that … favouritism.'

I gave her a sidelong glance. 'Go on.'

'It wasn't hard to make a middle-aged arsehole give me what I wanted. Especially an arsehole crippled by vanity.'

My jaw hit the floor. 'You didn't shag Wanker Wilkins?!'

'I didn't have to. All I had to do was … put the cupcakes on the tray and let him believe he might have the chance of … a little nibble.' She tossed her Kylie hair. 'Men! When will they *ever* stop thinking with their trousers?'

36

Portrait of a Lady

It'd been good to catch up with Will. And seeing Nat again had actually turned out better than I thought and I was genuinely happy to see her back on some sort of track. I made a promise to be a better friend to her.

But Intext and Brookhill weren't the only blasts from my past that week. Thornhill Hall was also on my mind after Veronica had texted again.

I remembered her last text and my promise made months ago – and now broken – to organise a trip to the Cotswolds to see them all.

I think it had been my very real connection to Cécile now, which made any contact with Camilla awkward to say the least, that had put any notion of a trip to Thornhill subconsciously out of my head. That's what I told myself, anyway.

But now, according to Veronica, Camilla was 'extremely frail.' I should have read the signs from her earlier text. Like the darling she was, Veronica hadn't wanted to apply any emotional blackmail. The fact that she was mentioning Camilla's health now made it clear how bad the situation really was. I felt scummy.

I still had a day's car hire to use, so I decided to motor up to the Cotswolds. It would be good to see Veronica again, and to taste Rosemary's scones.

Poor Camilla. I felt even more compassion for her now, at a distance of a couple of years, than I'd done after George's death. Her husband's affair with Cécile had been an open secret at Thornhill. This, and the knowledge that George still carried a flaming torch for his first wife, Arabella, must have made life at Thornhill all but unbearable for Camilla, a woman for whom prestige, station, public face were paramount.

These thoughts whirled around my mind as the car crossed the North Wessex Downs.

And I could still feel, in my chest, the aftershock of Will's revelation about David.

It wasn't long before the car was sweeping through the familiar gates at the edge of the Thornhill estate. The morning breeze had stiffened a little and the poplars that lined the avenue were bending, as if to salute my return. The snows of the previous week had pretty much disappeared – a few white crystals glistened like diamonds among the snowdrops.

Veronica looked worn down. She pulled me close.

'It's so good to see you. So good of you to come.'

'It's lovely to be back. How are things?'

She appeared to steady herself. 'It's been a bit … challenging.'

'Oh. I'm sorry. In what way? Too many bookings?'

'Erm … more like the opposite.'

This was a shock. When I'd left as Estate Manager a couple of years before, there'd been a healthy portfolio of corporate and private clients – shooting parties, team-building weekends, conferences, weddings. And I'd been confident that, when Veronica had agreed to take the reins, she'd be a safe pair of hands.

'What's happened?'

'I don't know. We're offering the same services. We have the same core staff and we still buy in plenty of experienced casual labour when we need it. But we've not been needing it.'

'I guess the whole economy's in a bit of a nosedive. Companies tightening their belts. Moving their operations abroad.'

'Will you have a look? At the business? See if I'm missing something. Doing something wrong.'

'I'm no management guru, Veronica.'

'Would you, though?'

'Sure.'

'Later. After you've seen Camilla.'

'How is she?'

'She just wants to see you.'

The lady of the manor was sitting in a high-backed chair in the South Drawing Room, her face tilted towards the sun. The light made her stretched skin look almost translucent. Her hair, once lush and well-coiffed, was thin and wispy. She was, Veronica had said, virtually housebound now. No more parties. No afternoon teas with her salon set. No more jaunts up to Mayfair to get her hair done.

She turned to see me and a wave of genuine warmth suffused her features.

'I cannot tell you how good it is to see you again.'

I knelt down and put my arm round her bony shoulders. 'I'm sorry it's taken me so long.'

She squeezed my hand. 'Nonsense. You have a life to live. And a thriving new career, I'm told.' If the thought of Cécile was a dagger in her heart, she hid it well.

'Well, it's different. A change.'

'We all need change. That's the key, isn't it? Not to get stuck in a rut. Keep moving. Adapting.' She looked at me with a frankness that was a little unsettling. 'That was *my* downfall, I think. I didn't adapt. In all sorts of ways. I had a dream and it came true quite quickly. Too quickly for me to realise it wasn't what I wanted. Or what I thought it was.' I didn't know how to respond to this confessional.

Ever the gentlewoman, she bailed me out. 'I'm sorry, darling. I don't mean I didn't love George.'

She'd never called me *darling* before.

'Or that I wasn't happy. I loved him perhaps a little too much. Was perhaps a little too happy. There was nowhere to go after those first glory years. Nowhere except down.'

I squeezed her hand and sat down in the armchair next to hers. It was only then that I saw the painting. The one that had hung over the fireplace in George's study. The one that had mysteriously disappeared after George had died.

Arabella. George's first wife.

Camilla's eyes followed mine. 'Looks good, doesn't it? I had it cleaned. I think everyone thought I'd taken a knife to it or something after he died, like some crazy raving Rebecca.'

That's exactly what I'd thought at the time and now I felt my cheeks burn with the guilty memory of that assumption.

'George adored her. And I adored *him*. This is one way I can show it. A strange way, perhaps. But what else can I do?'

'I don't know.'

We sat together, two women with no answers.

I asked her about the others. Rosemary's shortbread was still the best in the world, Camilla said, and all the guest reviews raved about the food. Robbie, the rather hippyish head gardener, was still marshalling the troops and keeping the grounds in top form. Camilla had heard from Kate, the cleaner, that Robbie had a new tattoo, although Kate had wondered how on earth the tattoo artist had been able to fit another one onto his already generously decorated body. And Kate herself had a new man. He was the captain of the village football team. Camilla hinted that Kate had quietly slept her way through the team until she'd made it to the top.

This was a novel experience for me – swapping gossip with Camilla. Her haughty, icy exterior seemed to have melted away with age. And she was strangely but charmingly affectionate. We sat for over an hour and she never let my hand go for a second during that time. She occasionally squeezed it with delight and now and again lifted her other hand to stroke my hair.

The experience put me in mind of being with my mother and there was something of Mum in Camilla when, after about an hour of conversation, she turned exhausted eyes on me and, with apologies, said she'd need to lie down. I helped her to her feet and she hung on my arm and we padded slowly across to the door.

'But I've loved this time with you. It's meant a lot to me that you'd make the long journey to see us all.'

Veronica met us in the large central hall and took Camilla from me – a light load. Camilla leaned in and kissed me softly on the cheek. 'Bye, darling.'

***

The Saturday evening traffic on the M25 was as hellish as ever and I didn't make it back to the hire car place in Golders Green until the guy was packing up. As I sprinted across to the office, the strap of my handbag snagged on a metal barrier and the contents spilled all over the car park – keys, lipsticks, perfume.

David Harwood's business card.

37

Suffragette City

Spring arrived at last.

It brought a sense of urgency to my morning commute. People had a bounce in their step, winter coats now shed in favour of lighter, paler fabrics. The shops were full of Easter eggs and chocolate bunnies, tempting us all to fall off the New Year diet wagon.

Those of us who hadn't fallen off on January 3rd.

Work was fine. Settled. No business trips on the horizon, no major new clients to fret about. Steady. Routine.

Nothing wrong with that.

I don't know why – perhaps I was feeling the need for a frisson of excitement – but one Friday evening, after a generous house measure of Miranda's vanilla-infused gin, I pulled David's business card out of my bag and dialled the number. Just an old friend checking in to say hi.

Two rings in, I started to feel like a fraud. And when he answered, and I heard the velvet vowels, I bottled it and hung up.

'Buggering bugger!'

Right, you silly tart. Behave yourself. What do you really think is going to happen here? The guy's recently divorced. Plus, if he'd wanted you, it would have happened already.

My phone buzzed and my heart stopped. David's number.

'Hello?'

'Jennifer?'

I'd always loved the way he said my name. 'Yes.'

'Did you mean to call me?'

'Yes. Well …'

'It's nice to hear from you.'

'Good.' I had a thought. 'How did you know it was me?'

'You gave me your card. I added your number to my contacts. I imagined … hoped … you hadn't changed your number. It *was* two years ago.'

'Yes.'

'So?'

'Sorry?'

'You called me.'

'Yes. I … wanted to check in with you. Say hi.'

'Hi.'

'Hi.'

'You've heard. About Sarah and me.'

I hesitated. And decided not to lie. 'Yes. I'm very sorry. That's what I wanted to say. That I'm very sorry.'

'It's fine. It is, as they say, amicable. It was clear, a few weeks in, that it wasn't what either of us really wanted. And we're both too … mature … to waste time living a life we don't really want. So we stopped. No hard feelings.'

'You seemed so happy. At your wedding. Which was a lovely day, by the way.'

'I'm glad you enjoyed it.'

'Sorry. Again. This seemed like a good idea at the time.'

'It *is* a good idea. Can I see you?'

'What?'

'I'm sorry. I've misread the signals.'

'No. No, you haven't. I'm just … surprised.'

'Are you?'

'Yes. I've always felt … But I wasn't sure *you* felt …'

'I did. I do. Feel.'

'Right. Good.'

'Yes. Can I call you? In a couple of weeks?'

'Yes.'

'The next two weeks are crazy full. And I want the time and space to properly enjoy the pleasure of being with you.'

'Then I'll look forward to your call.'

I went downstairs to share my news with Miranda and found her gawping open-mouthed at the TV, an open vac pack of Merchant Gourmet chestnuts in one hand and the remote in the other.

Look London was running a report on a kerfuffle at a community centre in Duckett's Green, two miles away. The centre was home to, among other groups, the newly formed Church Of The Mission Of The Everlasting Lord, which counted among its flock one Mad Mary. And now the council was closing the centre down – citing massive cuts to community budgets – and selling off the land to a developer throwing up 'executive apartments'. A group of protesters had chained themselves to the demolition company's security fencing. Naked.

Among their number one Mad Mary.

Miranda walked over to the drinks cabinet, pulled out two tumblers and emptied about five ounces of elderflower gin into each, followed by a splash of tonic. She handed me one.

'I mean … why can't she just bake cakes?' She threw back a belt of gin.

I sipped mine and it made my eyes water. 'Well, she's more … engaged than that.'

'Engaged! Why does she have to be bloody engaged? Why can't she slow down?'

'It's her way of staying young.'

'She's making *me* old. Before my time.'

'She wants to make a difference. She's an activist. She's Emmeline Pankhurst.'

'I don't *want* Emmeline Pankhurst as my mum. I want … I don't know … Mary bloody Berry.'

I put my arm round her. 'We can't choose our parents, though.'

Miranda turned apologetic eyes towards me. 'Oh, Jen. I'm so sorry. Moaning about my mother, when … To you. Of all people.'

'It's fine.'

On the screen, two female officers were helping Mary, modesty now restored by a foil blanket, into the back of a police van while she swatted at them with her bible. Miranda groaned and looked away and I looked at Miranda's striped leggings and badass cherry-red hair and couldn't imagine her growing old gracefully either.

Two days later, the incident, and Mary's prominent role in it, had made *The Tottenham Independent*. Miranda showed me her copy.

'My mother, the protester.'

A front-cover report of the protest was followed by a long opinion piece on council budget cuts that spread over the following pages. Mary had been let off with a caution.

I clocked a photo of Mary waving her bible in the air, triumphantly, in the manner of Che Guevara. 'At least she made page three. Quite an achievement at her age.'

Miranda was starting to see the funny side. 'I know. I'll never get her into a Knit and Natter group. She says they're for old people who like to talk about which bit of their body is falling apart. "The organ recitals" she calls them.'

'That's funny. She's very sharp. She needs a distraction that'll keep her brain active. Something that doesn't make her feel like a pensioner.'

'She's 74.'

'I know. But that's not how she sees herself. Which is great.'

'Is it?'

'Yeah. Absolutely. How would you feel if someone told you to stop working and take up stamp collecting? Or macramé?'

'I'd probably punch them.'

I pointed to the *Independent*'s photo of Mary. 'Well, that spirit, that strength of character that makes you feel like punching people. That comes from *her*.'

Miranda's eyes softened. 'You're right. I should cut her some slack.'

'We *all* think our parents are bonkers. That's how generations work. It's nature's way of telling teenagers to get away from these people and start a life on their own. Your mum just needs a project. I'll give it some thought.'

Miranda kissed me. 'You're lovely.'

I smiled. 'I know.'

That night, I sat with my laptop on the top of my lap and Googled stuff happening within a four- or five-mile radius.

With Mary's dodgy hip, Zumba didn't seem like a goer. And given that she'd used my iPad for a tea tray on more than one occasion, and once passed me Miranda's hairdryer when I told her my phone's screen was frozen, Computing Skills didn't seem like a smart move either.

Then, on my Facebook newsfeed, I happened upon a food bank. Looking for volunteers.

Perfect.

Community involvement. Social conscience. Activism.

***

Sonia ran tight ship on a shoestring.

'*Daily Mail* readers think food banks are just for homeless people. But we get all sorts these days. The working poor. People working two jobs who still, after London rent and travel, can't afford to feed themselves. We're a rich country. It shouldn't come to this.'

I mentioned Mary. Sonia had seen the report in *The Tottenham Independent* and was impressed. 'We need that kind of commitment to social justice. It's our lifeblood.' She paused for effect.' And if *you* feel like pitching in, we can always use an extra pair of hands.'

I said Mary would be in touch.

And I signed myself up for Tuesday evenings.

38

D Day

When the two weeks were almost up and I was beginning to think I'd dreamt the whole thing, I got a call from David.

Could we meet? What kind of meeting did I want? Might he be so bold as to suggest a weekend away? How about a place halfway between his Hampshire home and my North London hangout? Would Windsor do?

'If it's good enough for the Queen, how can I say no?'

I got to the hotel – boutique but old-fashioned palatial – a couple of hours ahead of the appointed time so I could hit the hotel gym.

The guy at reception found David's name and informed me that my room was next to Mr Harwood's.

Separate rooms. I admired the lack of presumption.

It was quite sexy.

Nothing like some good old endorphins to turn jitters into confidence.

I pulled on my pinkish retro LA Gear trainers and hit the treadmill for twenty minutes before doing some lightweight stuff on the machines. Then I sluiced myself off and hit the sauna to get the pores peachy, all the while listening to nineties power ballads to get me into sex-goddess mode.

After a luxurious shower, I spent three quarters of an hour applying my makeup and fiddling with my hair.

With ten minutes to go, I was starting to get jittery again.

Mini bar. One small glass of white before I meet him downstairs for cocktails.

Right. Get the black killer heels on, girl. Then knock him dead.

The heels were not in the wardrobe. *Hm. Still in my case, then.*

My new weekend case is one of those carry-on friendly jobs with a thousand ingenious inside pockets. I checked every one. Even the one that's big enough only for a spare lipstick.

No black killer heels.

Shitting hell!

My list of footwear choices was now short and comprised: my navy blue Converse high tops that (I think) look good with jeans and make me (I think) look down with the kids; my pinkish retro LA Gear trainers; the hotel's complimentary white bathroom slippers.

The man with the warm eyes and the velvet vowels – this man who'd been living in the corner of my mind for the last two years, whose face came into my head about every seven seconds – was standing at the cocktail bar with his back to the door.

I hadn't ever dared imagine we'd *ever* get to this point.

I touched his elbow and he turned to look at me.

There was a look of such intense emotion in his warm eyes that I thought for a second he might actually cry. Instead, he smiled.

'I've been looking forward to this.'

I smiled back. 'That's my line.'

He looked at my dress. The classic little black number. 'You look gorgeous. But then you always do.'

Then he clocked my pinkish retro LA Gear trainers and chuckled. 'Not sure it'll catch on.'

'I don't care. I'm a trailblazer.'

'Yes. You are.'

I don't remember much about the food, although I'm sure it was delicious. All I remember is a curious mix of excitement and comfort – the excitement of being with someone new, coupled with the comfort of being with someone you feel you've known all your life. A curious and delightful mix.

We stopped outside my door.

David looked me in the eyes. 'Can I just say that, despite your ridiculous choice of footwear, Jennifer Brown, I adore you.' He took both my hands in his. 'And, from the minute I first saw your face, I've wanted to do this.'

He pulled me gently towards him and gave me a long, slow, lingering, searching kiss. When we pulled apart, I blinked and tried to remember how to speak. After three or four seconds, it came back to me.

'Would you like to come in?'

'I was hoping for an invitation.'

'I was hoping you'd be hoping.'

39

D is also for Destiny

David and I had found each other.

It had taken a while, and there'd been some false starts – a major one on his part – but we were now where we had both wanted to be. There's a special kind of happiness in knowing that someone you've wanted desperately to be with has harboured the same strong feelings for you.

This weekend had made life good.

***

Then, suddenly, as I was driving back to London, it wasn't.

Veronica texted to tell me Camilla had died.

'It's been coming for a while. We've known that. But it still hurts. I feel like I'm only just getting to know her, the real her, after all these years.'

I could hear the tears in Veronica's words. And the news hit me like a brick, too. My last meeting with her had been lovely. And, like Veronica, I was sad for the times we *hadn't* had. The warmth of that last day with Camilla had made all the previous times feel like a lost opportunity.

***

I stood beside Veronica, Rosemary, Robbie and Kate on the steps of Thornhill Hall and we bowed our heads as the coach carrying

Camilla's body crunched slowly past us and headed for the small family chapel on the edge of the Thornhill estate, with us mourners falling in a few paces behind.

In the chapel, I thought back to her husband George's funeral, with its pomp, its military salutes and its dignitaries in attendance. Camilla's ceremony was a much more modest affair – just the core staff, me, and the surviving members of Camilla's salon set, the hoity-toity ladies Camilla had collected for her famous afternoon tea parties. Plus Jason, the stylist in whose Mayfair salon Camilla had spent shedloads of cash over the years. Her patronage had paid for his purple crushed velvet suit and silk cravat ten thousand times over.

We sniffed into our tissues as the vicar plodded over to his lectern. Then the chapel doors were thrown open and all heads turned to see Edmund, Camilla's desperately old and eccentric father-in-law, being wheeled into the chapel at a dangerous speed by a beefy carer in her twenties whose forearm tattoos would have given David Beckham's a run for their money. Edmund looked impossibly, distressingly frail as his hefty carer heaved him onto a pew.

After a rather thin rendition of *Abide With Me* played by an organist who looked like the instrument was something of a novelty to him, the eulogy was delivered by Erica Dickens, local councillor, wife of MP Claude Dickens and leading light in Camilla's salons.

When she paid tribute to Camilla's charity work, there were nods and murmurs of agreement. Then she switched to the subject of the tea parties and the charms of their hostess and the wonderful food Camilla had always selected and supervised. I glanced at Rosemary and she smiled. Then I thought I detected a chorus of suppressed titters when Erica waxed lyrical about Rosemary's meringues, which she declared 'whipped to stiff perfection.'

I knew I wasn't the only one in the room for whom the phrase had conjured up images of Camilla the Alley Cat, the 60s fashion model and Cat Girl at Soho's infamous private club, The Cat's Tail.

During my time as Estate Manager, one of the older guests at a shooting party had remembered her from his time as a junior at a merchant bank whose staff had been frequent clients at the club. It hadn't taken much Googling to piece together a media story involving Camilla, a Home Office minister and a portfolio of 'special services.' It was a notorious past Camilla had worked tremendously hard to leave behind and the client's willingness to reminisce had been swiftly shut down by George, ever the gentleman and protective (if not loving) husband.

Camilla was laid to rest beside George, squeezed in between her husband and his faithful labrador, Benson. The geography would have made her smile with satisfaction – she'd always complained to George that he thought more of his dog than he did of her.

After the interment, we stood around in the Orangery in little groups and I made polite conversation with the vicar and his wife while nibbling on dainty finger sandwiches and petits fours. It was the kind of do early Camilla would have wanted but I had the feeling it wouldn't have entirely pleased the sparkier, warmer Camilla I'd only caught a glimpse of near the end.

Rosemary pulled me away from the vicar on some flimsy pretext, handed me a brandy and dragged me over to the corner where she, Veronica, Robbie and Kate were huddled like some medieval cabal.

Rosemary was the one to speak.

'She could be a bit of a cow. We all agree on that. But she was also a star and a bloody good egg who didn't deserve a lot of the shit that came her way. And we loved her. And we drink to her.'

We raised our glasses. 'To Camilla.'

A reedy voice piped up, 'To Camilla.' We all turned to see Edmund in his wheelchair, the old fire in his eyes, executing a perfect 'long way up, short way down' salute, like the old military man he was.

I walked over to him. His lip was trembling.

'I did love her, you know.'

'I know.'

'And my son wasn't the husband he might have been. I accept that.'

'George was very fond of Camilla. And very protective of her.'

'It wasn't enough.'

I had no answer to that. Edmund changed the subject.

'But he knew *your* value. You were the best steward of this estate he'd ever worked with. He couldn't praise you highly enough.'

'I was grateful for the opportunity to work with him. I think it's a wonderful place. I was very happy here.'

Edmund patted my hand. Then he saw his carer stride over and cloud of irritation descended over his face. He turned rueful eyes towards me. 'Time to be a useless old bastard again.'

On the drive back from the Cotswolds to London, I thought about Camilla and her life and how it had backfired. And I remembered what my old Chemistry teacher, Mr Skidmore, had said about his own plans and how his world had suddenly been turned upside down by his wife's illness.

I wondered what lay ahead for me. Finding David seemed so right, it made me suddenly scared for the future. When something's so good, you worry you'll lose it. If it's already wonderful and can't get any better, the only thing it can do is get worse.

The only way is down.

Miranda was in the kitchen opening a bottle of Crémant de Loire. She poured some into two flutes and handed one to me.

'I know you've just been to a funeral but I feel like celebrating.'

'Celebrating what?'

'You. You and your gorgeous bloke. After all this time.'

I felt a smile spread across my face. 'I know. I've hardly had time to take it in. But it does feel … lovely.' I clinked her glass. 'Thank you. I'm very happy.'

She pointed to an oblong package on the kitchen table.

'That came for you.'

I ripped it open. Inside, an oblong box with a card attached.

Dear Jen. I thought these might be a good standby. For future weekends. D. x

There was a PTO, so I flipped the card over.

PS. I hope you don't mind but I took the liberty of checking your size with Will.

I lifted the lid and parted the tissue to reveal a gorgeous pair of killer black heels. Christian Louboutin.

I slipped them on. A perfect fit.

I was a real-life Cinderella.

***

We like to feel that we're in charge of our own lives. That we make our own choices. A lot of the time we do, of course. Will I get up now or press snooze? Will I have pasta for dinner again or mix it up with a risotto? Will I buy recycled toilet paper because its kinder to the environment or the dearer quilted stuff because it's kinder to my caboose? These are the things we have control over.

But the big stuff is different.

A letter from Montague and Maybole, Camilla's solicitors in Stow-on-the Wold, invited me to make an appointment with them at my earliest convenience.

Friday afternoons at Artisan Wines were pretty relaxed, and I didn't need much of an excuse to make the pleasant drive northwest to the Cotswolds, so I booked myself in for three o'clock and booked a car for a day.

I thought about the painting of George's first wife, Arabella, and the care Camilla had taken over its restoration, all of which she'd been at pains to point out to me the last time we'd met. And I remembered that George had once told me I reminded him of Arabella. In fact, he'd once given me, as a Christmas present, a gorgeous antique French brooch that had belonged to her. Had been her favourite piece of jewellery, in fact. If he'd confided all this to Camilla, perhaps the painting, too, had been bequeathed to me.

By the time I reached Stow, I was certain this was the reason for the solicitors' letter. I was deeply flattered.

I was ushered into Patrick Maybole's office. Camilla's solicitor shook my hand and waved me to an armchair.

'Sherry?'

'Erm … I'm driving. So perhaps just a small one.'

He opened a cabinet and took out a decanter. 'How *was* the drive?'

'Oh, fine. I've done it several times. Really like it, actually.'

'Good.' He handed me a glass of pale cream. 'Well, we have to observe the formalities, of course, so I'm afraid you need to make yourself comfortable while I read the whole document to you.'

I was puzzled. 'Okay. This *is* about the painting?'

It was his turn to look puzzled. 'Painting?'

'I'm sorry. I've been presumptuous. Camilla, the last time I saw her, mentioned a painting. Of George's first wife. And … because of things George said a couple of years ago … about how I … oh, it's not important. I just thought I might be … inheriting it. The painting.'

Patrick Maybole gave me a look that was part puzzlement, part shock.

'I'm sorry. I assumed you knew.'

'Knew what?'

'Well, you *do* inherit the painting.'

'Oh. Okay. Lovely. Thank you.'

'Along with the rest of Thornhill Hall.'

I felt like someone had driven a truck through my brain.

'What?'

'The hall. The estate. Everything. You own it. And the painting.'

The edges of the room started to swim and my eyes lost the ability to focus on anything for several seconds. Patrick Maybole touched my shoulder.

'I'm sorry. I didn't mean to shock you. As I say, I assumed you knew.'

'No. Why? When did she, they …?'

'The will was drawn up three weeks before George died. He talked to me a lot about you. In you, he felt he'd found the perfect person to take the place on. Look after it. Do the right thing. On his death, the title descended to Camilla, of course, but, having no children or other dependants, and with Edmund's health declining sharply, they were both in absolute agreement – no question about it – that, on Camilla's death, the title should descend to you.'

'This was all decided two years ago?'

'Yes. Over two years, now.'

In the car park, I sat behind the wheel of the hire car and stared through the windscreen.

Ten minutes later, I was capable of speech and I called Cécile.

Then came my second shock of the day.

Cécile had known before me. Had known a couple of days after the will had been drawn up. George had told her everything.

Suddenly it all made sense. The trip to Switzerland with bigwigs, the weekend in the country with the toffs, the important 'high net worth' individuals whose accounts I'd managed. All part of an elaborate and adorable plan to integrate me into her upper echelons, to prepare me for what she knew lay ahead.

Will's voice dripped mock outrage.

'Well, don't think I'm calling you *My Lady*. That's not going to happen.'

'There's no title, you daft bugger.'

'Right. Just a stately home filled with antiques and a couple of hundred acres of country estate.'

'*Seventeen* acres.'

'Oh, right. Positively bijou.'

'Will you and Kavi come and visit?'

I heard him smile. 'My darling mistress of the manor, you won't be able to keep me away. And believe me when I tell you this could not have happened to a nicer person. Because there *is* no nicer person.'

Then I told him about David. And he screamed.

Which made we want to call David.

'Goodness. Life-changing.'

'It doesn't change *me*. You know that?'

'I know that the you I know is not the kind of person who can be changed for the worse by anything. I'm extremely pleased for you.'

'Thank you. I'm extremely pleased to be with you. I am *with* you, aren't I?'

'I *hope* you are. And it is my very fervent wish that the situation continues.'

'We're a nice situation to be in.'

'Yes. We are.'

I took a deep breath and started the engine.

There would be challenges ahead. Responsibilities. A shift from employee to employer. Owner. Landowner.

My life so far had been a fairground ride. A ghost train now and again but most of the time a rollercoaster – twists, turns, thrills, the odd bit of screaming, hands in the air, good friends by my side.

It was scary at times. But it was bloody exciting.

And I didn't want the ride to stop.

Stay on board for the ride.

Jennifer Brown will be back soon.

https://jenniferbrownsjourney.co.uk/

About the Author

Author Angie Langley was born in Somerset and has lived in the south west of England all her life. Nowadays home is a 17th century thatched cottage on the banks of the River Avon in Wiltshire, a tiny piece of heaven and a true writer's paradise. *'Jennifer Brown Moving On'* is the second in a series of three books continuing the adventures of our heroine as she muddles her way through life's ups and downs.

Angie would like to thank you for buying her book and would be delighted to hear from you, so do please follow her via Twitter (@JenBJourney and @angielangley0) or by visiting her website: www.jenniferbrownsjourney.co.uk